THE FIRE
WITHIN
THE NIGHT

JD NELSON

To Nels, always Nels

CHAPTER ONE

For the two hundred and ninetieth day in a row, I slid the old-fashioned key home, turned the lock over, and felt a frisson of excitement in the pit of my stomach. I was living my dream.

Too bad that dream was sucking the life out of me.

At first, owning my own bookstore in the Upper West Side had been a delight; I met interesting people, had access to new books before they hit the shelves, and best of all, I answered to no one. I was my own boss. You'd think that I'd be happy, hell, ecstatic to come here every day. Yeah, right.

Every morning, I would drag my gangling, half-dead carcass through the fiction section and make a beeline towards the espresso machine slumbering behind the countertop. Damn, I envied that machine. At least, he could rest. I, on the other hand, hadn't had a good night's sleep in over nine months.

Throwing my keys next to the register, I took perverse pleasure in cranking up the machine. "Wakey, Wakey, Mr. Espresso. If I can't sleep, neither can you."

He didn't respond. He never did. But I wouldn't either if I were him. Who wants to wake up every morning to a red-eyed, sleep-deprived, crazy lady with a major case of bedhead? No one. That's who. Which was why I was still tragically single at twenty-five years old.

I managed to fumble a cup onto the countertop (after two attempts) and pump my favorite white chocolaty goodness into it without too much trouble. How did I do this in my zombie state? Practice. Lots of practice. And even then, it's a crapshoot. There had been several 'incidents' I'd rather not go into—ever. Let's just say that steam was as dangerous as fire in the wrong hands.

Ten minutes after the most successful coffee endeavor of the week, the jingling of the door chimes alerted me to my first customer of the day. I peeled my face off the glass pastry counter, attempting to appear as if I hadn't been drooling on the job. A peek around the New Release shelves revealed that my slacking off hadn't mattered.

Chase, my only employee, looked at me with piercing, reproachful blue eyes and stern hands set on her slim hips. "Is it impossible for you to wait on me? Aren't humans supposed to have some kind of biological imperative to make their lives better?"

I cringed at the familiar scolding tone. Chase was the only person younger than me that could make me sorry I'd used my own equipment—in my own store. Hate was a complete understatement for the way she felt when I touched 'her' espresso machine, and she wasn't too shy to tell me in no uncertain terms that she would soon tire of reprimands and head straight into kicking my ass.

"Sorry, Chase. In my defense, I was half asleep when I made this." I held up the cup and tried to look pathetic, which was sadly easy for me.

"Erin, you use that excuse every day!" she exclaimed.

"It's not an excuse if it's true," I grouched.

Her eyes rolled toward the ceiling. "Sure, it's not, honey."

Knowing that I was forgiven (until next time), I giggled and snatched my coffee off the counter before she could pour it out and make it the 'right' way. "I'm going to go through the thrift store finds in the back. Call me if it gets busy?"

"Will do, boss." She saluted and skipped behind the counter, her pink ponytail swinging with every step.

Still chuckling, I made my way to the back room to sort out the big box of goodies my new friend at the thrift store sent over the day before. Chuck was great about bringing me the antique books he'd find at the estate sales he attended. They never cost much—a quarter here, a dollar there, and I was happy to pay him for his time and the cost of the books. Some of them had been great finds. First editions and signed books were common in large estates.

On this particular day, there was a copy of Jane Eyre and Northanger Abbey on top of a huge book so dusty I couldn't make out the name. Without even knowing what the large book was, it was already a phenomenal haul. The Jane Eyre was a nineteen forty-six photoplay edition. It had been issued when the Orson Welles version of the film had been released and could easily fetch up to a hundred dollars in the store.

Excited, I picked up the two books on top and walked back up front. "Hey, Chase! Guess what?"

"Chuck came through with a great find? Good, now I can give you this perfect white chocolate mocha, and I won't have to hear your epic saga about how every cup of my special coffee you enjoy steals four dollars out of your pocket? Right?" She held out the cup. "Now, give me that swill."

"It's not swill! I can make a simple espresso drink, Chase. I am capable of that," I countered, indignant, though I knew she was a hundred percent in the right.

She shook her head and clucked her tongue. "It's so sad that you have deluded yourself into believing that, Erin."

I blew out a huff that lifted my black bangs up and traded cups with her. "I'm going to look at the other book. Can you get this one marked to a hundred and this one to ten?"

"Sure thing, boss! Let me know what the other book turns out to be. It's pretty cool looking—almost like a prop in a scary movie or something."

"Yeah, and you can let me know if a witch comes looking for a missing grimoire. I might need to borrow her broom to get all that dirt off it."

3

"I've been watching Mrs. Frank from around the corner," she said, whispering conspiratorially. "If anyone has lost a grimoire, it's her. Plus, I'm pretty sure she's hoarding black cats."

I giggled and toasted the air in her direction with my coffee cup. "Thanks, Chase."

"Anytime," she replied. In mock seriousness, she added, "And Erin, I do mean, anytime. Stay off my machine, will ya?"

"Sure," I lied. I'd learned soon after she was hired that there was no point in trying to reason with her. She took being right to a whole other level. Also pointless was reminding her who was making the payments on the building and its contents, that she had been issued a uniform, and that people could hear what you said about them if you say it to their face. Chase might be one of a kind, but she was obviously from another freaking planet.

Perfect mocha in hand, I trudged back to the stockroom and steeled myself for the painstaking process of cleaning what I hoped was a first edition of Moby Dick that would get the store out of debt and pay for the awning I was so desperate to replace. The sun shining through the windows seemed to become a little brighter every day.

To my disappointment, the last estate find was indeed an old spell book of some sort. Chase was right again. What a surprise. I rubbed at the red-leathered tome with gentle strokes until I could see crude runes etched in the cover—runes that were at complete odds with the handwritten spells in Old and Middle English I found inside. If the book was from the time that they spoke Old English, there was no way that this book could be as well preserved as it was.

Unless it was spelled.

I looked around the dark back room, my nervous eyes darting everywhere. I didn't believe in witchcraft and thought it was a definite bunch of nonsense, but I also thought it was best not to tempt fate—just in case. I'd seen a lot of inexplicable things in my life.

Chase, however, was precisely the kind of person who would be gung-ho to try any and every spell from the strange book. She had no fear, which was usually a quality I admired, but not in this situation. I couldn't let her know what the book might be. She'd have both of us turned into familiars or worse. No, the smart thing to do would be to take it to the occult shop down the block the next day. Maybe they would be interested in it. I doubted my crowd of little old ladies and business people looking for the latest Nora Roberts or James Patterson would give it anything but a look of scorn.

As usual, my fickle brain started to change its mind as the day wore on. I was becoming more and more intrigued the longer I thought about the book. So much so, I had to stop myself from going to look at it three times. It was almost as if it were calling to me, which was just silly. The rational part of my brain knew magic was nothing but a load of hocus pocus.

But by the time seven o'clock rolled around, the fear of tempting fate had vanished, and I was counting the seconds until I could inspect the book at length. With a promise to wait for her to make my coffee the next day, I shoved Chase out the door a full ten minutes before her shift was up, switched the lock closed, and raced to the back, turning on the overhead light and even lighting a few candles for good measure. If there was a power outage while I was messing around with the unknown, I did not want to be unprepared … and I was a teensy bit scared of the dark … and pretty much everything else.

Placing the heavy book on an empty table, I read through the passages, turning the pages with gentle fingers. Not for fear of damaging its worn pages, but because I was terrified of it. I'd watched plenty of movies where some inanimate object turns out to be a sentient being hell-bent on killing the poor, defenseless (and stupid) girl with her finger poked in it. That scenario sounded fitting for this book. Most of the spells were ominous, with warnings of dire consequences if the spells weren't correct when performed. Sometimes even death. I wanted to stay as far away from those as possible.

Regardless of the scary stuff, I figured, at the least, there might be a protection spell in the book a non-magical person could cast. I hated the short, solitary walk to my apartment every night. So far, the potential for danger had been more frightening than the actual trouble I'd had, but I wasn't naïve enough to think I could escape notice forever. Even in the Upper West Side, it's still dangerous to be a single woman on foot, alone after dark.

I'd almost given up on my fruitless search for any 'safe spells' to cast when I found one that didn't sound as if it would bring the world to an end, although, it didn't make a lot of sense. But, then again, what did make sense about this strange book? Taking a deep breath, I traced my finger across the page and whispered the words.

Tis fair and light, thy night.

Be not afraid, elves.

Fullsome fere come.

Thy moon will guide.

Wither ye go, thy magick shall be betwixt us henceforth.

The instant I spoke the last word, the bulb overhead glowed bright and shattered, raining shards of glass onto the candles, extinguishing their flames. I screamed and turned away from the table, frantically waving my arms in front of me to find the lamp near the door. Trembling, I flicked it on and glanced around for anything that might have changed, relieved when there was nothing. Laughing shakily at my foolishness, I blew the debris off the spell book and tucked it under my arm. I'd take it to the occult shop tomorrow on my walk to work in the morning.

Witchcraft! What was I thinking?

I wasn't alone. Someone was following close behind me. I could hear their soft, careful footsteps echoing off the empty street in time with my own. Even in my panic, I could see the inane irony in that I'd looked for a protection spell in the very book someone was now going to steal. Well, at least, it would save me a trip to the occult store tomorrow.

Stopping under the guise of checking my heel for a break, I dropped my purse and tote a few feet in front of me. I knew running was out of the question. There was no way I could outrun whoever it was in my heels. The shoes might do more lasting damage to my feet than the would-be thief. And this way, the mugger could just take my belongings and go. No one would get hurt, and I could go home and look up the closest car dealership to set up an appointment. I wasn't going to go through this again.

The problem with that idea was … he didn't go for it. Through the long, dark fringe of my hair, I could see a black-haired man in his late twenties or early thirties admiring the architecture as though he were waiting on a bus. Really? I risked a longer glance at the snug black t-shirt and jeans he wore, looking for a thankfully absent weapon, then brought my gaze back to his face. He was still studying the buildings as though he might sketch them out later when he had spare time.

I sighed. This could go one of two ways. One, this guy was waiting on a bus or taxi, and I was just being paranoid, or two, he was an attractive serial rapist/murderer/human skin wearer waiting on me to turn my back, so he could jump me and drag me to his cargo van. Which one was more likely? I had no idea, but I was about to find out.

Shaking my head at the insanity of what I was about to do, I picked up my bag, fished into the side pocket for the pepper spray Chase insisted I carry and started walking back in his direction. Crazy? Oh, yes. But I would rather face my attacker head-on than give him the opportunity to grab me from behind. I wanted a fighting chance.

Stopping about six feet away, which was still way too close for my comfort, I expected the handsome man to register some surprise that I was now within striking distance, or at the least, to become defensive, but instead, I found him staring into my eyes with question. And that question was, "What did I do to you to make you want to blind me with the contents of your aerosol can of pain, crazy lady?"

"W—why are you following me?" I blurted out, raising the can in a halfhearted attempt. I was feeling a little stupid. It was apparent he didn't mean me any harm.

The stranger's dark brows lifted in surprise. "You called to me, daughter of Odin."

His voice was unexpected, deep and accented with a pleasant Scandinavian lilt, but it was his face that was really remarkable. When he turned it into the light, I could see just how spectacular he was. I became tongue-tied for a moment as I tried to wrap my mind around my would-be attacker's flawlessness. A perfect aquiline nose, bright, expressive green eyes, and a sharp, strong jaw made for an exquisite specimen of a man. I'd never seen anyone as perfect as he was.

Realizing that I was making a puddle on the sidewalk with my drool, I blushed and addressed his statement. "I...uh...didn't call you. Wait. Did you say Odin? Like, Norse Mythology, Odin?" Confusion filled his face, and I'm sure my expression mirrored it. This may have been the strangest meeting between two people— ever. "I'm sorry. I don't understa—" I started again, then I stopped when I did. Everything made perfect sense. I called him with the spell I recited from the book! Quickly pulling the grimoire from my bag, I offered it to the handsome man. If anyone knew to whom the book belonged, it would be him.

He held out his tanned hands and took it from me without any reaction. "Where did you find this?" he asked a moment later, his face hardening with suspicion.

"A friend shops estate sales for me. I own the bookstore." I motioned down the street toward my shop, immediately realizing how careless that was. I'd just given him all the information he'd need to become my newest stalker. Why didn't I give him my social security number and mother's maiden name while I was at it?

He turned the book around in his hands. "Can you show me the spell you cast?"

I flipped to the spell's page then looked up to find he was staring at me, his black brows knitted together in concentration. "Um…it's there on the left."

Turning the book around, he scanned the text then let his appraising eyes roam over me again. "It seems that I and all of the elves on Midgard are now yours to command." His voice was guarded, but not unkind. Thank goodness.

"Elves…what?" I backed away from him. "I'm not a witch. I couldn't have cast that spell."

He smiled. "My lady, you are bestowed with an unbelievable amount of power, as are your brothers and sisters. It is well within your scope to hold this kind of magic, even more so with the aid of a summoning spell."

Brothers and sisters? My heart pounded with excitement. "What do you mean by brothers and sisters?" I didn't have any family, much like the rest of the foster kids I grew up with. Hearing that I could have a family was a miracle to me, no matter how odd the chain of events leading up to it were.

"Odin has had many children with many females." He paused as he watched a homeless woman pushing her grocery cart across the street. "Can we go somewhere that we will be able to talk about this in private and comfort? You are chilled."

That was true. I was freezing. However, I couldn't take him back to the bookstore or my home. That wasn't smart. A young woman disappearing with a dark, otherworldly stranger—yeah, I'd seen that movie, too. It doesn't have a happy ending. Racking my brain, I tried to think of somewhere that was secluded but public. I couldn't afford to make a poor choice here. Even if he turned out to be an elf, he could still be a rapist elf, and at over six feet tall, I wouldn't be able to fight him off.

"We can go to French Roast," I suggested. "I'd love a cup of coffee." And to be able to call the cops, if they were needed.

He flashed a set of perfect white teeth. "That is a good choice."

"It's a couple of blocks this way." I pointed to the direction he'd come from, glad I wouldn't have to turn my back to him. Either he was what he said, or he was mentally ill. I was really supporting the elf alternative. Not only would I be safer with him, but he was much too handsome to have been in or escaped from the mental ward.

The man offered me his arm as we began to walk toward 85th Street. I didn't take it, just kept walking. I wasn't born yesterday.

His lips quirked at my reaction. "My apologies. How easily I forget the distrustful natures of the females of Midgard. Although, I do not know how I could have. Emelie's personality is very similar to your own."

"Is Emelie your wife? I didn't see a wedding ring." I clasped a hand over my mouth, horrified at what had just come out of it. Did I just say that? I gave myself a mental slap in the face. I'd been hovering between the fear of him assaulting me and wanting to take his clothes off with my teeth since we'd met. I needed to pull myself together—quick. "Sorry, I don't know when to keep quiet."

"That statement is truer than you know," he said, with a cryptic smile. "To answer your question, no, Emelie is not my mate. My true mate is yet to be revealed to me. But even if I were mated, male elves do not wear wedding rings."

There was something clandestine about the bemused smile his face held after his answer as if he knew something I didn't. Huh? I didn't understand all the mate and true mate stuff he was going on about, but I heard the concept of him being single loud and clear.

His rich laughter rang out into the night, confusing me. "What are you laughing about?"

"It is your thoughts. They are at war with one another. Everything moves so fast; it is hard to keep up."

How long did it take me to go from zero to panic? Oh, about point zero-three seconds. "Wait. Let's back up. Did you just say that you could hear my thoughts?"

"Yes, quite clearly," he said, amused by my response to this news. "But you need not be embarrassed. I am complimented by your ... admiration."

There was a fleeting moment in which I wondered if anyone had ever died from embarrassment. Why couldn't he have mentioned that he was a telepath before I made a total ass of myself?

He stopped walking. "I promise you. That was not my intention."

I nodded without looking at him, trying hard not to lose my count of the sidewalk cracks. It was either that or obsess over every impure thought I'd had for the last few minutes. The way I'd been drooling over him, he probably thought I was some sort of a nymphomaniac.

"What is your name?" he asked, ignoring that last thought. "I am Jakob Väsen of Svartálfaheim,"

That made me glance up. "Jakob? Elves have regular names?"

Grinning (which on him was a mind-numbingly sexy sight), he added, "And regular lives, just with magic included."

"Where is Svartálfaheim? Is that another planet?"

"What is Svartálfaheim is the question you want answered. It is a world of the Norselands—just as Midgard is, but it is unlike the planets you know in your solar system. It is another dimension."

I was starting to understand what the term 'mind blown' meant. I was stunned. "What?"

"Midgard, or Earth, is one of the nine worlds that make up the Norselands. The others exist on a different plane."

Of course, he was from another plane of existence. I could have never found this perfect embodiment of my dream man on Earth. I almost wanted to check behind us to see if he had a line of women following him down the street. Surely, he would attract attention. "So, does that mean elves are aliens?"

He chuckled at the comparison and shook his head. "Not exactly. You have yet to answer my question. It is your turn."

Question? What question? Oh yeah, what's my name. "I'm Erin Doherty."

"Was your mother Irish, lass," he asked in a thick brogue, trying to lighten the mood.

I laughed and shrugged. "Doherty is the name the state of New York gave me. I've never met my biological parents."

He sighed. "I wish I could say that this is an uncommon occurrence with the children of Odin. However, it is far from it. The majority of them will never have the opportunity to meet their father, and there are a lot of his children who do not know either of their parents. I am interested to know who your mother might be. She cannot be a human. He has not ventured out of Ásgard in centuries."

"Ásgard? Is that another plane? Can you take me to meet Odin? Wait. Is it even a good idea for me to meet him? What do you think I should do?"

"Slow down, Erin. Let us take this one step at a time."

I nodded my compliance. "Sorry, I didn't mean to bombard you. You just have no idea how big this is for me. I have a parent. You're positive that it's Odin, right?"

Pursing his lips, he cast his troubled eyes in my direction. "Of that, there is no doubt."

I wasn't convinced. "But how could you know that already?

12

We met tonight."

He reached a hand out as if to touch my face. "May I?"

"Yes." My reply was breathless with the anticipation of his touch. What happened to that tough New Yorker with the fight or flight response from a few minutes ago?

Smiling at my reaction, he cupped my chin with his warm hand and tipped it up to peer into my eyes. "I did have my doubts when I saw you come out of your shop. Your eyes are not the color of Odin and his descendants; they are similar to my own. The giveaway is your signature. It is almost identical to your brother's. Soren is mate to the female, Emelie, I mentioned before."

I furrowed my brow in confusion and embarrassingly disappointment when he took his hand away. "Signature?"

It didn't go unnoticed. Barely keeping the smirk from his face, he explained, "Every creature of the Norselands has a signature—a sort of essence, if you will, that distinguishes them from each other. You have your father's classic signature."

I guess that couldn't be any stranger than any of the rest of what he was telling me. It was more than ludicrous. I couldn't be a demi-god. I didn't dare hope that his words were true.

"You can trust me, Erin. It is the truth. Odin is your father, and you have a village of siblings. You couldn't possibly remember them all. My friend Soren is the oldest of them, and there is a great chance that you are the youngest. How fitting it will be for him to show you to your new world," he mused, a slight curl at the corners of his mouth.

I tensed. My new world? What did he mean? He wasn't going to try to take me somewhere, was he?

"I do not mean to keep frightening you. It is unintentional. I thought that you might want to leave Midgard—I mean, Earth, to live on another world of the Norselands, perhaps Ásgard. It is closer to those in your family. Forgive me for the mistaken assumption."

I was starting to feel bad about him always having to apologize for being himself. He wasn't from here. I'm sure he was just as bewildered with my conduct as I was of his. Taking a bold step, I slid my hand into his much larger one and was shocked at the tingling sensation that shot up my arm. "There's nothing to forgive, Jakob. You never know, I might move there one day."

In other words, if he lived on Ásgard, there was a strong possibility that I would go there. I couldn't deny that I was attracted to him. Hell, that smile was reason alone to up and move to another dimension.

He brought my hand to his full lips, never taking his eyes away from mine. "I like the way you say my name, Erin. Your voice is a perfect accompaniment to your extraordinary beauty."

Rendered speechless by the deep, sexy delivery of his compliment, I was unable to articulate even the simplest of words. How I wished I could hide my impure thoughts, so I wouldn't ruin this moment. He would know how much I wanted to feel those lips against my own … and elsewhere.

He covered a look of surprise with a grim expression. "Let us go, Erin, before Soren murders me."

I was confused by his statement, but more than thankful that we were walking again. One more second at a standstill and I was sure that I would have tried to kiss him.

At that thought, Jakob turned his smile my way and gave my hand an almost imperceptible squeeze. I thought I might hyperventilate. Did that mean that he liked me, too? Taking a deep breath, I held it. He was right, I needed to slow down and take one thing at a time—my brain was overheating. Or was it just warmer? In the time it had taken us to walk to within a couple blocks of the cafe, the air outside had turned unseasonably warm. I took off my scarf and stuffed it into my coat pocket with my free hand, not wanting to let go of him quite yet.

"I should have warned you that I was going to warm the air.

Your hands were cold. I could not stand for you to be in discomfort."

"Can all elves do that?"

"No. Light elves can command nature-based magic, such as the ability to manipulate plants and animals, whereas dark elves excel at mastering the elements."

"That makes you a dark elf then, correct?" I had no doubt that he was an elf now. No human could perform that kind of magic. The telepathy, maybe, but warming the air? That was just...unreal.

"Yes. I am a dark elf." He glanced up ahead and returned the wave of a striking couple standing outside the door of the cafe. "Erin, do not be alarmed."

My voice trembled with fear. "Who are they?"

He patted the hand that was strangling his own, reassuring me. "I alerted Soren to the discovery of his sister as we walked. He insisted on coming to meet you in person. The female is his mate, Emelie."

Soren walked the half block to meet us and bowed a complicated bow that I was sure I could never duplicate. "I am Soren Vidar of Ásgard."

I took the opportunity to study his appearance as he spoke. He might have the same accent that Jakob did, but the similarities ended there. How unusual he was with his pale fair skin, white hair trailing down his back, and intense red eyes. There was no hope of him passing as a human.

Sheepish, I introduced myself to the intimidating man. "Hi, I'm Erin...um, Doherty."

His calculating face broke into a startling grin that almost seemed foreign against his harsh features. "Allow me to introduce you to my mate, Emelie. She has been looking forward to this moment for some time."

"Hi, Emelie," I offered, smiling at my new sister-in-law. I wondered if Soren meant that she could see the future. If looks were anything to go by, she might. Emelie didn't appear to be elven, like Jakob, or a human. In all honesty, it was pretty hard to believe that she had ever lived here at all, looking the way she did. She was petite, with blonde, flyaway hair and a kind smile that lit up her unheard of metallic silver eyes. In a word, she was stunning. How odd they were compared to Jakob and me. I was sure their arrival in the cafe would cause a spectacle.

"I can assure you, it will," Jakob said.

"Gosh, I am so sorry if you heard that! I don't mean anything by it. I just…" I broke off, horrified at my insensitivity. What kind of idiot forgets that her thoughts can be overheard?

Soren laughed. "It has been too long since we have been bombarded with stray thoughts, has it not, Jakob?"

Jakob chuckled. "It has. Two years too long, I would say."

In a blur, Emelie launched herself from Soren's side to engulf me in a massive hug. She swayed as she spoke. "This. Is. So. Awesome!"

Three seconds into the attack, I found myself struggling to stay upright when a tingle started running up the length of my body, feet first. When Emelie let go, I stumbled and thought I would pitch forward, but Jakob's lightning fast hands reached out to steady me. To my surprise, he made no mention of it, and I found myself appreciative for the first time in a while, that a man…err…male was willing to help me for nothing in return.

Jakob put his arm around my shoulders, pulling me tight into his side. I couldn't resist resting my swimming head on the soft black cotton that stretched across his muscular chest. Who could have? "Uh, maybe I should go home. I'm feeling a little woozy."

"Erin, allow me to see you back to Álfheim with me. I believe Emelie has given you an inadvertent boost of magic. You need to lie down."

16

Soren seemed irritated by Jakob's idea. "I can read her just as well as you can. There is no need for you to trouble yourself with her comfort or living arrangements. As her brother, I will be more than happy to do this myself."

"Be sensible, Soren. Long-term company so soon in your mating? That is not an ideal situation for a couple as … close as you are, and Emelie's old room is available for her."

I blushed at what Jakob eluded to and had an urge to cover my ears so that I didn't have to hear about my brother's sex life.

Soren caught his meaning and nodded his immediate acquiescence after seeing my expression, although he did it without any of the embarrassments I expected. "Fine, Jakob. Take Erin with you, but if you lay one hand on my sister—"

Emelie placed a finger over her mate's lips. "Soren, you know Jakob can control himself. It's Nils you have to worry about."

"You're right, little one." Changing tactics, he continued, "Jakob, I am making you responsible for her. Fenrir is not to come within five meters. Her beauty is sure to make her a target for his advances upon first sight."

"Nothing will happen. Besides, your sister can take care of herself." He smiled down at me. "She almost pepper sprayed me tonight."

"You did?" Soren asked me, laughing.

I answered from the safe cocoon of Jakob's arms, still feeling fuzzy from Emelie's magic. "I thought he might be a rapist."

Emelie burst into helpless giggles, and Soren arched an eyebrow. "I see your opinion of him has changed."

Had it ever! I couldn't think of anywhere I'd rather be. "Yes. I have no problem staying at Jakob's. So, I'll see you tomorrow morning?"

"Tomorrow night," he corrected. "I want to take a look at that book of yours in the morning."

"Okay," I loosened my grip on Jakob (with reluctance) and dug the book out of my bag. "See you tomorrow."

Emelie grabbed Jakob and me in a hug, singing out, "Group hug! See you guys tomorrow! I can't wait! Oh, call Chase and ask her to take over the shop for a couple days, before you forget."

I could still hear her tinkling laughter on the wind even after they'd disappeared. Whoa. That was unexpected. I looked up to Jakob, feeling safer than I'd ever felt in my entire life. "Why would I forget?"

Grinning down at me, he spoke. "It is sometimes better not to question Emelie. If she tells you to do something, you can rest assured that there is a reason for it."

"Can she see the future?"

"She is a Norn. She makes the future."

"Wow."

"Yes, it is a responsibility that no one would cherish, yet she does. Do not let her carefree personality fool you. She is dedicated to giving creatures whose fates she aligns the best possible future."

"I see, and Soren? Why is he so … scary?"

"Soren's long existence has been rife with strife. Your father's misdeeds and ill-treatment of his 'subjects' makes him hated among the Norselands. I am sure that has had some bearing on his character. I promise you have nothing to fear with him, or with myself." He reached into his pocket and produced a pale blue stone. Seeing my confused face, he explained, "I cannot travel using my own magic as Emelie and Soren do. It is not an ability gifted to the elves. I must rely on a shifting stone. You, however, will be able to travel without one—once you learn to control your magic."

I eyed the stone. "What should I expect?"

"You will see a blinding white light and then my chamber."

Closing my eyes, I gripped him tighter. "Okay, let's go to…uh, where are we going again?"

"My home is in Álfheim, the realm of the light elves. Hold on tight."

CHAPTER TWO

My first thought was that Jakob's bedroom wasn't much different from my own with its Spartan bed, desk, and dresser. My next thought? Unadulterated, sheer agony. I fell to my knees, my screams reverberating off the walls of the small room in time with the throbbing pain.

Jakob was frantic, wringing his hands, unable to help. "Where is the pain? Erin, please!"

"My back!" I hiccupped through my sobs, just as the door burst open and two unknown males tumbled in. One was dark, similar to Jakob. The other was how I pictured a Viking warrior, muscled and wild-eyed with a fair complexion and unkempt, blondish-brown hair reaching his collar.

"What the fuck is going on?" The rugged stranger asked as he strode toward us.

Jakob answered without taking his eyes off my face. "I am not sure. May I examine your back?"

The other male crouched down to where I was on the carpet. His bright green eyes were sympathetic. "I believe it is the valknut, Jakob. Is the pain in the right shoulder, *härlig kvinna*?"

"Hon är en vision av skönhet," the Viking added.

I wiped my eyes with the sleeve of my coat and took a deep breath. The pain was starting to recede. "Yeah, my right shoulder. What's a valknut?"

Jakob bent and helped me to my feet. "It is your father's mark, Erin. Every creature of the Norselands is born with it. Come with me."

He gave the other men a significant look, and they made themselves scarce so fast I wasn't one hundred percent sure if I hadn't imagined them being here.

Jakob chuckled. "You did not imagine them. That is my brother, Viggo, and my friend, Fenrir, who goes by Nils. We are house-mates."

"What did they say?"

"They said that you are a vision of beauty," he said, leading me into the adjoining bathroom and opening the closet to reveal a three-way mirror. He paused to gaze at my reflection for a long moment. "I will leave you to your privacy. You should be able to see the mark on your shoulder with the mirror."

He was leaving? I still had no idea what I was looking for. "Wait, Jakob. What am I looking for? Is it some kind of tracking device?"

A strange expression crossed his features. "One can hope that is not the case."

"Is my father really that bad?"

"He is much worse than you can imagine. He is a tyrant. The entire realm suffers as his playthings. It is a relief to me that you were fortunate enough to have green eyes. Had you not, you would be forced to endure the same disdain the creatures of the Norselands harbor for Soren and the rest of your siblings."

Well, that was beyond depressing. "Poor Soren. No wonder he was so serious looking." Being shunned because of your parent had to be as bad as it was for me having been excluded for being an orphan.

Jakob shook his head. "He is impervious to that sort of thing. When you are seven thousand years old, few circumstances will bother you enough to take notice of, which is why I want to leave you to look at the mark by yourself. I am certain that he would take action if he knew I saw you in your undergarments."

21

"I understand, but can you at least show me yours, so I know what I'm looking for?"

With an uncertain expression plain on his face, he turned his back on me and shed his dark jacket and t-shirt. "If that is what you desire."

My legs took me over to him as if they had a mind of their own. The need to touch his smooth bare back was overwhelming. Reaching up, I traced the overlapping triangles of his mark's design with my fingertip, enjoying the way his muscles tightened at the first stroke.

"Erin?" he inquired.

Jakob's impassioned voice was gruff with the same lust I was feeling. Unable to help myself, I leaned into him, resting my forehead on his back and breathing in his masculine scent. "Yes?"

"Do not do something you will regret."

Sliding my hands to his stomach, I placed a kiss in the center of his back, my lips lingering on his skin as I spoke. "Will I regret it, Jakob?"

He stilled my roaming hands with his own, turned to face me, and walked me backward until my back was pressed against the middle mirror. "That depends on whether you want to see me alive tomorrow, älskling. I was not in jest about Soren's anger." His voice was slow and slurred.

"Are you okay?" I asked, concerned.

On a heavy sigh, he breathed, "I do not know," and pressed his hard body into mine. I moaned out his name as he slowly licked up the column of my throat and whispered into my neck. "You are so perfect, Erin. I do not want to hurt you."

Opening my eyes, I pulled back to meet his hungry stare. His jaw was clenched in unnecessary restraint. "I want you, Jakob."

He bared fangs. "You know not what you ask for."

I gasped at his exhibition, more in surprise than fear. "You're a vampire?"

He threaded his fingers into my hair, burying his face in the dark mass. "The dark elves have been called many things, älskling. Gud, jag vill ha dig. Jag vill begrava mig själv i dig när jag tar en ven."

I didn't have to speak whatever language he was speaking to understand what he said. I wanted the same thing—even if that meant I was about to get laid by Dracula.

A pounding on the bathroom door startled us apart. "Uh, Jakob? Soren is on the line for you. He sounds kind of pissed."

Jakob gave me an, "I told you so," look and picked his shirt up to hold over the impressive bulge in his jeans.

"I'm sorry," I mouthed.

"No more than I," he acknowledged, leaving the room.

Our interloper stepped into the bathroom after Jakob's departure and grinned a knowing smile. "You have quite the dirty mind, Erin. I approve."

Another telepath? Well, isn't that just what the situation needed? I unbuttoned the top buttons of my shirt to examine the mark on my shoulder. "You liked that, did you, Nils?" I asked distractedly.

"I am a heterosexual male, aren't I? That bit about him burying himself inside you, while he takes your vein? That was smoking hot. You must be a naughty female to have evoked those words from our virtuous Jakob. He is so … saint-like. I, on the other hand, would be happy to do anything you set your dirty little mind on." His smile widened, showing the barest amount of fang. "Anything."

With a grimace, I straightened my top. "No, thanks."

Affronted by my not caring that he was more than a virile male specimen, he added, "I am also a wolf if that does anything for you."

"What do you mean, wolf?" Did he mean he was a werewolf? Holy shit!

"Yes, I do." He growled low, flashing his glowing yellow eyes.

I tamped down the urge to reprimand him for reading my mind again. Instead, I squealed in delight and pointed to the door. "Outside—now! I have to see this!" He looked confused, but I didn't care. A werewolf! How cool was that?

Jakob was in the living room, just hanging up the phone with Soren, as Nils led me out the front door and into the night. "Where are you taking her, Fenrir?"

"He's going to phase for me." I was giddy with excitement.

Viggo burst out laughing from where he had been sitting on the couch and followed us outside. "You already know the lingo? True Blood?"

"Yep," I agreed, returning his amused grin with an eager one of my own.

Nils harrumphed with impatience. "Naked male phasing over here."

"Oh, sorry, Nils." I ignored his now nude form and gave him a 'go ahead' motion. "We'll talk later, Viggo."

Jakob groaned. "It is almost as if you are already one of them. How could they have tainted you with their nonsense this fast?"

"Nonsense? Are you kidding? I'm at a fantasy creature camp. This is awesome!" I winked at him. "You're the hot camp counselor, by the way."

"She already has you figured out!" Viggo crowed. "You are the serious, somber one out of all of us." His animated face went blank. "Do you know what I just realized, Erin?"

"No, but it already sounds awesome!" Viggo was fast becoming one of my favorite friends—ever. His zest for life was contagious.

"You are a female!" he said. "We can reenact the getaway scene from Breaking Dawn Part II! Please, tell me you have seen it."

"Of course I have! Three times!"

Viggo put his arm around me and spoke with a serious face for a moment. "Mate me instead. Jakob is so boring. Trust me. It is a dreary existence without joy and mirth in your life."

"Just hurry up and phase, Nils. She needs to get back into the safety of the house!" Jakob demanded in exasperation.

Viggo leaned down and whispered, "See?"

A loud crack of bone (that sounded excruciating) pulled my attention from Jakob's brooding visage, alerting me that Nils was phasing into his wolf form. It was incredible. One second, there was a deliciously naked man standing across from me, the next, a huge wolf stood in his place. It happened so fast, if I'd have blinked, I would have missed it.

I walked to Nils. His tail pounded the ground in an enthusiastic wag. "Wow. You're a big scary puppy!" I rubbed his ears and hugged him to me. "I've always wanted a dog."

Nils shifted back into his normal form beneath my hands, and I snatched them away from his bare torso as if he was on fire. He sighed. "Well, that got me freaking nowhere."

Jakob shook his head at our theatrics. "Come, children, it is almost morning."

"Awwwww!" Viggo and I groaned in chorus as we followed single file behind him, snickering when he shook his head in disapproval.

Once back inside of the house, the group scattered. Jakob excused himself to do some research—a chore that Nils and Viggo deemed wholly insignificant when compared to the virtues of the God of War game they had been arguing over in the living room. I went in search of food. I should have followed Jakob and asked the million questions about him, the spell book and the Norselands that were on the tip of my tongue, but my hunger wouldn't let me move past the kitchen. I could barely think, let alone unravel the mysteries of the world…err…worlds… on an empty stomach.

Leaving the boys to their game, I went to the kitchen in search of food. My hope that I would find unusual fruits and vegetables, or maybe even animals, in the kitchen were dashed by the ordinary tomatoes, chicken, and milk inside their fridge. The pantry was even odder. It held at least ten jars and boxes of organic marinara sauce and spaghetti noodles. Why so much?

"It is Emelie," Viggo said in answer. "She is a bit of a freak about her Chicken Parm."

I smiled to myself. I was excited about the prospect of getting to spend time with my new sister-in-law. Emelie was obviously unusual, but I already knew we'd be good friends by her affectionate welcome. "That sounds good. Are you hungry?" I turned to search the island cabinets for a frying pan and found Viggo's hopeful, puppy dog face. "What?" I asked, wary of his expression.

"You can cook?"

"How else am I supposed to feed myself? I'm not made of money."

"Oh, sweet mercy." Dropping down to his knees, he bowed down at my feet in reverence.

"Get up from there, you weirdo." I giggled and pulled the chicken out of the refrigerator.

"What's going on?" Nils asked from the doorway, smirking at Viggo's still prone position on the floor.

I opened the drawers looking for the meat tenderizer and shrugged. "I'm cooking, and Viggo is practicing to be a jester when he grows up?"

"Holy shit!" Nils exclaimed, making me jump. "Jakob, you picked a good one. She cooks!"

The sound of Jakob's deep chuckle made me forget what I was doing. I glanced in the drawers not seeing anything but the private time we'd just shared.

Viggo popped up to his feet and handed me the utensil I was searching for. "Erin, you have got to learn how to block your thoughts. You are already worse than Emelie was. At least she wasn't thinking about making out with one of my brothers." He sighed. "Oh wait, yes she was."

I nearly dropped the jar of sauce I was pulling off the shelf. "Come again?"

Nils barked out a laugh and took off like a wolf after its prey. "I'm out."

Viggo grabbed a stack of plates out of the cupboard and followed him. "Sorry, I have to set the table. Emelie will have to fill you in."

"Are you kidding me?" I threw my hands up. "Leave me hanging, why don't you?"

"Sorry, poppet. I should not have said anything at all."

I pouted with my arms crossed, shooting daggers at him. "Fine."

He studied me a moment, then squinted his eyes. "That is not going to work on me, missy."

"It doesn't work on anyone! What does? Damn it! Now I'm dying of curiosity. And what the fuck is up with missy? Where's your walker, old man?"

He laughed "I doubt that you will die, you hateful bitch."

I grinned. "You never know. We don't even know what I am yet. I could be half-human."

"I would bet my inheritance that you are Odin's child with a dark elf female. Your eye color alone would mark you as one of us. Well, that and your great taste in vampire cinematography."

"Me? A dark elf?" I guess that couldn't be any more unusual than me being Odin's daughter.

"Yep, you a dark elf. Have you not noticed the similarities between us? We have the same nose." He left with the plates and came back for the silverware. "Thanks for making dinner, Erin. You have no idea how long it has been since we have eaten anything out of this kitchen other than breakfast. Nils cannot cook anything else."

"That's not true!" Nils yelled from the living room. "I can make lappkok."

"Nej, Nils. Du kan inte. Kommer du inte ihåg vad som hände förra gången?" Viggo replied in an exasperated voice, then winked at me. "He gets upset when we mention the 'incident'."

I could hear Nils' scoff from where I stood. "Whatever, Viggo."

Viggo shuddered. "It was horrific." Seeing the question in my eyes, he added, "Do not ask, Erin—ever. No need to have that bouncing around in your head."

He couldn't have said anything that piqued my interest more. "What language are you speaking?" I asked, trying to remember some of the words he'd spoken so I could look them up later.

"Swedish. We lived in Uppsala until recent events forced us to move here. We speak it when we are home out of habit."

"Swedish … ugh. I tried to learn how to say the numbers one through ten when I was younger. I'm not sure if it's even possible for me to pronounce the number seven. It's just a nasal noise."

He laughed and started back towards his game. "Do not worry. We will endeavor to speak English while you are here."

"Viggo?"

He stopped, reluctant to answer my question. He knew what I was going to ask. "Yes?"

"What does älskling mean?"

He winked at me. "Sweetheart, beloved—so many things, poppet."

I blushed. "Really?"

Nils poked his head in the kitchen and answered for Viggo. "Yes, and it's all fucking nauseating. I still cannot believe you're going to pick Jakob over me. There are thousands of dark elves. I'm one of a kind!"

Amused, I gave him a hug. "Don't be sad, Nils. I still wuv my wittle puppy!"

He rolled his eyes and muttered, "Fuck me. I'm getting drunk," as he shrugged my arm off and stalked away.

"All right, get out. Let the female cook in peace," Jakob said, from just outside the doorway. My heart palpitated in triple time when I heard the possessiveness in his voice.

"No one is moving in on your female!" Viggo shot back.

Jakob didn't respond to his brother, just seated himself across the counter from me and watched me work until Viggo stormed out in anger. Breaking the silence, I spoke first. "They weren't bothering me, you know."

"They are a distraction, and I am starving, Erin."

I looked up to find him fixated on me with burning eyes. The look on his face clearly conveyed that he wasn't hungry for food.

Dinner was tense. So much so, Nils and Viggo opted to eat in the living room rather than eat with us. It's not as if I could blame them. The heat between Jakob and I was scorching. My thoughts must be driving them all crazy. "Tell me about your family," I suggested to try and take our minds off of the elephant in the room.

"My mother and father have been gone for many years. I have my two brothers. Viggo, you have met. Kristian is in Svartálfaheim, another world of the Norselands. He serves as king there in my stead."

My mouth dropped open. "You're supposed to be a king?"

He nodded. "Kristian is keen on the throne, and I have no ambition to rule. I think it better to let him have his desire than end up with a dagger in my back."

"You think he would do that to you? To his own blood?"

Sighing, he spoke. "I have no idea what he is capable of. Two years ago, he was returned to his right mind after over a hundred years of possession by another. Kristian was long known in the Norselands as the Mad King."

"Huh," I muttered, lost in thought. It was too bad that Jakob relinquished the throne. I thought him being a king would suit him well.

He leaned in close. "Is that so?"

I swallowed hard. "Sure, you're kind, serious, and passionate."

"You think me passionate?"

"Yes," I exhaled.

Viggo chose that moment to step into the room and clear his throat. "I am heading to my room. See you guys tonight."

I stood to hug him. "Good night, Viggo."

He patted my back once before shoving me away from him. "Good day, Erin. Sleep well."

Bewildered, I looked at Jakob, who was standing across the table, furious and staring a hole in the back of Viggo's head as he walked away. "What was that about?"

Through clenched teeth, he said, "I do not want him touching you."

"Is that jealousy coming out?" I teased. "I'll give you a good night hug, too, if you want one."

"If you come any closer, you are getting more than a hug from me," he promised, ready to pounce. "Much more."

"I like the sound of that," I replied, daring him to make good on that statement with my eyes.

"Your brother, Soren, does not. He reminded me of my promise to keep you untouched when he called. As I knew he would."

"None of what you're saying is making me want you any less."

His hand snaked out to trace the line of my jaw. "You must stop this, Erin. Soren is my oldest acquaintance, and you are his newly found sister. Do you not see how this could be disastrous to our long friendship?" I feigned disappointment, even though I knew he would know what I was up to. "Try all you like, temptress. You will not win this."

Arching an eyebrow, I asked, "Is that a challenge?"

His brother's voice drifted in from the next room. "On second thought, I believe that I will go to the castle for the day. You guys are creeping me out."

"Not leaving!" Nils yelled from somewhere nearby. "No way am I missing this!"

Jakob walked to the doorway to talk to Viggo. "There is no need to leave. Nothing is happening in here."

"I am sure that you are right," Viggo assured him, sarcasm dripping from his words. "And yet, I am still leaving. Get up, Nils. You are going with me."

"Like hell I am!" Nils countered.

There was the muffled sound of shuffling, and then the front door slammed. The silence that followed, along with Jakob's irritated sigh, assured me that we were alone. Perfect. I shot Jakob a look of victory.

CHAPTER THREE

After helping me with the dinner dishes, Jakob made himself scarce again. He was hiding from me. It didn't matter. I would get my way—eventually. I guess that I should have felt guilty for making him a prisoner in his own home, but I didn't. I knew he wanted me in the same way I wanted him, and I didn't need his mind-reading ability to figure that out. It was in every intense move he made. He was coiled up, ready, and waiting for the right moment to strike. I just needed to find out what would push him far enough to bite—so to speak.

I took a long shower while I worked on my plan of attack, hoping that the noise of the water would hinder Jakob from eavesdropping on my thoughts. It was my best chance for privacy. I already knew that the first step in my strategy would have to be learning how to block my thoughts. There was no hope of getting anywhere with him if he had the upper hand. The second step? I needed answers. If I knew more about my surroundings and situation, it would be easier to figure out why Soren didn't want me around Jakob. I didn't buy that brother/sister respect thing. That sounded like a handy excuse if I'd ever heard one. The third step? Well, I didn't have one, but I was sure that I would figure out something. I had to. The instant attraction I felt with Jakob was too compelling to ignore.

Luckily, when I stepped out of the shower, naked and wondering what I would put on, I found that Emelie still kept clothes in her old room. Although she and I had vastly different taste, we were close to the same size. The unfortunate part was that almost everything in her closet was sweaters and jeans. I wore skirts and heels on a constant basis. I liked appearing professional at work. Since the day I opened the store, every day was a 'professional' day. So, I rarely had the opportunity to wear anything that might be deemed casual or comfy. I smiled to myself as I slipped on the jeans, finding myself excited about my new family, and also because tomorrow would be my first day off since Christmas. Hell, today might be the best day of my life. Sex would just be the icing on an already wonderful cake.

I found Jakob relaxed and bare-chested on the bed in his room, his laptop propped up against his stomach and knees. He didn't look the least bit surprised to see me. Big shocker there.

Joining him on the bed, I peeked at the screen. "You have Google here?"

"We have everything you have at home and more. Midgard is within our realm. Remember?

"Yeah, about that."

He closed the laptop and set it to the side. "Go ahead. I am ready for your questions."

"We might be here a while," I warned.

"I have nowhere to go. It is daylight outside."

"Oooh, you've answered question number four hundred and twenty-eight."

He laughed and folded his arms behind his head. "Allow me to answer questions four hundred twenty-five, six, and seven. No, I will not turn into a bat, nor do I have to take blood to survive; that is for pleasure and mating purposes. Also, garlic does not affect me in any way." He paused and frowned. "I cannot believe what you are thinking Erin. You can see that I do not sleep in a coffin and even if I did, I would never fuck you there."

My eyes shot to his. I could tell he was uncomfortable with what he'd said. He hadn't meant to use such coarse language with me. However, I thought it apropos. I wasn't thinking of white picket fences and making love. I wanted hot, primal, unforgettable sex with Jakob. I wanted him to fuck me so good that it would make me want that white picket fence.

Jakob looked as if my thoughts were sending him into overload. "For the love of the Norse, Erin!"

I grinned a Cheshire cat smile and changed the subject. "Tell me about Soren and Emelie. How long have they been together?"

His face showed distrust. He knew I was up to no good. "Two years. Emelie has overcome much to be mated to your brother."

"How so?"

"Many years before Emelie was born, her mother, Wist, who was a Norn herself, changed her fate to be aligned with my brother, Kristian's, so that she would be allowed to mate Emelie's father who was fated to my step-sister, Viveka."

I repeated what he said in my head to try to grasp all that. It was a mouthful. "Why did Wist do that to her own daughter? It's just so cruel." It was like, Disney Princess cruel. Poor, blonde, and beautiful Emelie can't ride off into the sunset with her true love because her wicked mother made her marry a mad elf instead. I doubted that I'd seen that particular one on DVD before.

He smirked. "You have a strange, human mind, Erin. It amuses me to see what you will think of next. Disney Princesses...Emelie will be thrilled at the comparison."

I smacked his arm. "Don't you dare tell her! You just keep going on with your history lesson, Professor."

"Where was I at before you started abusing me? Oh, yes. How could Wist change Emelie's fate? We will never know what the circumstances were that led to Wist changing Kristian and Viveka's fates. Perhaps, she was evil, or Ander's life was at stake, or maybe, she was in love with him and did not want to see him marry Viveka. No one knows. The one thing we do know is that Kristian could not stomach Anders, who was a light elf, on his father's throne. In an attempt to keep the crown, he allied himself with someone who could obtain a Norn, a creature the Norselands wanted dead for many reasons. Good reasons, I might add."

"What creature?"

"Freyr. He is known as a god in your Norse Mythology."

"I remember him. He's the guy that's always depicted with a sizable…uh, phallus. Makes perfect sense to me. I say that a male with a big penis can't be trusted. Now, those are words you can live by."

"Yes, Freyr is known for his…fertility." He looked almost unsettled. "Erin, I cannot understand your way of thinking. Are you in jest? You smile as if you are. However, your thoughts tell me that you believe in the theory."

I pondered his question for a moment. "Both, I guess. But I shouldn't limit that to males with large penises. I don't trust any male—large or small." I winked, then grinned at his discomfort. There was no doubt that he fell into the large penis department if he was worried enough to ask. Which pretty much cinched that best day of my life thing. Hands down.

He looked more confused than ever. "I see."

Laughing at his bewildered face, I asked, "Do you?"

"No. Not at all. I said before, your mind is a strange place."

"What's sad is that's the fourth time someone has told me that this week, and they can't read my mind."

"That, I can believe."

"So, how did Mr. Fertility's actions start the war?"

"Kristian sought out Freyr's doppelgänger—a creature whose treachery was famous throughout the Norselands. It was a dangerous, foolish thing to do. The real Freyr was our master once. We were given to him as a gift—as slaves."

"What? Wait. There was never any doppelgänger at all, was there?"

"You are wise for one so young. No, it was Freyr. Kristian made a grave mistake when he allied himself with someone so evil. With his mind possessed by Freyr, Kristian called off the union between the elves. Years later, after Emelie was born, Freyr had

Kristian start a war. He couldn't risk the elves becoming strong now that he was so close to getting what he lost."

"So, did Emelie go through with it…the mating to Kristian, I mean?"

"Yes, she did, the moment she came of age. It has been a great relief to have peace between the elves, though ties are still strained, especially with the young who have never known a life without war."

"Was he still possessed by Freyr when he mated her?"

"Yes, for a day, maybe two. Freyr was imprisoned long enough to break the spell."

"You're kidding? How long were they mated?"

"A couple of days. The council demanded it annulled because of the illicit fate bonding by her grandmother, Myrgjöl. fates are not allowed to be changed by anyone unless sanctioned."

"Is the council the government here?"

"Most consider them a council of peers, but yes, they do govern the Norselands to an extent."

"Your step-sister must have been upset about losing her mate. And even more so after they annulled Kristian's mating to Emelie anyway."

"The crown was the important thing to Viveka. When she found out that she had lost it to Kristian and Emelie, she went mad and did the worst thing possible. She started her own alliance with Freyr."

"What? If you can't beat them, join them?"

"So, it would seem. We believe that she joined forces with him in an attempt to control the elves in one way or the other."

I lay down next to him and stared at the ceiling. "And those two are still out there on the loose?"

"We captured Viveka at the same time as Freyr but did not

realize that she had the power to shapeshift herself into another creature, taking on their appearance, as well as their unique signature. Now that we have that information, it is a matter of time before they make a mistake and we imprison them again."

"That does not make me feel all warm and fuzzy."

"Nor should it. It is no coincidence that a spell book containing a way to rule over all of the elves found its way into the hands of one of Odin's daughters."

I hadn't thought about the spellbook being planted, and he was right, but I didn't want him to be. It made me happy to think that the spellbook coming into my life was part of my fate. It had led me to Jakob or vice versa.

"Erin." His voice held a warning.

I held up my hands. "Okay, okay. No more of that."

"Good. Now, do you have any more questions?"

"Where were you while all this was happening to your kingdom?"

"I was … away … for most of the time."

"And when you weren't?"

"Erin, Kristian orchestrated a plan that started a war between the elves that lasted the entire twenty years it took Emelie to come of age. I would be a fool to stand in his way of this when I do not want it."

"Your people…uh, elves, wouldn't have been subjected to a king that makes deals with the bad guys if you had stood in the way."

"Are you reprimanding me for my inaction?"

"No. Well, maybe. I just think that you should have stopped him when you saw how he was manipulating the situation to his favor."

"There were…I had my reasons," he stammered, his demeanor

becoming defensive.

I pursed my lips. "I hope they were good ones."

"In the end, they were not, and there is not a night that goes by that I do not regret that. I was blinded to the truth."

I yawned and nestled into his pillows. "All this makes me thankful to be ignored by my parents. I could have ended up a pawn too."

"But, thankfully, you did not. Is there anything else that your inquisitive mind wants to know?" His smirk was telling.

"Why don't you tell me? You already know, don't you?"

"Do you think so little of my gift? Your thoughts are as auditory to me, as they are also visible. I know about your 'three-step plan'."

I sat up. "I wouldn't have to plan anything if you'd get with the program."

He urged me back down, keeping a possessive hand at my neck. "I am in a program. It is the 'do not get killed by your best friend for deflowering his baby sister' program."

"There's one thing wrong with that program, Jakob."

His eyes widened. "You have not been chaste?"

"I'm twenty-five. That's practically middle-aged for a human woman."

He looked thoughtful. "I suppose."

His expression concerned me. Would he reject me because I wasn't pure?

"No," he assured me, his fangs slurring the enunciation of his words. "Your brother is the single reason I am not tearing Emelie's clothes off your body and marking you as mine." He paused to trace my bottom lip with his thumb. "I have not been 'pure' for the last forty-five hundred years."

I shivered under his touch. "Forty-five hundred?" I meant for it to come out as a question, but it was more a statement of wonder. If he was that ancient, I had good faith that he would be somewhat of a sex-god, and that made me want him more.

His grip on my neck tightened as he tensed. "Erin, you need to go to your room—now. Before we do something that we regret."

"If you taught me how to block, you wouldn't be subjected to my thoughts," I reminded him, breathless with want. I still couldn't figure out what made him so tempting to me. Sure, his looks and that sexy accented voice doesn't dissuade from the temptation, but it was more than that. It was about who he was as a male, and what he said with that beautiful voice than how attractive they made him. How could I not crave him? He was perfect.

"You would still be thinking those thoughts, Erin, and I am not yet sure that you can keep your hands to yourself, or that I want you to."

I leaned up to bestow a lingering kiss on his cheek. "That sounds promising. Good night, Jakob."

"Good day, älskling."

I stopped at the door. "Viggo told me what älskling means."

"I know he did," he said, and left it at that, presumably to keep me up for the rest of the day with cryptic phrases that I'll never be able to understand.

I lay awake in bed for hours after I left Jakob. I couldn't seem to relax. Maybe it was because it felt so strange being in a foreign land, or perhaps, it was the fact that he was sleeping shirtless in the next room. I couldn't hear any noises coming from there—thank goodness. I'd be driving him mad with my incessant thinking if he were awake.

Unable to bear my restlessness for another moment, I threw my feet over the edge of the bed and started for the door. I had to do something other than lay in this room and think—anything else.

Jakob was standing poised to knock when I opened the door. I smoothed down my bedhead. "Uh, hi."

"Nope, get back in there." He spun me in the direction of the bed with ease, his naturally austere persona replaced with an aberrant, mirthful disposition.

"But I can't sleep," I complained.

"Yes, you can," he disagreed, grinning and pulling me across the room by my hand. He climbed under the covers of my bed and held them up for me. "Get in."

I slipped in next to him. "This is so not how I thought our first time would be."

He dragged me into his body, molding himself against my back. "You are hilarious. Now, go to sleep."

Sleep? Was he kidding? I could try, but with him so close, even a coherent thought seemed a stretch at this point.

"You are not trying hard enough."

I turned around to face him. "You know, I did give you the opportunity to teach me how to block."

His white teeth gleamed in the darkness. "So you did."

I waited on him to elaborate.

"I am not going to. I am trying to sleep, as you should be."

Pouting, I asked, "Don't I, at least, get a good night kiss?"

His eyes popped open. "You are relentless, Erin. Go. To. Sleep."

I gave him a soft, unexpected peck on his lips. "You came to my bed half-naked. You don't see how that gesture might have been misconstrued as you wanting to have sex with me?"

He moved to trap me beneath him. "Make no mistake, älskling. I want to take you. I have wanted you since the moment you called me."

Arching against him, my body begged for what he offered. I was so ready. He placed blistering hot kisses along my jaw and whispered soft, foreign words against my neck. "Please, Jakob," I pleaded with him.

Dragging his lips across my cheek to my mouth, he licked my lips open, all of his earlier control lost when I responded in kind. Panting, he pushed himself up on his knees to try to compose himself.

"Jakob?"

I cried out in surprise when he used a combination of his fangs and hands to rip the front of Emelie's sweater open. "If we do this, Soren cannot know, Erin. Promise me." His voice was hoarse with restraint.

"I promise," I responded without hesitation, and then took a deep breath—and another. I was so desperate to have him inside me. I would've agreed to anything.

"Erin? Your eyes, they—" He broke off in alarm.

I could see the reflection of blue flames in his eyes. "What is that, Jakob? Am I on fire?"

No sooner than the words left my lips, a fire ignited inside of me. It licked down my arms and legs as if someone had put a match to gasoline. I screamed, and Jakob sprang into action, picking me up to run to the bathroom. Lowering me into the tub, he turned on a spray of freezing, cold water.

Within seconds, the flames were out, but my skin remained untouched. "What just happened?" I asked, through chattering teeth.

He turned the shower off and pushed the wet hair back from my eyes. "You are a fire-walker, älskling."

"Why didn't the fire burn anything?"

"What you produced is a magical fire. If you had concentrated long enough, you could have burnt the house to the ground. There can be no doubt that you are an elf now. Fire-walking is a rare elven gift. There are maybe a hundred in all of the light and dark elves combined."

"I'm gathering that sex is also a rare elven gift."

He laughed and handed me a towel. "You are wicked, Erin. You alone would lament the loss of sex when you have just realized that you have been bestowed with a much-coveted power."

"Yippee," I muttered, dropping my head back against the porcelain rim of the bathtub to stare at the ceiling. What else could happen to keep us apart?

"I will get you some dry clothes."

I didn't spare him a glance as he left. This whole thing had been so messed up—a complete disaster. I'd hoped for a romantic night that I would remember with fondness, not a night where the highlight was me setting myself on fire and ending up a drowned rat.

"Do not be so dramatic, Erin. You look just as beautiful the way you are now as you ever do." He frowned. "Wait. That did not come out right."

Accepting the shirt he held out, I stood and shed the ripped sweater. I didn't have any dignity left. "The bra is coming off," I warned.

"I hope so."

Surprised and inspired, I unhooked the front of my bra and let in fall into the tub.

His breath whooshed out. "You are perfect," he whispered.

Well, that was encouraging. "Are you sure you want me to put on this shirt?"

"No, though I know it isn't right. I am not sure that I can stop myself. The temptation is unbearable."

Taking advantage of this unheard of lapse in Jakob's

judgment, I slipped the jeans over my hips and stepped out of them, straightening just in time to catch him adjusting himself. I gave him my best bewitching smile and stepped out of the tub towards him.

"What are you up to, Erin?"

I sashayed past him to the bed swinging my hips provocatively. "What do you mean?"

He was hot on my trail as I climbed into bed and under the blanket. "Erin, what are you doing to me?" He motioned to the hard sex that was by no means concealed by his boxer briefs. "You are enjoying seeing me suffer, are you not?"

I looked from his eyes to his erection and held my thumb and forefinger up, grinning. "A little bit."

He groaned. "Mischievous little elf. How shall I punish you?"

"I could think of a couple hundred ways."

He walked to the other side of the bed and climbed under the covers, pressing himself into my back as he whispered into my ear. "I am sure you can, but you know, I think making you wait to get this cock between your thighs will be punishment enough."

I gasped in mock horror. "You wouldn't."

He slid his hand across my ribs to cup my breast. "Would I not?"

I moaned in satisfaction. I wanted his hands all over my body.

He trailed his fangs across my shoulder. "Where do you want them, älskling?" He trailed his fingers down my stomach, inching lower as he spoke. "Here?"

"Yes," I sighed, moving against his fingers and reaching for his erection.

He hissed when my hand grazed the fabric. "Careful, Erin. We cannot get out of control."

I was way past losing control. His talented fingers already had me on the edge of orgasm. "Please," I begged him.

Growling, he pierced my shoulder with his sharpened canines, and everything went black. I thought that I'd been struck blind. Then, everything came barreling back in fast-forward as I reached my peak, screaming out his name.

It was a minute or two before I could even speak again. "Jakob?" I was hoarse and sagging against him.

"Hmmm?" He licked my shoulder and bit down again.

I sucked a pleasured breath through my teeth. "How opposed are you to mating someone who isn't your true mate?"

"You are the one—my fated. I feel it when I look at you, when you touch me. It cannot be the spell."

I knew how he felt. It was as if we had a force-field around us, a magnet of sorts. I turned to face him. "Are you sure?"

"At first, I thought that my desire for you was false, that it was your beauty or the book that was causing the attraction, but now, I am positive that is not the case."

I took a deep breath, in anticipation. "What's changed?"

"Everything, älskling."

I could feel his heartbeat pounding against my sensitized skin. Turning over, I put my ear to the light hair on his chest. "Your heart is racing."

"Your blood has made me intoxicated, and your thoughts are…arousing. He chuckled. "You are not the innocent female I thought you were when we met, Erin."

I was trying hard to ignore the need to take advantage of him while he was still rock hard. "Are you disappointed?"

"No. My concern is that Soren will be provoked to murder me if he finds out about our involvement. We must keep what will be between us a secret—for now."

I swallowed hard. "What's going to be between us?"

He spoke without taking his eyes off of mine. "When we are allowed to be mated, nothing will keep me from doing things to you that will make me hard as steel when I reflect upon them."

My breath caught.

He smirked. "You have nothing to say?"

I had plenty to say. First and foremost on my mind was, "Why won't you fuck me?"

Laying back, he sighed. "Do you think that I do not want to? All of the blood in my body has circulated to my dick!"

"And that's exactly why we should do something about it. It could become a medical problem."

He was intrigued. "What do you suggest? Wait. Damn it. Do not answer that. We cannot, Erin. We should not have done what we have already."

"Why not? Who's going to know?"

"I will. Think about it in terms of Victorian times on Midgard. It is much the same here. If I make love to you and we are found out, it will taint your honor, and you will be shunned by our kind."

"There's no one here to find us out Jakob, and I'm pretty sure that when I go back to Midgard, no one will care if we had sex there."

His expression became serious. "You will not be going back to Midgard. I will not be persuaded otherwise. I cannot protect you there." He paused to gauge my reaction. "I understand if you are upset by it. It will be hard to leave your life behind."

"Honestly, I'm not upset at all. That bookstore is killing me. Yes, I love it. But working twelve hour days, three hundred and sixty-two days out of the year, is starting to take its toll on my sanity." I stopped. "How am I going to support myself while I'm in Álfheim?"

"I will support you, Erin. It will be my privilege as your future mate," he said, a little offended.

I straddled his waist, sighing when he cupped my breasts. "Do you know what my privilege is, as your future mate?"

"No. Indeed, I am almost afraid to ask."

Leaning down to nip him on the lips, I started working my way down his stomach, breathing in the scent of spice on his skin, embedding it into my memory, between every descending kiss.

He laced his fingers into my hair, tightening them to stop me. "Erin, please. If you do not learn to block your thoughts today, Soren will strike me down for what you are trying to do."

I gave up and sat down beside him. "Why can't we just tell him about us if we're true mates?"

"We will. It has been one day. Give him a chance to become reconciled with the fact that you will be mated to any male first."

I brought his palm to my mouth, kissing the center. "I don't want any male. I want you."

"That just reaffirms the fact that I must teach you to shield your thoughts. We cannot delay. What do you have up there, a card catalog? The level of organization is incredible. I could pick out anything I wanted to see."

"So, my mind is a loose cannon? Is that what you're saying?"

"Yes." Smiling, he moved to the foot of the bed, folding his legs beneath him. I pulled on the shirt he gave me in the bathroom, mirrored his position, then waited...and waited. He didn't say a word, just stared at my face.

Confused, I waved my hand in front of him. "Are you still there?"

His cunning smile widened. "Yes."

I narrowed my eyes in distrust. "Why are you smirking?"

"I am waiting for you to realize that you are naked from the waist down."

Glancing down at my exposed bottom half, I snatched the

pillow into my lap. "I did not mean to do that."

He tapped his temple. "I know."

"Then, why didn't you tell me sooner?"

"I was enjoying the view?"

"You are as bad as Nils!"

He shook his head, horrified. "There is no way that could ever be true."

I giggled. "That bad, huh?"

"You have no idea." He lowered his gaze. "Do you want to put on something? I am ready when you are."

Lowering my eyes to the straining bulge in his lap, I lifted my brows. "I can see that."

He tackled me to the mattress, placing passionate kisses on my lips and jaw on the way down. "Do try to control yourself, you naughty elf."

I sighed in genuine discontent. "If I must."

He kissed me again with a resolute look on his face. "You must."

I traced the ridges of his back with my fingers. "Fine. Let's do this." And by do this, I mean, hot, enthusiastic sex.

Laughing, he asked, "Do you think it is within your power to ignore your preoccupation with my penis for a few minutes? I have something important to teach you."

"Oh no. I'm not making any promises. You do realize the aforementioned penis is in a most favorable spot between my legs, right?"

"Believe me, I could not be more aware of where it is, but in the interest of my safety, I am asking you to try to control yourself."

I pretended to give it deep thought. "I could give you three, maybe four minutes."

"How magnanimous of you." He shook his head and made an unsuccessful attempt at hiding his smile. "I will start off by pushing a boost of magic into your system to help you along. Are you ready?"

As I started to tell Jakob the exact thing I wanted pushed into me, he put his hand over my mouth. "Do not say it. I am in agony."

I could so relate to that.

Intertwining the fingers of his right hand with my left, he nodded, and I felt an immediate tingling that ran up my arms and made my hair stand on end. It was a delicious feeling.

"Make a conscious effort to keep me out, Erin. Close off what you do not want me to see or hear. "

"Okay." I squeezed my eyes shut and focused on keeping my thoughts private, though I knew that it would be easier said than done. It was almost impossible to think of anything but the weight of Jakob between my legs.

"Perfect!" Jakob exclaimed, scaring the life out of me. "It took Emelie all day to learn what you have just done in one try. Try to keep me out for as long as you can."

I smiled. "If it keeps you where you are, I can do this all day."

Jakob shook his head and sat up on his knees. "You are evil, älskling."

"It's hereditary, I think."

"That, I believe."

After several more successful attempts, I gave up on not yawning. "I'm fading fast, Jakob."

"Sleep. Just remember what I have taught you in the evening when you wake up."

"I won't forget." Imagining that my secrets were locked tight in an impenetrable bubble was as easy as, well, imagining that my secrets were locked in an impenetrable bubble. I couldn't believe that Emelie had had trouble learning this. It was so simple.

"You cannot, älskling." His worried voice matched his expression.

"You know, you're making Soren sound a little scary."

He wrapped his arms around me and kissed my neck where he'd bitten me. "He is fair and just. You have nothing to fear."

"But?"

He sighed. "But, because we are not mated, we are not allowed to act on our impulses, no matter how intense the attraction is between us."

"I'm kind of okay with keeping this a secret."

"I am glad to hear you say that, because next time, I will not stop—even if you are on fire."

CHAPTER FOUR

In the evening, I was awakened by an earthquake, or what I thought was an earthquake. When my eyes snapped open, Nils was the first thing I saw. He was holding out a shifting stone while shaking the bed with an urgent bouncing of his foot. "Wake up! Soren is here," he hissed.

Jakob disappeared with the stone just as I jumped out of bed and ran, half-naked, to the dresser for another pair of Emelie's jeans.

Nils watched me yank them on. "What are you doing to our resident do-gooder, Erin? This is the kind of thing that I would get caught doing."

"Are you going to tell Soren?"

He burst out laughing and put his arm around me. "I live for shit like this. You have no idea how long I've waited to have ammunition against the altar boy."

"Not one word to Soren, wolf. I don't care what you do with the information, as long as it doesn't get back to my brother. I mean it."

He held the door open. "I'm starting to think that Jakob is perfect for you. Both of you are little old ladies—always worried about something going wrong.

"It's called caution, Nils."

Grinning, he said, "Caution? Nope, never heard of it."

That did not surprise me.

If Soren suspected anything out of the ordinary, I couldn't tell. He sat on the sofa, dressed in an average pair of faded jeans and a University of Oslo t-shirt, his cool demeanor normal—for him

51

anyway.

"Was your night pleasant, sister?"

"It was. Well, it was after I got the valknut tattoo thing. Jakob taught me how to block my thoughts and Nils phased for me. It was fun." My lips stretched into a manic smile. I needed to reel it in a bit.

Unperturbed, Soren returned my smile. "I am glad that you enjoyed yourself. However, I am afraid that what we will be doing this evening will not be nearly as enjoyable. Father has requested your presence at his castle."

My excitement over meeting my father for the first time was extinguished with Jakob's entrance. His face was horrified.

"Are you insane, Soren? You cannot take her there."

"He has asked to see her. It is best not to make him ask again."

Nils huffed. "This doesn't feel right."

"No, it does not," Soren agreed. "However, if the escapees are in league with Odin, this may be our best chance at finding out what they are planning."

Jakob was appalled. "By risking your sister? It is a dangerous move to make."

"Is it that dangerous?" I asked.

"No. Let us go," he answered, distracted as he took my hand. It was obvious that Nils and Jakob were making their opinions known in a silent conversation.

"Guys, come on. The sooner you let us go, the sooner we will return." I tapped my foot, impatient to get it all over with. "We'll be back pretty quick, right?"

"Yes. I will keep in contact, Jakob, should we need your assistance."

Jakob nodded, but I could tell he didn't want me to go. His troubled face was the last thing I saw as we materialized to Asgard.

The trip to the forest surrounding Odin's castle was the work of a moment. As soon as the blinding, bright light faded from my vision, I looked around in wonder, over the moon to see a world so different. Álfheim seemed to be similar to Earth, but Ásgard was surreal. Everything from the plants to the towering trees had a hazy, almost shimmering quality. It was magical. There was no other word for it.

Soren pointed at the monstrosity of a castle dominating the landscape ahead. "Odin's castle."

"Are we walking?" The distance to the castle was at least five miles if I was lucky. I'd never make half that in the heels I was wearing.

"Yes. I thought it would give us an opportunity to talk."

"Sounds good," I said, putting on a fake smile. His hopeful face was so adorable. I hated the thought of disappointing him, even though I was pretty sure that he would have to carry me halfway into the trek.

An unusual smile lit his features. "I find that I am excited to learn more about you. All of our other siblings are at least a thousand years old. It is refreshing to meet one so young." He extended his arm. "Tell me about your human life in Midgard."

I took his arm, then jerked my hand away. "You're vibrating."

He laughed. "So are you. Your magic is bursting to get out."

He could say that again. "Yeah, I know. I set myself on fire this morning."

"Are you injured?" He stopped, looked at my hands and touched my face.

"Oh, no. I'm fine. I'm a fire-walker. At least, that's what Jakob said."

Soren's face was unbelieving. *"Did you say a fire-walker?"* His voice came from inside my head. *"Speak to me using your thoughts."*

"That's what Jakob said," I sent at him, hoping that I'd done it in the correct way.

Soren nodded and looked around. *"We are going to experiment."*

I was wary. *"What do you mean?"*

He gathered a handful of leaves and put them in a pile on the path. *"Stand back."*

A sharp crack sounded a moment before a bolt of lightning struck the leaves, and they burst into flame.

"See if the fire burns you."

I shot a crazed look at him. *"Are you out of your mind?"*

"I will heal you, should you become injured. Rest assured."

"Okay." Leaning down, I reached for the fire, holding my breath. It was warm, but not unpleasant. It kind of tickled. I glanced up at Soren in awe and laughed with joy. *"Wow."*

He shared in my jubilation. *"You are amazing, sister! See if you can pick up the flame in your hands."*

I didn't have a clue how to do what he asked of me, so I gave him a blank stare and waited for instructions.

His crimson eyes glowed with excitement. *"My apologies, your lack of fear makes me forgetful of your ignorance. I believe that you will adjust to the Norselands with ease."*

Lack of fear? I was terrified of everything, from the spooky moss covering the trees to the glittery quality of the air surrounding us. Most of all, I was afraid to meet my Father.

"I can see by your expression that I have been mistaken."

"I'm sorry. I am trying to be brave."

Hugging me into his side, he said, *"There is no need to apologize, Erin. I have asked too much of you already."*

"No, let me try."

Nodding in approval, he gave me the go-ahead motion. *"Just scoop it up into your hand, if it does not obey."*

"Obey?"

"Yes. You are mistress of the flame. It shall be your constant companion. I can see it in your eyes even as we stand here."

"I hope you do not plan on taking the fire-walker to your father, Víðarr."

We both spun to see the owner of the tiny voice that caught us off guard. I was surprised to find a small female, dressed in an elegant gauzy green gown. Her brunette curls were pinned up high on her head in dual purpose—to avoid the delicate, gossamer wings that were beating madly to keep her at our eye level and to hold up the elaborate jeweled crown she wore.

Soren pulled me down into a kneeling position with him. "Queen Layla, we thank you for the gift of your company. Allow me to introduce my sister, Erin of Midgard."

She flew to Soren's eye level and frowned. "Midgard you say?" Her voice was pleasant, but her expression said otherwise. "Why have I not heard of this sister in my own domain?"

Soren stood and helped me to my feet. "She was found on an excursion by Jakob Väsen, a mere day ago."

"The elf king?"

"No, your majesty. Kristian Väsen is the ruler of the dark elves. I speak of his brother."

Her frown deepened. "Do not trifle with me, Son of Odin. Kristian Väsen could not lead himself out of the mouth of a dragon, much less rule the whole of the dark elves."

Soren agreed, without a second's hesitation. "Yes, your majesty."

The queen turned her attention to me next. "I am the queen of Älvornas Rike, the land of the faeries." She paused. "Erin, you are from my own beloved Midgard. May I ask your opinion on males who do not honor their promises?"

"I think—" I started and then stopped. I didn't know how to answer her.

"With the truth," Soren urged in my mind.

"I believe that a man...I mean, male, is as good as his word, your majesty."

She harrumphed in Soren's direction. "I see who got the brilliant mind in the family." To me, she just gave a bright smile and said, "Call me Layla. Any creature who is wise enough to know the truth of that statement so soon in their existence should have the right."

I smiled and curtseyed. "Thank you, Layla."

She floated to my shoulder and stage-whispered into my ear. "Now that we are sisters in friendship, what would you say if I told you that your brother has not kept his promise to a dying friend—his best friend?"

My brother's sigh told me that he was guilty of her accusation.

"What is the promise?"

Soren's voice was full of disdain. "I am trying to keep my promise to Cedric. His true mate is hidden and quite mad. You know this, majesty."

In the space of a second, Layla grew to our height and poked Soren in the chest in anger. "Don't you dare take that tone with me, Víðarr! You've had two years to do this one simple thing."

"Simple thing? Are you the fucking mad one?"

I sucked in a shocked breath. "Soren!"

Her calm demeanor didn't waver. "Might I suggest that you use your sister to find her? She is a fire-walker, I believe."

The anger faded from Soren's features. "You are right. Why did I not think of that? How can I thank you, majesty?"

She feigned deep thought while twirling a lock of her brunette hair around her finger. "Stop being yourself?"

I burst out laughing, and she joined me. Similar to Jakob and Viggo, the faery queen was pretty down to Earth for someone belonging to royalty.

"That is a helpful suggestion, Layla. Come, Erin. We must take our leave."

"That's Queen Layla, son of Odin. Take care that you do not make us wait too much longer. My humor grows short."

"I understand. You have my word," he said, dipping into a deep bow.

I followed suit. "Goodbye, Layla."

She hugged me. "Goodbye, my new friend." She looked past Soren to the two steel-faced but beautiful male faeries carrying a pale green shifting stone. "Take this stone with you as a gift of our friendship. It will help you until you can find your own magic."

I took the stone from the two tiny males. "Thank you. This is too generous."

One of the faeries whispered in Layla's ear. "Not at all, Erin. Soren, please take your leave now. Loki has been alerted to your arrival."

No sooner than the words left her lips, Soren grasped my arm, and the forest disappeared.

Emelie's smiling face greeted us when we arrived at their apartment. "Hey, nice outfit, Erin."

I struck a pose. "You like this? I borrowed it from my sister-in-law." I grinned. "I just love saying that!"

She grinned back. "I love it just as much as you do! Can you believe we've been married for two years, and he hasn't introduced me to any of his thousand or so brothers and sisters?"

"That's terrible," I said in mock horror, giving Soren a stern shake of my head. "You should find a new mate, Emelie."

She picked at the sleeve of her top and looked over to him in distaste. "He was an awful choice."

"That is quite enough, you two." Soren kissed her cheek, and they shared a quick, secret smile. They complimented each other so well. No matter their vast differences, they were perfect for one another. I hoped that, in time, he would approve of Jakob as my mate. I wanted my own compliment.

Emelie showed us into the kitchen where she was busy making gingerbread cookies. "I'll make tea while you tell me how the meeting went."

"The meeting did not take place. We were stopped by Queen Layla, who advised us against it."

"Uh oh. Did she mention Cedric?"

"She did. However, she was helpful instead of cryptic today."

I smiled and hopped up onto a bar stool with a flourish. "That's because we're super best friends now, and you're a male who reneges on his promises." He rolled his eyes at my crowing. I responded by sticking out my tongue.

Emelie made herself comfortable next to me. "Sounds as if she wasn't too happy."

"She wasn't. She made herself big and poked Soren in the chest. It was pretty awesome."

"What the hell did you do?"

"Nothing, little one. She was just agitated. It is normal for her." He shot me a squinty-eyed, 'Shut your mouth, or I'll kick your ass' look.

If Emelie's rolled eyes were any indication, she wasn't convinced, but she kept quiet about it. "What else did she say?"

He sighed. "She said that Loki had been freed from his imprisonment."

Emelie stood up, her eyes shimmering pools of mercury as she had a vision. "Odin is desperate. He knows, Soren."

"What does that mean? Who is Loki?" I'd heard of him, of course, but knew nothing about his history. My coming here really underscored my need to learn the sagas of Norse Mythology. How I wished I'd devoted more time to it in my reading. Maybe then, I wouldn't feel so woefully uninformed and unprepared.

"It means that shit just got real," Emelie told me, going back to work on her cookies.

"Little one, don't scare her. No one is in any danger within the rebellion. It is true; Loki is a trickster. A more cunning male than him I have never known, but he will not go against us. His actions will be against the one responsible for the wasted millennia he spent in pain."

"Pain?"

His brows lifted. "You have not heard that ridiculous tale of the goddess Skaði punishing Loki by placing a serpent over his head? It was once thought that if his mate did not catch the poison before it dripped onto him, Midgard would tremor with the intensity of his pain."

"No offense, Soren, but Norse Mythology is weird. I know little about it."

Emelie shot her fist up in triumph. "Yes! See? It's not just me. Those stories are mega-creepy."

Soren continued without acknowledging her as if he was accustomed to this kind of outburst from his mate. "Apart from the earthquakes, it is an accurate storytelling. That is a rarity among the sagas. Some do have a bit of truth behind them. However, a good portion is fiction."

"I don't like this, Soren. Why would he think it necessary to send Loki after Erin?"

"If Odin has recalled Loki from his torture, there has to be an important reason for him doing so. Baldur was a favorite son, and there is no doubt that fortune was on Loki's side the night of the murder. Odin may have spared him, but he will never trust him again. What I would not give to find out what Father is up to."

"Damn it! Why can't I see it? What kind of Norn can't see the freaking future? And don't you dare give me that practice makes perfect crap, Soren, or so help me, these gingerbread men will be the last cookies baked in this oven."

Someone needed to stop the madness. Cookies were at stake. I laid a hand on my brother's arm. "She's threatening you with cookies, Soren. I think you should heed the warning."

"I would not dream of mentioning that practice does indeed make perfect," he said, with a mischievous grin. "That would be cruel."

"For Pete's sake!" I yelled, not quite loud enough to cover Emelie's cursing. "Think about your loved ones. We all suffer from a cookie shortage. Some of us more than others."

"In that case, I concede. My mate's magic must be obstructed by an unseen source. A binding spell, perhaps."

The whites of Emelie's eyes were hidden under a sudden silver sheen of her magic. "Soren," she started.

He took her hands. "What is it, love?"

"I'm seeing Freyr and Viveka."

"Can you see where they are hiding?"

She furrowed her brow in concentration. "I can't make it out. The vision is clouded by darkness. I only see a tall, crudely built stone building."

Soren stood when her eyes cleared. All traces of his earlier humor were gone. "This changes things. We need to call a meeting and make a plan of action. Emelie, will you contact Nils, Jakob, and Viggo?"

"Of course," she said, getting up. "Come with me, Erin. You're looking a bit peaked."

A blush filled my cheeks. "Sorry, everything seems to move so fast here."

She laughed. "Not to alarm you, but all of this is because of you. We haven't had this much excitement in two years."

"Great," I mumbled, my voice dripping with sarcasm.

She held out her hand. "Come on, you need sunshine and girl talk. Stat."

I couldn't have agreed more. "That sounds great. You'll tell me about the fire-walker thing later, Soren?"

"Of course. Go have your girl talk. I'll be here, still trying to figure out what girl talk is when you get done."

I grinned and gave him a quick hug. "Thanks."

Emelie led me to a bright sunroom at the back of the apartment that displayed a good portion of Ásgard. My father's castle was a speck in the distance from here, and I was almost sad that we didn't get a chance to travel through the forest. It was amazing, even from this distance. I sat on a large chaise with Emelie and stared out into the expanse. "This place is beautiful."

"It is. Soren chose a beautiful place for us to live. This apartment actually sat vacant for a few decades while he waited on me. Isn't that romantic?"

"Unbelievably romantic."

I could tell she was excited to have someone to talk to, but I couldn't help but think how heartbreaking it must have been for Soren to have this empty reminder of his true mate when her mother united Emelie's fate with the king's.

Whether it was her magic or the guilty look on my face, she saw right through me. With narrowed eyes twinkling with mirth, she put her hands on her hips. "They told you about Kristian, didn't they?"

"Kind of. They told me to ask you for specifics."

She shrugged. "Let me guess. Viggo?" When I nodded, she continued. "There's not much to tell. Kristian is a sweet male, but he's not my true mate. You should meet him. He's handsome and single."

Oh my God, she was trying to hook me up with my almost-boyfriend's brother. I tried not to squirm. "Uh, I'm not looking for anyone right now. Thank you for thinking of me though."

"Let me know if you change your mind. I'm seeing you with a Väsen. I can sense the signature in your future. What about Viggo?" She wiggled her eyebrows. "He's...nice."

I cringed. "For a brother, maybe."

"Huh. I thought for sure it would be one of them."

I wondered why she hadn't made the connection between Jakob and I. Jakob would have been the logical next choice, but she didn't mention him at all. I guess it's possible that she thought his serious demeanor didn't mesh well with my free-spirited ways. But, somehow, I didn't believe that was what it was, especially with her own mating having striking similarities to my own situation.

Emelie thought about my future for a minute more and then shook her head as if to clear it. "I know you have questions, so I'm just going to let you ask me anything you want, and I'll answer to the best of my ability. Just don't tell Soren. How does that sound?"

"Awesome. The first thing I want to know is what Soren discovered from the book.

"Not much. The one thing that we know for sure is that it came from Odin's library. He isn't in the habit of loaning out important artifacts, so we assume that either Freyr or Viveka stole it while they were there on a visit and left it with you because you alone have the power to cast the spell. How they knew that you would have that power is the mystery."

"Wow. How crafty of them."

"That is Viveka to a tee. I suspect she holds more of a role in this than Freyr even realizes. Why would she go to all this trouble to serve under him? That cannot be what her ultimate goal is. There's no way."

"How did they know that I was Odin's daughter? Do you think they know who my mother is?"

She nodded. "They must. Viveka knows a great many things that she shouldn't because of her talent. She even lived among us, disguised as my great aunt Katrine, for a short time. That is where the promise to the faeries comes in."

I almost fell off my seat; I turned to her so fast. "What!"

She picked up a box of tissues from the table and put them in her lap. "Viveka came to us disguised as Katrine when Soren summoned her to help me cope with my new Norn abilities. My great-aunt was a Dis," she explained. "They're kind of like assistants to Norns. Anyway, Soren's friend, Cedric, seemed to fall in love with her, and she acted much the same way. Her attention was consumed by him. We had no idea she wasn't who she said she was. What reason did we have to believe anything else?"

"That she is able to do that is scary. How can you ever be sure anyone is who they say they are?"

"You can't. Soren doesn't enjoy hearing me say this, but I think, for a moment, she forgot that she was there against us. I saw her after Cedric was mortally wounded by Freyr. She was grieving for him as a widow would. It is the one time I've ever felt pity for her."

"How did you find out she was an impostor?"

"That is the most amazing part. We didn't have a clue until after we captured Freyr and Viveka and put them in a cell. Not even twenty-four hours later, we have her on camera shifting back into Katrine's form and freeing him."

"You haven't seen them since?"

"Not a peep in two years."

I sighed and sat back. "I am never sleeping again."

She gave me a sage look and nodded. "That would be safest."

"So, how do the faeries fit into the story?"

Plucking a tissue out of the box, she wiped her eyes. "Cedric was a great friend to the faeries that lived in the garden of Soren's ruined estate in Sweden. We buried him there. The faeries just want to make sure Cedric's memory is honored by Soren keeping his promise to save his true mate. Soren, of course, wants more than anything to be able to fulfill the promise, but how? We don't even know where she is."

"Save her? From what? Herself?"

Emelie's eyes widened. "I'm an idiot. The faeries are known to be vague to the point of ridiculousness. Why did I not think of this before?"

I was confused. "Think of what?"

She got up and grabbed my hand. "Come on, we have to tell the guys, now."

Lost, I followed her lead and tried to look as if I knew what the hell was going on.

Soren stopped talking in mid-sentence when we entered. "Emelie, what is it?"

She was so excited she could barely speak. "Erin, she—she figured out the riddle! It's so simple. It was staring us in the face!"

"Darling, I have no idea what you are talking about."

"The faeries! They're vague."

Soren was mystified. "Yes, love, they are."

"I mean that 'saving her' is vague. What if they mean for us to save her from herself?"

"Shit."

I looked up for Nils' when I heard his voice and spotted Jakob sitting in a dark corner, smoke curling upward from a lit cigarette between his fingers. My eyes couldn't have found him faster if he were sitting in a spotlight. I drank him in, wanting so much to kiss his lips, to feel his hands on my body.

To my disappointment, Jakob only nodded to me as if we were passing on the street. It was obvious he knew how to play it cool. Me? I knew how to drool and draw hearts around his name in my journal. I was pathetic.

Soren was thankfully oblivious to my reaction. He was ecstatic. "Erin, you are a miracle! Jakob, you know Viveka best. Go to Uppsala and see if you can find her."

"Where do I start? She could be anywhere."

I spoke up. "Emelie said she was in a crudely built stone building."

"Yes, a tall one," she elaborated.

I paced the room, thinking. A tall, crudely built building in Uppsala, what would that be? The answer came to me out of the blue. "The temple at Uppsala! Wasn't the temple built for humans to worship Odin, Freyr, and Thor?"

"Yes. How did you come up with this idea?" Soren asked, amazed.

"I read a book on human sacrifices once." They all gave me looks of disconcert. "I own a bookstore. I read a lot. Stop looking at me."

Soren started barking orders. "Jakob, forget Viveka, look for the temple. Start with the original site. Nils, find your father, and then meet up with Jakob. I will visit my brother, Thor."

"How amazing," I said, sitting down before my weak knees buckled under my weight. How could I have forgotten that Thor was my brother, too?

Soren huffed. "He is not that amazing. Trust me."

Emelie giggled at her mate's reaction. "You're cute when

you're jealous, Soren."

He ignored the smattering of laughter around the room. "Viggo, can you stay with Emelie and Erin?"

"Stay with two beautiful females instead of fighting the bad guys," he said. "I thought you would never ask."

In under a minute everyone was gone. Viggo clapped his hands together. "Let us go shopping. Those heels have to be killing your feet, Erin."

I was so happy that I hugged him tightly. "You're a mind reader."

"True," he bragged. "Which means that I cannot help but notice that you learned how to block. Come on, female—spill. What's going on between you and Captain Serious? He's smoking today. That means something big must have happened last night."

"What?" Emelie screeched. "You and Jakob? Oh. Holy. Shit!"

I smacked Viggo on the shoulder. "It's supposed to be a secret! What's the point of even teaching me how to block, if you're just going to blurt things out?"

He winked. "We are all girlfriends here. No one is going to out you to Soren. Give us the scoop."

Sending a questioning look Emelie's way, I couldn't stop the smile that spread across my face when she gave me the 'hurry up and spill' motion with her hands. "He thinks that we're true mates."

They both froze.

"He said that?" Viggo asked, in a voice that was way too calm to be normal.

The atmosphere in the room had turned serious. I didn't understand what I'd said to cause it.

"Uh, Em lay your hands on Erin and see what you can see."

She held her hands out, and I didn't hesitate to put mine in hers.

"Come on Em, tell us something."

Her silver eyes shimmered in the firelight. "Damn it! It's a Väsen. That much I know. I keep seeing the castle, but that puts you with Kristian."

My heart full of hope deflated.

"Don't get discouraged. My visions aren't perfected just yet. Maybe Jakob will be king one day."

"Maybe," I agreed, but I didn't believe it. I remembered what Jakob said about not wanting to get stabbed in the back by his brother.

"Yeah, Erin. I could see you as the queen in the future.

"Sure, the dark elves would just love to have a daughter of Odin as their monarch." I rolled my eyes.

Viggo thought it over for a second. "It may not be a complete disaster."

I threw my hands up. "Let's go get me a pair of sneakers, or sandals, or whatever elves wear on their feet before my blisters have blisters."

Viggo smiled. "I'm a one problem at a time type of guy anyway."

CHAPTER FIVE

Displaying oddly shaped fruits and vegetables, strange animals, and many tables of magical potions and contraptions, the marketplace was precisely what I'd hoped it would be. Viggo obviously felt the same. He was a kid in a candy store, flitting from one stall to the next, though the villagers stared at him as if he had a second head.

"Erin, they have ambrosia! You have to taste it before you go! So delicious!"

He ran off before I could say anything. "Does he act like this all the time?" I whispered.

Emelie watched him with a loving smile on her lips as he bartered for an amulet in a good-natured, animated way. "Yes. He's adorable, isn't he?"

Bemused, I watched him leap with victory after he out-haggled the male. "How is he still single? He'd be snapped up in a minute on Earth."

"That's not the way it works here. You're expected to wait on your mate, no matter how long it takes. My grandmother, Myrgjöl, said that his mate is to come soon. He's pretty lucky. Soren waited six thousand years for me. Can you imagine how horrible that must have been?"

"No, I can't. I'm twenty-five, and I already consider myself a spinster," I said, laughing at Viggo's high-pitched reaction when he saw a baby dragon for sale. "Viggo's mate has her work cut out for her. He has more zest for life than I've ever seen."

"That he does." She shook her head in exasperation as she saw him bow dramatically to yet another group of dark elf females, causing them to giggle and fawn over his purchases. "He makes me tired just watching him."

After a few minutes, Viggo looked over at us in apology and convinced the females to go about their shopping so that he could return to us.

"Nice of you to join us," I griped.

"Finally!" Emelie added.

"Is my allure to the opposite sex making you jealous, or is it that you want to be the object of my affection, poppet?"

"I just want shoes." I'd long since given up wearing the heels and was now walking barefoot through the grass behind the stalls.

He put an arm around both of us. "Fear not, my surly friends. I found the perfect elven slippers for her majesty. You do not think I stopped those females for any other reason, do you? Who else would know better where we could get the most comfortable shoes for your dainty little feet?"

I was ashamed of my short temper. "I'm sorry. I didn't mean to get testy."

Emelie threw Viggo's arm off of her shoulders and glared in my direction. "Are you freaking kidding me? Don't you dare believe that bull!"

I narrowed my eyes at Viggo and stepped out of his reach. "You jerk!"

He feigned innocence, walking ahead of us in the pretense of pointing out the correct booth, the sedate smile never leaving his lips as he held up a pair of dark blue flats. "Look at these, Erin. They are so you."

"I think we can take him," I whispered to Emelie. "You and me, together; we can kick his ass."

She linked her arm with mine. "We'll hash out a plan tonight. Count on it. He's had this coming for a while."

Two goblets of ambrosia, four new outfits, and three pairs of fashionable elven flats later, we collapsed onto the sofa at

Emelie's. "I'm not sure if I want to thank you for taking me to the market or not."

Viggo was affronted. "How can you say that? Look how beautiful you are in your new clothes. Midnight blue suits your new eye color."

"New eye color?"

Smiling, he led me to a mirror in the hallway. "I cannot believe you are a fire-walker. Your eyes have been alight with flame all evening, poppet. You didn't notice the villagers staring?"

"No." I'd thought that they were all staring at Viggo's comical personality. "Should I hang out in the bathroom, just in case I catch fire?"

Emelie giggled at my ignorance. "This is hilarious. I wish I had a camera to capture the look on your face right now."

"You're super helpful, Em. You know that?"

"If you do not project it outward, we should all be fine," Viggo assured me, smirking.

I examined the wavering glow of my eyes. "Have you known many of us?"

He shook his head. "Not at all. It is a rare gift, and it is even rarer to keep the gift throughout one's lifetime."

"I don't understand."

He leaned against the wall and watched me watching myself with interest. "Magic is a privilege, Erin. If you abuse it or use it for evil, you will lose it. Maybe not right away, but it will leave and never return."

I pursed my lips. "If that's true, why haven't Viveka and the Freyr lost theirs yet?"

"We have no idea what Viveka might or might not have lost. The one magic that we know for sure that she has is her ability to shapeshift. As for Freyr, he has an endless amount of artificial magic. I am afraid that capturing him will not be good enough this time. Even the council agrees that his death will be a blessing to all of the Norselands."

The thought of Viggo fighting against that kind of power scared me. "Is it you, Nils, Soren, and Jakob alone?"

"No, there is also Kristian and his right-hand man, Axel. Emelie and Myrgjöl help out on occasion, as well."

"Why isn't the council looking for them too?"

He laughed and shook his head. "You still do not understand the way it works here. Your father owns the council. He rules everything here—every single thing. That is why there is a rebellion. The others of the Norselands do not have the strength or resources to take down Odin. We do. Soren chose his warriors well. We all bring something to the table that will defeat Odin."

I raised my eyebrows in interest. "What do you bring? I'm pretty sure charisma isn't a superpower."

He smirked. "I deserve that, but I am going to be offended anyway."

Unconcerned, I walked back to the sofa and slipped off my shoes. "You started it, lover-boy."

Emelie came out of the kitchen with a pitcher of water and a bag of chips. "We don't have time for this bickering. We have all night for that. Right now, we're going to behave and watch the episode of Supernatural that I DVR'd while we were gone.

Viggo grabbed the remote. "Move over fire-girl."

I flipped him off with a smile.

Emelie laughed at our exchange. "You and Soren could be twins, Erin. You are so much alike."

I wondered how true that was. Would Soren sleep with my best friend and keep it a secret? I glanced over at Emelie and knew that if my best friend were her, the answer would be a resounding yes.

After the episode was over, Viggo excused himself to read. With our similar taste in fiction, I wanted to know what book he was reading and would have followed him out if Emelie hadn't caught my attention.

Yawning, she stood up and stretched. "I don't know why I'm so tired today."

"I'm right there with you," I concurred, rubbing my aching feet. "I didn't get any sleep last night."

She slapped her forehead. "Oh, that's right. I forgot that Soren told me that you were asleep when he arrived on Álfheim. It must be because we grew up on Midgard. I just don't feel right if I don't get at least a couple hours a night."

Oh, please don't let her be saying what I think she's saying. "No one else sleeps here?"

"On a rare occasion. We're the weird ones."

I covered my face with my hands and buried my head in my lap. "Noooooo!"

"What is it, Erin?"

I'm sure my face showed every ounce of chagrin that I felt. "That means that Jakob listened to about four hours' worth of me obsessing over him yesterday morning when I thought he was asleep."

She whistled low. "That … is … embarrassing. But, if he's into you as much as he says he is, he enjoyed it. Soren heard my every thought for days when we first met. He must have thought that I was so sad. I was already in love, though all I had of him were old photographs from decades ago." She looked off as if remembering a fond memory. "I think I knew before I met him that he would be the one. Does it feel that way for you with Jakob?"

I thought about it for a second. "At first, I was just attracted to him, but after about ten minutes, I struggled not to touch him and had complete confidence that I would be content to spend the rest of my life with him."

She groaned. "You know I can't interfere, right."

"Riiight, but ..." Was she going to help me?

"But, I'm going to tell you something that you should know."

I braced myself for the worst. "Okay, let's hear it."

"I don't think this is going to be a deal-breaker for you. You can relax. I was going to say that if you decide to pursue your relationship with Jakob, there will be an obstacle."

An obstacle? That could be just about anything. "What sort of obstacle."

Her eyes glazed over. She was seeing another vision. "All I can say is that you need to decide whether or not Jakob is worth the work that it will take to be his mate."

I didn't need time to answer that question. He was worth it, no matter the obstacles. "He is. I can feel it."

She grinned and laced her fingers with mine. "Somehow, I knew you'd say that. I saw the way he looked at you this evening. I do not doubt that Soren did, too. I'm warning you. Soren will not be keen on you dating anyone so soon after your arrival, but I will try to remind him that our love was quick to blossom, though I cannot promise he will listen. He is so stubborn, and even more so since ..." She broke off, looking worried.

"Spill, Emelie."

She sighed. "Odin's death has been prophesied."

"No," I said, in disbelief.

"It's not going to be immediate, but you may well be the last of his sisters. He wants to make sure you're taken care of."

"That's sweet of him." It was sweet. No one had ever loved me enough to care about that before.

"Soren is a good male underneath it all, and I'm glad to see him take an interest in you, however problematic that may be to your predicament."

I gave her an impulsive hug. "Thank you for doing this."

She patted my shoulder. "It's no big deal. We're sisters now."

I was sure that my smile was soggy. A sister—how much I'd wanted one. "Shit, I'm going to mess up this makeup."

"No! You can't mess it up. Jakob is going to go crazy when he sees you."

"I don't know. It could be an improvement." I'd never felt so made up in my life. Viggo had gone overboard with the elven makeover tonight.

"You look stunning. Did you see the males staring at you as we left? Their tongues were hanging out!"

I waved her away. "Now you're just being silly."

"I am sure that there was one male with his tongue out."

"He was getting it pierced! You are so weird!"

She shook her head. "You, too? Why does everyone say that? I don't see it!"

"So, you're a seer who can't see?"

"Shut up."

Jakob returned to Soren's in the wee hours of the morning. I wouldn't have been any wiser if Viggo's shrill voice hadn't woke me.

"What the fuck are you thinking, Jakob?" he asked.

Creeping over to the kitchen door, I listened for Jakob's response.

"I do not have to tell you what I am thinking, brother. You can see with your own eyes that I have found a stunningly beautiful elf that happens to be my true mate. It is a blessing. I will not look at it as anything else."

I grinned at the stunningly beautiful part. Jakob was a keeper.

"Yeah, well, that 'beautiful' female in there has feelings," Viggo hissed. "If you so much as make her cry, you are going to need a body cast."

"What the hell, Viggo? What has gotten into you?"

"I could ask you the same. You are a stranger to me. The Jakob I know would not take advantage of an innocent."

"I am doing nothing to her innocence, Viggo. She has already been unchaste with a mortal."

All right, that was enough of that. I peeked inside to see Viggo and Jakob mere inches apart, their faces contorted with rage. "Uh, can we keep the unchaste thing between us, Jakob? It's not the kind of thing I want circulating back to Soren."

He spun in my direction with a mortified expression that morphed into lustful awe the second he saw me in the doorway. "Forgive me."

I acknowledged his apology with a shrug of indifference but sighed inwardly with sharp relief. He approved of my makeover. "It's okay. I know you were just proving a point."

Disagreeing, he shook his head. "It is no excuse. I should not have shared something so private without your permission. My temper got the best of me. I apologize."

"In that case, as penance for the heinous crimes you have committed against my honor and reputation, you have to kiss your unchaste, could-be mate."

"It would be my pleasure, älskling. Permit me to say that you are ravishing tonight." He stepped closer, smiling down at me as he cupped the back of my head to pull me into his embrace.

I would have come to him without restraint. I'd craved the sight of him since he'd left. "I missed you," I said, standing on the tips of my toes and pressing my lips to his.

Viggo groaned. "Mark my words, you two. This will not end well."

The next afternoon, I woke feeling great and ready to take on anything—except for Soren. He hadn't come back from his meeting with Thor before daylight, and though Jakob had tried his best to convince me to spend the day with him in Álfheim, I didn't want to risk leaving without checking with him first. He'd almost caught us both half-naked in bed yesterday. That was way too close of a call for me, so instead of cuddling up with a sexy male, I decided to start my day with magic.

After taking a quick shower, I dressed in another of my new outfits with a spring in my step (which is considerably easier in elven shoes) and took myself to the sunroom to practice. Last night, Viggo immersed me in the elven culture, and I loved it, even the makeup. I wanted to explore that side. It was the single, solitary magic that had made an appearance thus far, so I might as well try to use what I know I have.

Viggo was already in the sunroom when I arrived, his bare chest and feet evidence that he had just rolled out of his bed. "Why aren't you burnt to a crisp?"

He answered without looking up from his book. "UV protectant windows, but I've had Em's blood, too. It allows me to see the sun at any time. It is a light elf thing."

"That's cool, I guess."

"It is not as cool as it sounds. Biting Emelie is..." He shuddered. "It is just not pleasant."

I sighed and sat next to him. "I can see how it would be awkward."

"What?"

"I can see how—"

"The sigh," he interrupted. "What is going on with you?"

"I'm just being ridiculous."

"Nothing new there," he remarked, still not looking at me. "So, what is it?"

"It doesn't seem fair that her blood lets you see the sun, and all mine does is get you doped up. I feel like I have nothing to offer Jakob."

He glanced over at me. "How do you ... never mind? Do not tell me. That way, when Soren finds out about this and goes into his murderous rage, I will not be involved."

I snatched the book out of his hand, glanced at the cover, and threw it onto the table next to me. "You're already involved, Viggo.

"Hey! I was reading that."

I gave him an exasperated look. "How many times have you read it? Twenty? Thirty times? You can read Twilight anytime. I'm going to practice magic, and I need help not to burn the place down. You in?"

He grinned. "Oh, yes. That requires interaction."

I pursed my lips. I didn't trust him. "No funny business. I still owe you for yesterday."

Jumping up, he walked to the center of the room. "I would not dream of it, poppet." He stroked his chin in thought for a moment and then snapped his fingers. "I believe I will teach you the way my father taught me. We will start with the easiest magic— elemental magic."

"Do you mean elements from the periodic table or elemental as in weather and stuff?"

He nodded. "Yes and no."

"Okay ... what? I'm already confused."

"I mean fire, wind, and water."

"And Earth, right?"

"That is the human interpretation, but yes. There is also spirit, though it is unheard of in this age, and weather. It is not common magic, but I think you might be able to master, at the least, lightning. Your brother has a great affinity with electricity. I am sure you will, too."

I was more than dubious about that. So far, I hadn't been able to do much. "How much of this can you do?"

"All of it, except for fire. It is rare, remember?"

I joined him in the middle of the room, a smug grin on my face. "Ha! I can do something you can't do. Behold my awesome power."

He rolled his eyes. "Yes, you have the awesome power to set yourself on fire. I will endeavor to contain my jealousy and move on with my life."

"Shut up and teach me," I said, with a withering look of disdain.

"Promise me that you will not be disappointed if you cannot do this right away."

"I won't." He arched a brow. "Okay," I conceded. "I will be upset, but I'll get over it. Let's do this!" I was excited to learn something that I could control on my own.

He flung a hand toward the water pitcher on the windowsill and a tennis ball sized sphere of water floated out of the top. It zipped over to hover between us. "Your first test is water. Any other time, I would tell a student that this method is an excellent way of extinguishing flames, but you do not have to worry about that, do you?"

"Jealousy is so unbecoming, Viggo," I teased him.

"So is smugness, poppet. Now, pay attention—if you can."

I almost refrained from flipping him off—almost.

He grinned. "Okay, now that you are paying attention, I want you to concentrate on moving the sphere." Noticing my dismay, he added, "Do not worry. If you fail, I will catch it before it ruins the carpet."

I closed my eyes. I hoped he had paper towels handy. "What's the first step?"

"Clear your mind. Think of nothing but what you want to accomplish."

"Okay." I thought about the water, what it would weigh, and how it would feel in my hands if I were able to hold it in its current form. I could almost hear the water singing to me, telling me what to do in its own way.

"Erin! Reel it in a little!"

I opened my eyes to find six of the same sized spheres of water floating between us and laughed. "I did it!"

"Yes, you did. You are still doing it."

"I am?"

He chuckled. "Unless there is someone here I do not know about, you are. It is obvious that you have water under control. Can you combine these and send it back to the pitcher?"

He might as well have asked me to walk on the water. I didn't have a clue how to start. I wasn't even sure how I was holding the bubbles up. Staring intently at them, I urged it together, pleading with it to do what I wanted. Like a bullet, the water combined and shot across the room and into the pitcher.

Viggo's mouth dropped open. "I hope that we never become enemies, Erin. You are more powerful than any elf I have ever seen."

"Are you including yourself in that?"

"I will never answer that question."

I giggled and bounced on the balls of my feet. "What else you got?"

"Take it easy. It gets harder from here on out."

"We'll see."

"Have ego much?"

Putting my hands on my hips, I scoffed. "This isn't ego. This is confidence."

He mock-cringed at my reprimand. "Yes, Ma'am!"

"Damn, straight," I said, but then lost it and burst out laughing.

"What's going on in here?" Emelie asked from the doorway, still in her pajamas and holding a glass of orange juice.

"We're practicing magic," I answered, excited to show her what I'd learned.

"How's it going so far?"

I could tell that she was trying to get the story from Viggo. "Don't bother, Em. He won't tell you that I'm a natural, but I will."

She looked to Viggo for confirmation, and he nodded. "She nailed water on the first try."

Emelie set the glass on the coffee table and threw herself on the sofa. "That's so unfair! I was terrible when I started trying my magic."

"Awwww, Em. You were not so bad."

She cut a look at him.

"Okay, you were terrible. The worst I have ever seen."

"Thank you. All right Erin, let us see how you do with the soil of Ásgard."

I turned back to Viggo. "What do I do?"

He grabbed a sack of potting soil and dumped most of it out onto the marble floor below the windows. "I want you to split the soil into two separate piles. Use the same principle as the water and concentrate on what you want it to do."

Nodding, I walked to the pile, thinking about how I would do that with my hands. That's when the ground started shaking.

"Stop, Erin!" Viggo screamed, over the deafening rumble.

I thought about the ground being still, and the shaking subsided.

Emelie was on her feet looking harried. "Are you kidding me? You're not a natural. You're an elf on steroids!"

Viggo's eyes were wide as saucers. "I think we should go outside to practice air and fire."

Emelie ran from the room, yelling, "I need a coat! Don't start without me!"

Three minutes later, Emelie met us outside, grinning from ear to ear. "Okay, let's do this."

"How do you feel about moving the wind?" Viggo asked me.

"Fair to partly cloudy, with a chance of tornados?"

"Do not dare to think of a tornado! All I want you to do is move the scattered leaves in a pile. That's it." He said all of this without letting go of the porch railing or Emelie.

"Okay. Thanks for the vote of confidence, by the way." I rolled my eyes and then stared at the leaves, thinking about what they'd look like merrily spinning, end over end into a small pile, and with a mighty gust, the wind picked up in all four directions. It whipped my hair into my eyes, blinding me.

Viggo's humored voice sounded in my mind. "The leaves are in a pile, Erin. You can stop the hurricane now."

That task was much more straightforward than I thought it would be. As soon as I had the thought, the wind died down to a light breeze and then stopped altogether.

Emelie clapped her hands together. Her cheeks were pink from being windblown. "That was so cool!"

"That was crazy!" Viggo corrected. "Erin, your main concern needs to be focusing on scaling your magic down. Odin's blood has made you powerful beyond belief. I have never seen anything that could compare to you in all of my years."

"How many years would that be?"

"Let us just say that that I'm younger than Jakob but older than Kristian."

"Kristian isn't that much younger," Emelie added, a smiling, mischievous look on her face. "Don't let Viggo fool you. He's a baby when compared to Jakob."

"Huh. I didn't think that there was that big of an age difference between you two. Is it weird for you to be so much younger than your brother?"

"Is it weird to be seven thousand years younger than Soren?" he asked.

I laughed at myself. "Oh yeah, I forgot. It doesn't feel weird at all for me. Not in the slightest."

"That is good to hear, sister," said a deep voice behind me.

I spun around to see Soren's approving smile. "Guess what I can do?"

His red eyes met Viggo's green ones, and he quirked an eyebrow in question.

"She is a walking natural disaster," Viggo assured my brother. "Show him, Em."

Emelie put her hand on his bare forearm and his eyes silvered with her magic. "This is what I saw. Viggo will have to tell you about her water ability."

Soren's eyes cleared. "That will not be necessary. I can see that Erin has unrivaled power. My own power may be eclipsed by hers."

"At least we are starting to gain an advantage over Odin. With Erin and Emelie, we may free the Norselands yet!" Viggo boasted.

"Viggo, it will be a long time before I agree to send my mate and sister into battle. Regardless of the magic they possess, they are both still novices at their craft."

"Whatever!" Emelie said crossly. "Bring Odin, Thor, Viveka, any of them on. Erin and I will take care of them all by ourselves."

Giddy with excitement, I agreed wholeheartedly. "Hell, yeah! Let's do it!"

Soren sighed. "Relax, all of you. Not one of you is even going to consider anything as rash as taking on Odin or his servants right now. I mean it."

Viggo and I saluted at the same time, and when we saw each other, we burst into helpless giggles.

Soren pursed his lips and shook his head. "You two are too similar."

"They are, aren't they?" Emelie spoke more to herself than her mate.

Soren glanced at her with concern. "What is it, little one?"

A bad feeling filled me. Most likely because Emelie was aiming an agonized look of sympathy toward me with her silvered eyes. "What is it? Why are you looking at me with the sad eyes?"

"No. She cannot be," Viggo said, shaking his head in disbelief. "She just can't."

They were driving me crazy! "What? Stop the mind-speak and tell me what the hell is going on!"

Viggo's face was incredulous. "They believe that you and I are kin. But, it cannot be."

Their faces swam in my vision. "What did you say?" I couldn't have heard him right. I couldn't have heard that Jakob and I are related. Shame and revulsion racked me. "No. I can't be." I couldn't … wouldn't believe it. Not until I had proof, not if I valued my sanity.

Emelie's calm voice spoke in my mind. Don't worry about Jakob. Viggo has a different mother.

Viggo's voice spoke next. You're safe. Don't worry.

Soren cast a suspecting glare at Viggo and me. "Is there something going on between you two?"

"No!" We yelled in unison.

He didn't look convinced. "Tell me what is going on here, Emelie."

"Soren," she whispered, looking torn. "I can't."

"Em," he pressed. His tone was not one of amusement.

"I'm not sure if I can tell you. It might interfere with her fate. I have to be careful."

The disapproving look he gave her made us all squirm. He knew we were hiding something. Something big. "Fine, you three. Have your secret. But know that I will find out before long. I hope that it will not be too late to salvage the situation." He directed his attention to me. "Erin, let us see you practice your fire abilities. It will soon be nightfall."

"Sounds good." More than delighted at the change in subject, I walked away from them and readied myself for instructions.

"Wait a minute!" Emelie called from the porch. "I just planted that grass. It'll never grow back right."

Viggo rolled his eyes. "All right, you heard Better Homes and Gardens over there. Erin, will you step this way." He couldn't contain his wide grin as he led me to the fire pit.

"Are you serious? You want me to get in there?"

He snickered. "Yep. Get in there."

I stepped in and turned to face them, feeling silly. "Okay, what now?" They were beside themselves with laughter. Viggo even had his cell phone out to take a picture. "You guys suck. You know that, right?"

Emelie sobered. "I'm sorry, Erin. Come on, guys. Tell her what to do, so she can get out of there."

Viggo pocketed the phone. "Since I do not have fire magic, you are kind of on your own here, but from what I have heard, you carry the fire within yourself. It is up to you, how you get it out."

"Okay." I breathed slow deep breaths and thought of the blue flames that I'd seen reflecting in Jakob's eyes. Without delay, I felt a sudden rush of warmed wind and looked down to see my body erupt in bright blue flames from my feet upward, consuming me until I was covered head to foot. I couldn't hear the words that my family was speaking, but their faces were both awestruck and worried.

I yelled over the din. "What is it?"

They motioned to the reflective glass of the sliding doors. I gasped at what I saw. The outline of my body and the hair whipping around my head were visible through the flames, but my clothes were just a memory. I wasn't just covered in flames. I was the fire. I closed my eyes and concentrated on burning brighter and hotter, amazed at my transformation.

"Erin!" I could barely hear the frantic words Emelie was shouting over the sound of my roaring magic. Glancing over to see what the commotion was about, I spotted Jakob. He stood, uneasy but fixated, next to the house. I met his eyes with my own, smiling when he mouthed, "You are beautiful."

In the split second my attention lapsed, my fire began to burn in erratic bursts, changing color and sparking closer to the apartment. Soren, noticing the change, followed my eyes to Jakob, then hurled himself in his direction to question him, his face the picture of rage.

I threw my hands over my ears to block out the roar of the fire and Soren's yelling. "Stop!"

The fire reacted to my emotions, burning a blistering hot white, and then it exploded outward, raining tiny brick pieces from the fire pit over the lawn. Emelie and Viggo stood there stunned, a fine layer of dust coating their shocked faces. Neither seemed able to move.

Nils chose that moment to pop into existence with a strange male. Taking in the chaos with wide eyes, he strode to the water hose, turned it on, and doused me to extinguish the out of control flames. "For fuck's sake!" he said in confusion and anger, and then he turned to Jakob and Soren, who were still arguing. "What the fucking fuck? Stop fighting! We have more important shit going on."

Emelie seemed to unfreeze after Nils's string of profanity and rushed to cover my naked body with her shawl. "Shit. Shit. Shit! What am I going to do?" she mumbled to herself as she led me into the house.

I didn't answer, just continued the baffled teeth chattering I was doing.

Snapping out of her internal debate, she led me into the bathroom. "I'll get you something to put on. Wait for my instructions on what to say to Soren, okay? You and Jakob need to have the same story."

Weary from the magic, I let out a heavy sigh. "Why can't we just tell him?" I didn't understand the need for all this secrecy. What a perfect waste of time.

"I know that that seems to be the best way. I agree with you, but Soren?" She frowned. "He's from a different time. In the ancient days, what Jakob has done was punishable by death. And as your brother, he is well within his right to deliver that justice. Soren considers what he believes Jakob is guilty of as the ultimate in betrayal. It is a matter of your honor. And even more so, since..." She chewed her lip. "Jakob will tell you later." She tapped her head. "I'll be in touch."

"Okay."

Emelie interrupted the lamenting I was doing over the fact that everyone had seen me naked when she spoke in my mind a few minutes later. *"Soren has calmed. He no longer believes that you and Jakob are a couple."*

I fought the urge to cry and/or bang my head on the shower wall. This was the exact opposite of what I wanted.

Emelie's tinkling laughter filled my head. *"No, it's not. It's quite genius if I say so myself. You get to stay with Jakob at his house this way. Otherwise, you'd be locked in a tower in a faraway land."*

I pictured Jakob climbing my hair in Rapunzel style.

"Exactly."

"I hate that we're lying to Soren." And I did. I'd known my brother for a couple days, and already there were secrets. And I really didn't want to drive a wedge between him and his mate over some secret love affair that I should have the balls to tell him about myself.

"Soren is so stubborn. He forgets that when I was betrothed to Kristian, we were fooling around, just as you and Jakob are."

"That hypocrite!" I shook my head at Soren's double standard and pulled a towel from the rack.

"Yep. That's why I don't feel guilty for lying to him. He's being the definition of overprotective. You couldn't find a better male than Jakob, and he knows that."

"Let's hope he remembers that when he finds out the truth. And speaking of remembering, can you remember to stay out of my thoughts?"

"I wish I could, Erin. Believe me. I want to stay out of everyone's thoughts. Some more than others."

"Nils?"

Her laughter filled the connection. *"You nailed it. It's just ironic that it took me so long to block my own mind. Anyway, are you out of the tub?"*

"I'm about to get dressed. Why?"

"We need to talk about your mother, and you still need to…ah…meet Nils' father, Loki. Soren doesn't trust him, but I see him being an intricate part of the war against Odin. Whether my mate likes it or not, he is part of the rebellion now."

That explained the stranger with Nils. I sighed in exasperation. How was I ever going to look him in the eye after he saw me naked? Viggo, Nils, and Soren, too, for that matter. Every one of them saw me in all my glory.

"It'll be fine. They won't mention anything about it. I've threatened dismemberment of their favorite part."

"Remind me never to piss you off."

She laughed. *"Good call. I'll see you in a minute?"*

"I'll be right there."

CHAPTER SIX

Everyone was assembled in the living room when I emerged from the bathroom, clothed and warmed. Conversations were being had, but none of them out loud. That wasn't suspicious, or anything. I wondered what could be so important that they were using mind-speak to discuss it and then remembered the other part of what Emelie said. We needed to talk about my mother.

"Hi," I offered, and as soon as their solemn eyes were all diverted to me, I asked, "Who is it?"

There was no beating around the bush. Jakob answered, with zero hesitation. "Viveka."

I tried to appear nonchalant, but inside I was as crushed as any little girl would be to find out that her dreams of a faerytale life were dashed. I couldn't believe my luck. Both of my parents were megalomaniacs with the goal of ruling the Norselands. Wasn't that just peachy?

Viggo was the first to break the silence. "I am sorry about the 'marry me' comment, poppet. I did not realize it would turn out to be so creepy."

In a flash, the pieces came together in my mind as if it were a puzzle. Viggo must be Viveka's half-brother. It was no wonder we were so alike.

Nils chortled with glee. "I'd forgotten that you said that to her. Awkward!" He wiggled his eyebrows at me. "I'm still not related."

"Nils!" Soren reprimanded.

"I know, I know. She's your sister. Whatever."

Jakob, like most of the others, had been silent since he'd revealed my parentage. I wondered what his reaction to all of this was but couldn't bring myself to look at him. It was an impossible task. What if he had undesirable feelings about semi-dating his step-niece.

"Who wants to tell her about her family?" Emelie suggested, attempting to lighten the mood around the gigantic elephant of awkwardness in the room. "It's not all bad, right? I think I remember Viggo saying that his mother was the best female he's ever known."

Viggo nodded. "You are right, Em. You would have loved your grandmother, Alva. She was more than a mother to Viveka and myself. She was a friend to the entire kingdom and is still mourned as having been the best of all the queens of Svartálfaheim. It is a pity that she is not here to see her only granddaughter. You are her image. I cannot believe that I didn't notice it before tonight."

Nils shuddered. "You saw her naked, dude."

"Shut up, Fenrir!" Loki admonished, in a thick accent. "No one noticed her nudity, save you."

I sent him a silent thank you, and he nodded in acceptance and offered the chair next to him for me to sit in. When I was settled, I asked, "Loki, isn't it?"

"Yes, I am father to Fenrir and mate to Sigyn," he answered with his strange inflection. "The loss of your grandmother was a great one. The news of her death was spread far enough to reach me in my imprisonment." He smiled as if remembering a memory of her. "Her sharp tongue and intolerance for evil made her the most popular regent in thousands of years."

I grinned. She did sound similar to me … if I were Mother Teresa.

"I have agreed to tell Odin that you have escaped my grasp," Loki continued. "Now that I have seen you and know how much you favor Alva, I know that it is the right decision. She would skin me alive for not helping her granddaughter in a time of great need."

Breathing a sigh of relief, I hugged him. "Thank you."

"How can we trust you, Loki? You never do anything without payment of some sort. What do you want?" Jakob's deep voice was saturated with contempt.

Nils's hackles were instantly raised. "Do you think that after thousands of years of torture by Odin's hand—"

Loki held up his hand to silence his son, his young and handsome face marred with concern. "Calm yourself, Fenrir." Turning to address Jakob, he spoke simply. "I have joined the rebellion. Have your Norn examine my intentions if you do not believe me. Revenge against the Alfather will be mine."

"And you should have it," I agreed. "I'd be pretty pissed at Odin too."

"It is good that you have taken after your grandmother," Loki said to me in answer—as cryptic as the rest of them usually were.

I shot a meaningful glance at Jakob, and he nodded his reluctant acquiescence to the situation. "I hope your words are sincere."

"They are, Prince Väsen. Upon what is left of my honor, I wish nothing but goodwill to the rebellion and a reign of terror upon Odin and his servants."

Soren interrupted the tension with a question of his own. "What of the temple, Jakob?"

With a last untrusting look at Loki, he answered, "It is as we thought. They are replicating the temple and gathering sacrifices as we speak. I could not find the exact location, but it is the talk of the villages on Ásgard, Álfheim, and Svartálfaheim. They fear for their livestock and their children."

I gasped in horror. How could I have forgotten the passage I read about the sacrifices? "Did that really happen?"

"Yes. Every nine years for thousands of years. Of course, back then, they didn't have to resort to kidnapping and stealing; the creatures of the realm volunteered the sacrifices."

"Why didn't I see this?" Emelie lamented.

Soren put a consoling arm around her. "Perfection takes time with all magic, little one. In a century or so, you and Erin will be feared across the land."

She pouted. "Shut up."

"What about our brother, Thor?" I asked. "What did you find out from him?" I'd been fascinated by the blond warrior since I was a child and, now that he was my brother, I was ten times more intrigued.

"Our brother, Thor, is an imbecile content to ride on his father's coattails," he spat out, distaste plain in his voice.

Whoa. I hadn't expected that. Was he jealous of his father's close relationship with Thor, or was it the notoriety that his younger brother had?

Soren turned his crimson stare at me. "Do not trust Thor. He is anxious to meet you. Nothing good can come of it, I assure you. To remain our father's favorite, there is no limit to the number of evils he's willing to perform. Why he cares to, I will never comprehend."

I guess I can scratch that jealousy theory then.

Jakob subtly inclined his head. It was a reminder that he'd told me about how little upset Soren to the point of action. I should count myself lucky to have him take an interest in me. Otherwise, Odin might have found me first.

"So, Thor is a part of this temple rebuilding?"

"Oh, yes. It is not a surprise, as he was one of the gods worshiped in the original temple."

Loki spoke up. "Thor indicated to me that he is more than unconcerned with the implications of his actions. He desires his father's throne, nothing else. How Odin does not realize his treachery, I do not understand. It is almost as if he is bewitched."

Emelie stood. "Are you guys saying that Thor is with Viveka and the Freyr in this temple thing?"

Nils, who had been sulking on the sofa since his father's reprimand, finally spoke. "And Odin. My father and I can find out."

"Do it, then," Soren consented. "Just be careful."

"I don't get it," I wondered aloud. "How does my mother fit in all of this?"

"I believe that she is tolerated because of you," Jakob explained. "Your power rivals Odin's, which makes you the perfect weapon against the rebellion. I believe they think your sentimental human-born ways will make you an easy target for Viveka's manipulating."

I heard his underlying message loud and clear. I was born to be a pawn in the war between Odin and the rebellion. "Fuck that. I'm with you guys, no matter what."

Viggo patted my knee in an absurd, fatherly way making Nils cringe. "Good girl."

"Fenrir, can you grow the fuck up?" Jakob's tone was scolding.

Viggo's eyes twinkled with amusement. "Never mind that, Jakob. There is a better way. Soren, did Nils tell you that he stripped down naked in front of Erin when he phased?"

Soren's immediate rage was palpable, however calm his words sounded. "Is that true, Fenrir?"

"I've seen penises before," I interjected, trying to diffuse the situation. Judging by the horrified expression on Soren's face, this might not have been the best choice of words.

Snickering, Nils checked his watch and pulled out a shifting stone. He could care less that his life was about to come to an end.

"I have to go. Call me when we have a plan." He disappeared without another word.

Soren huffed and sat back in his chair. "Is no one a gentle-male anymore?"

Emelie settled herself into his lap and kissed him intimately enough that we all felt uncomfortable. "Not many, my love. I missed you."

I pointed at the door, looking to Jakob for an excuse to leave.

Standing, he announced, "If we are done here, Erin and I are expected at the castle for dinner."

Soren just nodded, never taking his eyes or hands off of his mate.

Loki stood as well, looking as if he wanted to be anywhere else. "I, too, must leave. I will keep myself open to contact, should you decide that I am worthy of your trust."

There was no reply from either of them. Bewildered, I followed the males outside, where we all shared a half-nervous, half-creeped out laugh.

Viggo pulled out a pale red stone and disappeared without preamble. He looked shaken by the affectionate display. Loki didn't speak, either. He just tipped his head in a polite bow and faded from existence amidst a wisp of smoke.

Now that we were alone, I wrapped my arms around Jakob and inhaled. I loved his scent. I craved it.

"Shall we go, älskling?"

"I'll go anywhere with you, Jakob."

He kissed the top of my head. "Erin, you are everything to me."

We shifted to a deserted garden next to a massive stone castle. Even in the dim light, the shadow of the building was formidable, as was the tall warrior fast approaching us with a broadsword hilt peeking out from behind his shoulder.

"Axel, how do you fare?" Jakob called out.

The strange-eyed, handsome male inclined his head. "I am well, Prince Jakob. The King is expecting you."

"Thank you." He motioned to me. "Allow me to introduce you to Erin."

"Ah, the daughter of Odin." He bent his short-cropped dark head in my direction and pressed his arm across his heart. "You bear an uncanny resemblance to our beloved Queen Alva. Does she not, sire?"

"That she does, and it is for good reason. She is daughter to Viveka."

Axel's yellow, reptilian eyes bore into me. "How unfortunate. I am sorry."

I nodded. "Thank you." He and I were of one mind on that subject. Twenty-five years of high expectations are not easily forgotten.

He smiled at my thanks, exposing his secret to me. He wasn't a dark elf. His mouth was a nightmare of sharpened teeth. I took an involuntary step back. "Jakob?"

"Do not scare the female. She is new to the Norselands, Axel."

His disconcert was apparent, but he apologized nonetheless. "My lady, I did not realize that the illusion had slipped. Please do not be frightened of my appearance."

Jakob, noticing that my eyes were still locked on the snake-like features Axel was trying to hide, tucked me in closer to him. "Erin? Can you still see Axel the way he was before?"

"Nothing's changed from the moment we've met," I answered, feeling as confused as ever.

Jakob was astonished. "I see the illusion, Axel."

He looked from Jakob to me. "You see through my disguise?"

"All I see is a tall guy with yellow eyes and some dental…um…anomalies."

Axel chuckled. "That is a kind description, Erin."

"Is it rude of me to ask if you are a dark elf?"

"Of course not, my lady. I am not a dark elf. I am son to Loki and the Giantess, Angrboda. You may know me by my name, Jörmungand or the Midgard Serpent if you are learned in Norse Mythology?"

"I'm pretty ignorant of my heritage," I explained. "But I do know that if you are a son of Loki, that makes Nils your brother, doesn't it?"

"It does. However, I would be interested to know if Fenrir views me as such."

What was an appropriate comment to that statement? Being around for only two days, I didn't know either of them well enough to contribute.

Saving me from the awkward silence, Jakob spoke up. "Please tell Kristian that we will arrive in a moment."

He inclined his head. "Of course, my prince. It was a pleasure, my lady."

"Likewise," I called out after his retreating form. When he was out of earshot, I turned to Jakob with a hundred questions on my mind. First and foremost was, "Did that go well?"

Jakob laughed and pulled me into his embrace. "With Axel, if you are still breathing after a meeting with him, it went well. He is impulsive. Steer clear of him, would you?"

"Since you asked in such a nice way," I purred, snuggling into his warmth. "Is there anything else you want?"

"A great many things, älskling."

I raised myself on the tip of my toes to press my lips against his. "Name it, and it's yours, Jakob."

"Do not tempt me. I suffered without your smell, your taste, your beautiful smile last night. I believe that you will be my undoing."

I locked my wrists behind his head and kissed him again, deeper this time. "Sounds fun. When do we start?"

The deep sigh he gave as a response sounded troubled. "I have something to tell you, Erin."

"I have something to tell you also," I countered, nipping his lip with my teeth.

"What would you have me know, my love?"

Letting my hands skim under his shirt and onto his muscled back, I said, "I am really, really glad that we're not related."

"Are you, kitten?" he teased.

"Kitten?" I pushed him down onto the garden bench behind him and straddled his lap. "I'm not feeling too kittenish tonight, Jakob. I missed you."

In a moment of clarity, Jakob looked to the darkened tree line in the distance. "Erin, we should not do this here. There are too many witnesses."

Looking around, I didn't see anyone, so I assumed he said that to dissuade me. "I don't care about witnesses. I care about you. I want you, Jakob."

He pulled me tight against him, burying his face between my breasts, and taking a deep breath before speaking again. "Which part of me interests you?" His voice was barely above a growl.

Pushing my hands into his thick, black hair, I wrenched his head back, running my lips along his neck, before saying, "Every part."

His half-opened lids sprang up in surprise. "Taste me, Erin."

I didn't comprehend his words right away. I was lost in his scent and the feel of his possessive hands resting on my waist. "Wait. What—" I stopped mid-sentence, stuck my fingers in my mouth, and found … fangs. Embarrassed, I put my hand over my mouth. "I'm sorry."

"You are very becoming, älskling," Jakob assured me. "Do not apologize for what is natural to you. Indeed, to all of us. Almost every species of the Norselands has their own version of fangs. Blood is a common element in our rituals and ceremonies. We do not fear it as human communities do."

As relieved as I was that he found this natural, and even beautiful, I still had reason to worry. My mouth was watering with the urge to bite him. I couldn't think of anything but the blood coursing through his veins. The feeling was so strong within me that I could taste the coppery tang of his blood in my mouth already.

Jakob cupped the back of my head and brought my mouth to the unmarked smoothness of his neck. "Take me as your own, Erin. I beg of you."

I didn't hesitate, sinking my teeth into the side of his throat, and moaning with the pleasure his blood brought me as it coated my tongue. I thought that it would taste coppery, of rust and salt, but it didn't. It tasted of the sweetest wine and had much the same effect. It was decadent. I didn't want to ever stop drinking and wasn't sure if I would have if I didn't get too lightheaded to continue. I pulled away, my head swimming with his magic flowing through my bloodstream.

"Erin," His eyes burned into mine.

I sighed. "Don't say that we shouldn't have done this." Nothing had ever felt so right to me.

"Never. I wanted to say that even if this turns out to be a disaster, and we are not allowed to mate, I love you."

Stunned, I searched his face and found nothing but sincerity. "Am I drunk, or did you just say you loved me?"

He kissed me. "Both, älskling."

"I am, aren't I? It's your fault. You're just so damn tasty." His body jerked beneath me when I scored his skin a second time, then he relaxed, tracing slow circles onto the bare skin of my back. He was enjoying this, too.

"I'm going to have to carry you into dinner if you don't stop, Erin."

I licked the last drop of blood from his wounded neck feeling boneless and sated. "Too late. Besides, I think we should skip dinner and find a bed. You have a bedroom here, don't you?"

"Yes," he answered after some hesitation. "Are you ill?"

"Not at all." I reached down and palmed the bulge between us. "I want you."

"And you shall have me—after dinner," he assured me through gritted teeth. "Kristian will be affronted if we do not dine with him tonight. He has ordered this dinner for you. I told him of your interest in the native cuisine."

"Fine," I pouted.

The corner of his mouth quirked up. "One more thing, my love."

"What?"

"Tomorrow, I will tell your brother of our impending mating.

"Are you sure it's wise? Emelie said it was a bad idea. Soren is going to be super pissed. What if he tries to stop us?"

His expression hardened, and his grip around my waist tightened. "Let Soren try to keep us apart. I welcome the challenge."

I leaned back. His words were spoken with fierce intensity. Who was this male? "I don't think Soren will object too much. I mean, come on, he's your best friend. Who could he trust more? Just ask for my hand or something."

He brushed my hair back and caressed my cheek. "I wish it were that simple."

"Why isn't it?"

"Erin, I—" He paused, struggling to find the words.

Fear tightened my stomach. "It's bad, isn't it?"

"Please, hear me out, Erin." His face held a familiar expression. I knew this look. It was a guilty, beseeching, lying, cheating kind of expression, not the mien of a noble male. How many times had I seen it? Too many.

"Will you divorce her, or un-mate her, or whatever the equivalent is here?" I thought it best to get everything out into the open. For once in my life, I didn't care if the male I was dating was mated. I might as well know what I'm up against.

"You already know?"

I shook my head. "No, but this isn't the first affair that I've found out I've been a part of. It is, however, the only one I've ever intended on staying in."

He enveloped me in his arms, his relief emanating in waves. "Please, allow me to explain my abhorrent behavior. I want no more secrets between us."

Pushing him away, I stood. "No specifics, Jakob. If I know who she is, then it will make me a mistress. I can't have that burden on me. I just need to know how long it's been since you've been with her and if there will ever be a time when you'll be tempted to return to her."

He answered without a moment's hesitation. "It has been two years since I have been with her as a mate. Before that, she and I had not seen each other in over a hundred years. She is much changed from the elf I fell in love with thousands of years ago. There is no chance of me returning to her."

He'd been with her for thousands of years? How could I ever compete with that?

"Erin?"

I stared out into the darkness, seeing nothing through my tears. "I just need a minute."

His arms encircled me from behind. "I am sorry. I realize that what I am asking you to do is something no female of worth would do or should be asked to do. Forgive me, älskling."

I sniffed, trying to hold it together. "Why didn't you tell me on the street the night we met—when you told me that you hadn't found your true mate? That would've been the perfect time to mention it."

"I did not want to lose you. Not when I had just found you."

Pretty words. I wondered how true they were coming from his lips.

"Trust me, Erin. Please."

"I trust you implicitly with my safety, Jakob. It's my heart that I'm afraid you'll be careless with." Once a cheater, always a cheater. Isn't that the saying?

He spun me in his arms. "I swear to you. You are my female henceforth. I will find a way to annul my mating. Emelie's grandmother, Myrgjöl, can help us. After all, it is because of her that it wasn't taken care of two years ago."

Hope filled me. "You tried to get out of the mating?"

"It was either my happiness or Emelie's freedom from the council. I would make the same choice again if I had to. A lifetime of servitude for the council is something I would not wish on an enemy, much less kind, sweet, Emelie."

"Of course you wouldn't." Though I was still more than conflicted about the situation, the fact that he'd tried to break their mating made me feel a little better. We still wouldn't be able to tell anyone or go anywhere, but at least we'd be together.

He tipped my face up and kissed me, his eyes earnest. "I know what you are thinking, Erin. This will not last forever."

"Promise me."

Tugging me closer, he held me tight in his arms. "I swear to you. I will make this right."

"I love you, Jakob," I confessed. "Please, don't break my heart."

Jakob's green eyes crinkled with his smile. "What is that expression, älskling?"

"Determination." What else could it be? I couldn't go back to my life at the bookstore after this, and I couldn't be without him. I'd made my choice; I would do everything I could to make sure Jakob and I would be together.

"I may never be worthy of, or deserve you, Erin, but ..." He pulled an ornate, black-stoned ring out of his pocket. "Be my mate and wife—even if no one can know that the ring is mine."

I held my shaking left hand out to let him slide the heavy weight onto my finger. "It's beautiful, Jakob."

"It was my mother's. I meant to give it to you after the first night we spent together, but Soren's early arrival made that impossible. I know my mother would approve of you. She said that the important thing is to fight for what you believe is right. I know that you and I are right." He placed my palm over his heart. "I can feel it here."

I sank into his arms, tears flowing freely. "I love you. I'd be honored to be your mate. I don't care how long it takes. We have an eternity."

He spoke into my hair. "I would do it this instant if I could."

I snuggled into his broad chest. "I know."

A bell sounded from inside the castle, making us both remember where we were. "That is the dinner bell. We should go."

I straightened my clothes and ran my fingers through my hair. "Do I have blood on my mouth?"

He chuckled. "Do I have a gaping wound on my neck?"

I stood on my toes to get a better look and frowned. The bleeding had stopped, but it still looked terrible. "Uh…what's your definition of gaping?"

"That bad, huh?"

"I could try to heal you. Soren has that talent, right?"

"No, love. I do not want to risk it after what I saw you do today. You need to learn control before you attempt that."

I shrugged. "Suit yourself. Should I take the ring off? Surely, your brother will recognize it."

"Kristian will not care. He harbors an intense hatred for my mate." He offered his elbow. "Shall we?"

"I'm a little nervous. He's the king. I've never met a king before."

He rolled his eyes. "And what am I, just a lowly prince? I did tell you that I was to be king, did I not?"

"Oh, yeah." I grinned. "Hey, that makes me a princess and a princess-to-be, right?"

"It does, and this will be your home, should you choose to live here. It is tradition."

My home? A castle? Never in my wildest dreams did I think this would have ever been possible. "Let's go, my prince."

I stayed close to Jakob, almost clinging to him as we walked through the hallways. The castle was intimidating, to say the least. Cavernous and silent, it reminded me of something out of a gothic novel, in spite of the obvious attempt to lighten the castle's drab stone walls with rich tapestries and paintings.

In complete wonder, I asked, "This is where you grew up?" It was unbelievable that anyone could have spent their childhood in this enormous place. I can imagine it took ten minutes just to find a bathroom.

"No, love. I was born a few millennia before the castle was built, though I have lived most of my years on the land it stands on. There have been many happy memories here."

I continued to stare at him long after he stopped talking. A few millennia, a thousand years … he said them as if it was nothing special to be forty-five hundred years old. To me, it was amazing. He didn't look a day over twenty-seven. Well, make that thirty when he's being serious—which is most of the time. "So, it's safe to say that you know your way around this place, huh?"

His green eyes twinkled with humor. "Yes. You examine me, älskling. What are you filing away up there now?"

"Just thinking about our age difference," I answered, then wondered if those words were a little too honest.

When I didn't elaborate, his brow lifted in question. "Will you not tell me your thoughts?"

No doubt, he was thinking that I was unsure about our mating as a result of the age difference, but that was so far from my mind. Not one of his self-perceived 'faults' was going to be a deal-breaker. He meant everything to me. I just hoped that he felt the same way in return. I had to wonder since he was so reluctant earlier in our acquaintance, if it weren't for the true mate thing, would he have taken a second glance at me?

"Erin?"

Resigning myself not to overthink it, I tapped my temple with what I hoped was a beguiling smile. "Don't worry, Jakob. There are good thoughts up here. *And delicious thoughts and naughty thoughts,*" I added silently.

He trapped me against the wall, his wicked smile and scent overpowering my senses, making me weak in the knees. "I am intrigued, älskling. Tell me about these naughty thoughts."

"Allow me to show it to you," I said, meeting his hungry green eyes and opening my mind to him, showing him what I was thinking … and wanting.

Growling, he dragged my body into his, digging his fingers into my shoulders with urgency as he took my mouth in a hurried, desperate kiss. "I will give my brother thirty minutes with you. That is all. This hunger is consuming me, Erin. I think of nothing else."

My breath hitched and then became shallow. I couldn't seem to take my eyes off his. The way he drew out my name made me shiver down to my toes, and that commanding tone had me on the verge of orgasm already. I wanted him now. Dinner could wait until tomorrow as far as I was concerned. I sent him another thought of him between my thighs, our bodies slick with the sweat of our exertion.

Tracing my bottom lip with his thumb, he hissed, "You romanticize what I am about to do to you, Erin."

My brain stopped working after those words. Breathless with anticipation, I glanced around us for any horizontal surface that we could use. "I can meet Kristian later," I suggested, slipping my fingers into the waistband of his jeans.

He licked his lips, exposing long, white fangs. "Erin, you need to eat. Trust me. You will need all of your strength today."

CHAPTER SEVEN

After two more attempts to prolong us from going to dinner, Jakob managed to drag me to a dining room the size of my apartment. Already seated at the long mahogany table were Axel and a finely dressed elven male that must be the king. To my surprise, they both jumped to their feet when they saw me enter. That was interesting. I'd expected someone as important as the king to consider me beneath the consideration of formality, what with me being the new mistress and all.

Axel was at my elbow to escort me in seconds. "Allow me to seat you, Lady Erin."

"Uh, okay." I was flustered by his invitation. I still wasn't a hundred percent sure that he didn't scare the daylights out of me. Sweet Lord, those teeth were truly nightmarish. Nevertheless, he appeared to be a real gentle-male. I approved of that. An old-fashioned male was hard to find. Just ask any woman living in New York City.

Jakob, however, did not appreciate Axel's good manners. His loud growl of warning sounded before he even had a chance to touch me. I shot Jakob a quizzical look and shrugged to Axel. "I guess Jakob will be seating me. Thanks anyway."

Kristian watched the encounter with fascination. "My brother, Axel was being polite."

Jakob nodded his acquiescence and muttered his apologies to Axel, though I didn't think he meant a word of it. His eyes still tracked every move the astonished male made.

I watched the tense interaction between the two for a moment but found it difficult to keep my eyes on their reactions once I was seated. My attention kept wandering to Kristian. Who could blame me? On top of him having the same thick black hair, build, and bronzed complexion as his older brother, he had the dreamiest purple eyes I'd ever seen. Emelie was right. He was smoking hot.

The king, noticing my scrutiny, lowered his head in an abbreviated form of the same strange genuflect Axel had performed in the garden earlier. "Jakob, you did not mention that she is so much like our beloved Alva. It is an amazing likeness."

"I did not notice the similarities until her lineage was revealed," Jakob admitted.

Kristian's shrewd eyes found the ring on my hand and then lifted to meet my face. "No doubt, you had other things on your mind."

I was sure my face was as red as a tomato. The marked look that accompanied his words was one that said he was appreciative of a little more than my commitment to his brother. Was this normal behavior for him?

A glance at Jakob held no explanation. Still absorbed in keeping a watch on Axel, he smiled at what his brother alluded to. "I have been a bit preoccupied. I ask, of course, that you do not speak of this to Soren. I plan on revealing all to him tomorrow."

Kristian inclined his head. "You do not have to ask, Jakob. I am the soul of discretion." Making his approval even more evident, he joined us on the other side of the table and took Jakob's forearm in what I assumed was a show of solidarity. "Congratulations on finding such an extraordinarily beautiful elf. I am relieved that you will have a proper princess at your side." His happy expression soured, becoming full of scorn. "One that understands that you have to make sacrifices for love."

I was surprised by the ferociousness of Kristian's words. Sure, Jakob had mentioned his hatred of his mate, but this was more than hate. This was someone who ached for revenge. She must have done something awful.

Jakob smiled at his brother. "Thank you, Kristian. It means a great deal to me … to us, having you as an ally."

"Of course, brother. I have not forgotten the part that you played in bringing Emelie into my life."

"It was nothing that you would not have done for me," Jakob said, with earnestness in his voice. "You are my brother."

"For the love of the Norse," Axel huffed. "Can you two save the 'I love you. You love me' shit for later. I'm starving over here."

I couldn't hold back my laughter. "Yeah, if you two ladies are finished, some of us are on a schedule here. I pointed to the clock in the corner of the room. "You have twenty-seven minutes, Jakob."

"Twenty-six, my love," he corrected.

Kristian reached out to take my hand, his canines fully extended. "Sorry about the delay," he lisped. "I am Jakob's youngest brother, Kristian."

The king was breathtaking up close, in the literal sense. My breath caught as I accepted his warm hand. The combination of his amethyst eyes and full lips was more than alluring. It was lethal. "It's great to meet you," I replied, not even comprehending what I said. "Erin Doherty, daughter of two psychopaths."

"And I, you, lovely one," he growled, his lips curling upward into a half-smile, hiding all but the tips of his fangs.

"Take care, Kristian," Jakob warned, catching on to Kristian's little diversion. "Use your influence over her again, and I will be taking your place as king tomorrow." His angry eyes softened as he cupped my neck with his hand and leaned down to kiss me. He lingered close for a few seconds before kissing me again, this time, with intensified passion. "Twenty-five minutes, älskling."

I began to believe the validity of the old adage, 'be careful what you wish for' when the first course of dinner was served and the desired (or so I thought) exotic cuisine sat in front of me. I was perplexed by the squishy yellow berries, but even more so by the turquoise and black melon balls. They were bizarre.

Jakob moved his chair closer to mine. "Let me explain, before you cast them aside, älskling. I know that you will love them. These are the fruits from which ambrosia is made."

"Thanks," I whispered, brushing my lips against his stubbled cheek. "But, you better explain fast. You have twenty-one minutes left."

He forked a turquoise sphere and held it to my lips. "Open up, little elf."

I accepted the forkful he offered, wanting to please him with my obedience, but food wasn't on my mind. He was far too attentive, too beautiful, and way too damn sexy not to desire. Just thinking of the promises he'd made for after dinner made me certain that I wasn't going to make it to dessert, or maybe even the next course.

We were so into one another, whispering and sitting way too close to be appropriate, that neither of us remembered that there were others in the room—until Kristian cleared his throat to gain our attention. "It will not matter how many allies you have, Jakob. Soren will kill you for this. Whether he knows or not, if this affair gets out, you are a dead male, as is his right as her brother. You would not want this for a female of your own blood. How could you condemn her to this?"

"I love her," Jakob answered. "She is my true mate. I care not for the consequences I may face in this."

Axel shook his head. "It is good that you do not, my prince. After what I saw in the garden, I would not be at all surprised if your affair is front page news by tomorrow. This will be a huge scandal. I believe that you should prepare yourselves for Soren's arrival in the morning. The guards will not be able to stop him."

Kristian sat back, dejected, though his face still held a smile. He was enjoying this way too much. "The heart wants what it wants, does it not, brother? That is the tragic way of life. Please know that you are both welcome to stay in the castle, indefinitely. Assuming you survive, of course. Nils and Viggo are welcome, as well. We are all family, are we not?"

"We are," Jakob agreed, looking distracted. I cringed as guilt racked me. Axel's words were plaguing him. Why didn't I listen when he tried to stop me? Now we were as good as found out, and it was all my fault.

He squeezed my hand, trying to reassure me. "It is good to know that we are welcome, Kristian, but let us not be rash. We may have been unseen. Nothing is certain yet."

Axel was unconvinced. "We shall see."

"I am sure that Jakob is right," Kristian said, dismissing the topic of conversation in exchange for a slice of delicious smelling bread.

"Right," I agreed. "Let's not make it a big deal, until it is one." Now, if I could only convince myself of that.

Kristian passed a slice of bread to me. "Try Evangelina's bread, Erin. She is the most wonderful cook."

Taking what he offered, I put it on the edge of my plate. "Thank you?" I didn't know what the right response was. Jakob's hands were gripping the edge of the table as if he wanted to strangle his brother, but his face remained passive.

Kristian, however, had a benevolent, innocent expression that was just begging for Jakob's reproach. "What ails you, brother?"

Agitated and looking murderous, Jakob asked, "Why are you giving my mate food from your hands?"

Axel rose in preparation so that he might defend his king. "Sire?"

Kristian waved him down with a grin. "Axel, Jakob's attachment is new. He is not himself. Ignore his outburst."

When Kristian inclined his head to me, still smiling like the little devil he was, I could see how Emelie could have been attracted to him. He was so handsome, it was ridiculous, and he had a persona that lit up the room. He might have appeared reserved and cordial upon first appearances, but after knowing him for ten minutes, I could see that he didn't stand on ceremony … and that he might be just a little evil.

Jakob was fuming. "You are trying to anger me, both of you, but I will not play this game with you two tonight. Ignore them, Erin. They lack the ability to grow up, even after centuries of existence."

Kristian shook his head. "Game? No, Jakob. There is no game. I am trying to prove a point. You cannot be this possessive and attentive to her in public. A creature would have to be blind not to know that you two are a couple. If Soren does not know by now, he will once he sees you two together."

"Be that as it may—" Jakob started, before getting interrupted by the staff with the next course. "We will finish this conversation later."

The king smirked. "As you wish."

After a few minutes into the next course, I realized that my thoughts about Kristian were right. In a brazen attempt, he was using his flair for magnetism to try to lure my attention from Jakob, who was busy explaining the strange, vivid orange soup. Axel, too, was trying his own version of hypnotism on me. I gave them a clear, stern 'it would be wise not to piss me off' look and brought my gaze back to the gold-rimmed tableware. I shouldn't have wasted the energy. It caused them to double their efforts. Try as I may to resist them, their influence soon won over. Even with Jakob occupying my every thought, when I heard Kristian's accented voice, my eyes drifted to his beautiful mouth on their own volition. Axel's was just as captivating. His deep voice snapped my attention to him like a gunshot on the rare occasions he spoke. I couldn't fight them. I didn't know how. With their combined capability to enthrall without lifting a finger, it was a wonder that these two hadn't already conquered the whole of the Norselands.

Jakob wasn't ignorant to all of the frivolity they were enjoying. In fact, my wandering eyes had his possessive nature enflamed to a breaking point. I knew this because every few seconds his control would slip, and I would hear tiny wisps of the nonverbal tongue lashing Kristian and Axel were getting.

I allowed him a minute or two to release his well-directed anger, then I stood and excused myself from the table. He followed my lead, with a questioning look. "Älskling?"

"Just a minute," I promised, walking back to the two tricksters and summoning every bit of influence that I could. I hoped that I was blessed with the talent, or at the least that the spell book would help me with Kristian, who stood as I approached the table.

"Lady Erin?" he inquired, confused by my return.

I curtseyed so that they could both see the cleavage that Jakob would soon have his hands on and smiled a seductive, persuasive smile. "Thanks for dinner, boys. It was fun." I lowered my voice. "But not as much fun as what I'm going to be doing for the next four to six—" I broke off, looking behind me to where Jakob stood and corrected myself. "Make that eight to twelve hours."

With a saucy wink, I made my way back to Jakob, who smirked at Kristian and Axel's open-mouthed faces and said, "Good day, gentle-males."

I didn't make it two feet out of the dining room doorway before Jakob captured me in his grip, threw my protesting form over his shoulder, and strode down the corridor without missing a beat. Amused at this new aggressive behavior, I slid down to wrap my legs around his waist, smiling when he cupped my bottom to support my weight. If that wasn't a massive step in the right direction, I didn't know what was.

"Where are you taking me, caveman?"

"First bed that I find," he growled through gritted teeth. He was a male on a mission—hallelujah.

"Well, you've just passed it," I said, spying an elaborate four-poster, which would be more than sufficient, through a couple of open doorways.

He shook his head without looking. "Any bed but that one. That chamber belonged to the harem."

I could hear car brakes squealing to a stop in my head. "Did you just say harem?"

Observing the revulsion I exhibited with a sigh, he stopped walking. "Erin, my father was from a different time. Long ago, it was a common practice for wealthy families to keep a harem."

"And yet, that doesn't make it any less disturbing," I pointed out. "How did your mothers cope with sharing his, um … affection?" I unwound my legs from his waist and slid to the floor to peek into the room.

He looked horrified. "Can we not talk about my parent's sex life right now?"

I mimed locking my lips and tossing the key. "Is it something straight out of Arabian Nights in there? Are there chains and whips?"

Jakob walked over the partially opened door and pushed it the rest of the way open. "Look around. I know you will not be satisfied until you see it."

He was so right. Not that I would tell him that. Walking past him into the room, I found a large, lavish parlor with two identical doorways on either side of a huge golden mirror. I wasn't expecting the sheer amount of extravagance that the room boasted. With furs, silks, and lavish carpets that would feed a small village for hundreds of years, the females of the harem had lived in luxury beyond even what the king enjoyed. I looked to Jakob in amazement. "This is bliss. Where do I sign up?"

He closed the space between us, molding his rock hard chest against my back. With his lips against my ear, he whispered, "You would be at the king's disposal for sex and blood at any given moment."

I shivered, forgetting how to make syllables come out of my mouth. "Wou—Would I?"

Silent, with slow, methodical touches, he wrapped my long hair around his fist until it was taut within his grip, then tugged me upward, lifting me onto my toes. "Night after night of meaningless sex, being drained to the point of weakness as a reward, is that something you would want for eternity?" His voice was dangerous and deep, bordering on a growl.

Answering him without pause or humility, I said, "If you were the male, yes, it does."

His muscular arm snaked around my waist, pulling me flush against the hard erection behind his zipper. Inhaling a slow breath, I shuddered as he nicked the tender nape of my neck and licked away the small bead of blood that welled there. "They would call you a blood-whore, Erin."

"So be it," I told him, ignoring the clear double meaning in his words. I knew he was attempting to spare me the shame of being his mistress. He didn't want me to suffer. However, on this, I wouldn't be swayed. "I will have you as my mate, Jakob. In any capacity."

"Take off your clothes," he commanded, before dropping the captured length of my hair and spinning me to face him.

With frightening intensity, his eyes burned into mine as a sudden, strong gust of wind blew the door shut, making my heart race anew. I didn't think, just obeyed him. My fingers flew to my top, nimbly unfastening each button with an efficiency that I owed more to my perpetual lateness than skill. My bra followed the shirt in the same expeditious manner. Jakob issued a guttural, approving growl as he ripped his t-shirt from his shoulders and kicked off his boots with hurried motions.

He was so beautiful, sculpted so perfectly, that when he pushed down his jeans to reveal his heavy erection, I froze, struck dumb. It had been a long time since I'd seen someone of the opposite sex this undressed—a looong time. And even then, they never looked like Jakob did.

A sexy chuckle roused me from my hypnotic state, bringing

my attention back to his face. "I want you naked," he reminded me.

More than happy to oblige, I let the flimsy, sheer fabric of my pants drop to the ground, and then hooked my thumbs into the sides of my panties to slip them over my hips. "As you wish, master."

"Master," he scoffed. "You think to win my favor with pleasantries, do you, female?"

I stiffened with fear and desire as he prowled around me. There was no other word for the sleek movement he made as he circled me, memorizing every inch of my exposed skin with his sharp eyes. He was a wild animal on the hunt. "I am just eager to please you, sire."

"Are you, Erin?" he asked, his face hard and hungry. "Are you eager for me?"

"Yes," I admitted, trembling under his stare, though I wanted so much to hold my head high and keep my poise perfect for our little game.

His voice was hoarse but controlled as he spoke. "Bedroom, female—now, before I take you here on the carpet."

Not moving, I dared him to make good on the threat. "Anything you desire."

With a low groan, he dragged me to the floor, forcing my thighs open with his body and kissing me so roughly, I knew he would bruise my lips. I didn't care. He tasted of the wine we'd consumed at dinner, exotic, sweet, intoxicating, and just as overpowering. Arching into him, I offered myself. "Fuck me, Jakob."

With his face tight from agonized need, he gripped his generous length, angled its broad head toward my ready wetness, and plunged into me with a growl and a flash of clenched, white fangs. Though I'd anticipated it, the exquisite shock of him pushing inside me drew a sharp cry from my lips that echoed off the walls of the room.

Jakob stilled within me, looking apologetic. "Erin?"

"Please, don't stop," I moaned, seizing his gorgeous, muscled ass and digging my nails into the firm flesh to urge him on.

"Never," he groaned, his eyes never leaving mine.

Lost in his stare, I began to contort my body to keep up with the punishing thrusts he delivered. The roar of the fire within me drowned out the sharp cries and incoherent words that sprang from my lips, over and over, until I came to my screaming completion. Collapsing hoarse, breathing hard, and boneless from pleasure on the carpet, I was in awe. "That. Was. Incredible."

He returned my loopy smile with a devious one of his own, while not too subtly reminding me that he was still rock hard and deep inside of me. "What makes you think this is over, by any means?"

I giggled. "Oh, my mistake. Carry on then."

"I intend to," he assured me, pushing deeper into my warmth.

"I love the sound of that," I confessed, my laughter fading into gasps as my body reawakened with every slow stroke.

His fangs glinted in the light of the chandeliers as his lips curved in amusement. "The sound alone?"

"Jakob, do you see anything in my ridiculous sex faces that makes you think I'm not enjoying myself with you?"

His smile widened. "No."

"Exactly."

He rolled us over so that I straddled his hips. "Your sex faces are not ridiculous."

Attempting to be the 'sultry vixen,' I leaned forward and nipped hard at his bottom lip, drawing blood. "They're not?"

"No," he groaned, pulling my hips back down as he thrust upward. "They are not." Moving a long lock of hair over my shoulder, he captured my breasts in his hands, first raking his tongue across a hardened nipple, then sinking his teeth into the flesh. Caught off guard, I hissed, my body moving by instinct to follow the quickening movements he made as he licked the blood from my skin. "Do you have any idea how sexy you are right now?" he asked, getting to his feet with impressive ease and pressing my back into the huge mirror that dominated the wall. "The breathy little moans you make, the flush of your cheeks, my blood on your heart-shaped mouth—you are ravishing, älskling." His hands tangled in my hair as he dragged lips, hot as embers, across my own, the blood coating them coaxing my fangs out of hiding. Bringing his hand to my mouth, he offered his palm. "Take my blood. Make me your mate. Even if it is only symbolic. I will not suffer another night without you in my bed."

Trembling, I held out my hand. "Jakob, there is nothing I want more."

Relieved, Jakob drew my hand to his mouth, biting down on the pad of my thumb until two twin beads of blood welled to the surface, then dragged it down his bottom lip, leaving a crimson trail. "Erin, my älskling, I accept you as my true fated mate. Let us never be parted."

Smiling, I laid a kiss in the center of his palm before biting down and mimicking his actions. "Jakob, I accept you as my true fated mate. Let us never be parted."

With a look of unadulterated love, he ran the back of his knuckles down my cheek and took my lips in a hungry kiss, before jerking away to gasp out and grind his teeth against an invisible pain.

"Are you okay?" I asked, pushing his hair back from his forehead. I didn't feel any pain, just an intense connection pulsating between us.

"The pain was not my own. It is hers," he explained, bringing his solemn eyes to mine. "I feel … you, Erin. You are my heaven. Your scent, your taste …" He pressed deeper into me. "I crave you."

"And I, you," I whimpered, almost unable to string together two coherent words as I began to lose myself in the pleasure he was bringing me. Again and again, he pushed into me, each time harder than the last, until I cried out, sinking my teeth into his shoulder to revel in the dark spice of his magical blood. After a few draws, I threw my head back, moaning out in pleasure as my elemental power swirled around us in a whirlwind of lust and want. Growling, he sank his hands into my hair, taking my mouth in a brutal kiss and driving himself faster and harder until he roared out his release, spilling deep inside of me.

"Wow. That was …" I panted for breath.

Jakob leaned a forearm against the glass and rested his forehead on my shoulder. "Insane?"

I smirked. "What? Most elves don't get mated during sex … against a mirror … in a harem?"

He lifted his head to look at me. "Älskling, no one has ever gotten mated without a Norn—ever. It is an impossibility."

"Nothing is impossible, Jakob. Not now." I kissed his healing bottom lip and tasted blood. Mine or his, I didn't know. We were pretty much covered in it. "Where's the nearest shower?"

He gestured to the room on his right. "Through the door and down the hallway."

"You seem pretty familiar with the layout," I said, suspicious of his intimate knowledge of the harem. "You didn't come here in the past for a little entertainment of the carnal variety, did you?" Please, say no.

"There has been no one else," he assured me, picking up on the tinge of jealousy that tainted my words. "You have forgotten that I was mated for centuries upon centuries."

"So was your father, and that didn't stop him," I pointed out.

"I swear to you that I have never used the harem for sex. Until tonight."

I smiled. "Well then, it was a pleasure servicing you, your highness."

He ran his fingers down my ribcage and the sides of my thighs, coaxing a purr from my lips. "The pleasure was all mine."

Threading my fingers through his thick, black hair, I brought his mouth to mine, then lifted myself off of his erection and slid to the floor before he could convince me to postpone washing the harem from my body. "Are you coming?"

"I will be in a moment," he answered, as he eyed my naked body with interest. He was wicked.

I raised an eyebrow at his innuendo, and then laughed when he mimicked me. Damn, he was sexy. I will never, even if I live a million years, get tired of that devilish smile of his ... or the way he feels inside me. Just thinking about the perfect way we'd fit together made me want to turn right back around and beg him for round three ... and four, maybe five. Hell, I may never leave this room.

"We have to eat, or we'll starve," Jakob reminded me, kissing my fingertips.

I sighed, rolling off of him and snuggling up to his side. "Yeah, but what a fantastic way to go." After round three in the shower and four and five in the harem's bed, food was the last thing on my mind.

"You are insatiable, älskling."

"For my mate, I am," I said, kissing his nose. "So, this food you mentioned? Do I have to leave the room to get it?" The harem proved hard to leave. Indeed, it was so hard that I was thinking of asking Jakob if we could take the room as ours when I moved into the castle. Besides the to-die-for bathtub built for six, it had a balcony unlike any I'd ever seen. As big as the room itself, it was decorated with vines upon vines of night-blooming roses and moonflowers, all intertwined around the wrought iron railing, filling the air with their sweetness. It was a little piece of paradise, and without too much prodding, I convinced Jakob to spend an hour before sunrise in the lounge chair with me, wrapped up in a blanket to watch the night sky. Well, watching when he wasn't being naughty. My mate was a bit insatiable himself.

"I can have someone bring food to us if you desire. That is if you are okay with the staff finding us in here."

Cringing, I shook my head. Anyone finding out we were here was a bad idea. Soren would flip his lid if he found out Jakob besmirched his sister's honor in the harem. "No, we should go, but first," I looked around. "I need pants."

"Go without them. No one will be about at this time of day."

Incredulous, I stopped my search. "Are you suggesting I prance about the castle naked from the waist down?"

His brows lifted in amusement. "As enticing as that would be, Erin, no. I am suggesting that you wear the robe from the bathroom."

I blushed. Of all the idiotic things I could have said. "You know, I think it might be entirely possible that you've fucked my brains out."

He laughed at my embarrassment. "I do not think that is possible."

"Oh, yes it is. Just take a look in this empty head."

Standing to pull on his jeans, he said, "No thanks. I prefer to remember your mind the way it was—compulsively worried and preoccupied with sex."

I scoffed. "Any woman would be preoccupied with sex with you in their bed, brains or not."

"That statement is a hundred percent not true," he assured me, bemused at my fawning over his sexual prowess—which was extensive.

"Uh, sure it's not," I teased. Although, I wasn't sure if he was being modest or truthful. The one thing that I was sure of was that I'd be making the walk of shame to the kitchen wearing a goofy smile along with the robe from the bathroom. "Ready?"

He opened the door with a flourish. "After you."

"Why, thank you, kind prince."

"Of course." Once in the hallway, Jakob pointed to the end of the long corridor. "I want to show you something before we eat. Do you mind?"

"Not at all." The castle looked to have, at least, five-hundred rooms. We could explore all day and still not see everything.

"The gallery is just off the staff's entrance. It will not take a minute."

He opened an ornate door and led me inside. My eyes were drawn to the heavy gilded frame of a life-sized painting as soon as we entered. It took one glance at the cruel indifference that marred the beautiful raven-haired female's face to know that she was my mother. "Is it a good likeness of Viveka?"

Jakob wrapped his arms around me from behind. "It is. The artist has captured her beauty, utterly."

Still somewhat stunned, I stared at my mother for a few moments more, taking in everything I could. "She is perfect—a vision."

His heavy sigh tickled my ear. "Erin, that beauty does not extend to her heart. Do not be tempted to trust her because she gave birth to you. She has done unspeakable things."

"Unspeakable things? Like what?" I knew he wasn't exaggerating. He'd used the real name-stern voice combo. That only happened when he was serious about something.

"She joined with Freyr in torturing my brother to near insanity. For over a hundred years, she drove him mad with the thought that he was a rapist when, in fact, he had done nothing. That was two years ago, and the last time anyone has seen her."

Well, that explained the apology Axel had given me outside. My mother was as horrid as everyone had warned. Great. Did I win the parent lottery or what?

Nudging my shocked form along, Jakob led me to the adjoining chamber to show me another painting. I sucked in a breath. It was my grandmother, Alva. The female was almost an exact replica of me. The one difference was the rich chocolate brown of her eyes. They had a twinkle of humor in them as if she had a secret joy that she could not share. I walked closer, amazed at the incredible likeness, devouring every inch of the painting, looking for dissimilarities. I found few. We even had the same fingers...and jewelry. In the portrait, she was wearing the ring I now wore. Turning to Jakob, I held out my hand. "I thought you said that this was your mother's ring?"

He nodded with a half-smile. "And it is. Alva was my mother for so many years that I have lost count. How I wish she were here today. This castle was once alive with magic and the sounds of a loving family. Now, it is a tomb. I fear when Alva drew her last breath, the kingdom did, as well. It is a pity that you see it as it is."

Smiling, I blinked back tears. For the first time in my life, it felt like I had some connection to my family.

Jakob pulled me into his embrace, resting his head on my shoulder. "Älskling, I did not bring you here to upset you."

"I'm not upset. I'm not. I feel like I'm home."

I could feel his grin as he kissed my neck. "You are, Lady Väsen, you are.

In the staff kitchen, which was still four times bigger and ten times more luxurious than my own, we found Kristian with a bottle of tequila and an embittered expression.

"Hi," I offered, sitting across from him. "What's the good word?"

Violet eyes glared at me. "What good is there without a

mate?" he slurred, leaning on the wood table. "I have lived an eternity without a female to call my own—an eternity of waiting, hoping, seeking, of wanting. Even after Emelie promised my mate was soon to come, still, she has not arrived. I grow tired of the trial, tired of life."

My word. I don't think anyone could have anticipated that kind of response out of the dark elf king. Jakob was standing stunned at the counter, a loaf of bread in one hand and a jar of mayo in the other. He hadn't known how much his brother was suffering either. Switching places with Jakob, I took the sandwich supplies and pushed him toward his downtrodden brother. Kristian was in a lot of pain. I didn't think kind words from me were going to cut it, so I took a knife to the bread instead, all the while wondering how soon she was destined to arrive. If I could just ask Emelie, I bet she'd know.

Oh, wait. I can. *"Emelie?"*

She answered right away. *"Hi, Erin! How's it going?"*

"Not great. Kristian is drunk and wallowing in some serious self-pity," I told her.

Her tinkling laugh filled the connection. *"Kristian doesn't drink."*

I watched him take another shot. *"Well, he does today."*

"Are you serious?"

"Dead serious. I think seeing Jakob with me might have broken him."

She sighed. *"I was afraid of that. He has been so lonely."*

"Yeah. So, you think you can put a pin on that true mate of his before he does something more drastic?"

"Of course, I'll be right there."

"We're in the staff kitchen."

"Hi," Emelie said, making us all jump.

Kristian was on his unsteady feet so fast that his chair fell backward. "Emelie, my mate, where is she? I can bear it no longer."

She held her hands out to him without preamble. "We'll find her now."

Jakob and I smiled at each other as Emelie's eyes silvered over. I knew without asking what was on Jakob's mind. He was eased by his brother finding his mate, and not because of the guilt he felt in finding his own true mate, but because he knew Kristian needed her so badly.

"Her name is Shannon," Emelie told us. "She's human and from ... oh." She paused, looking weirded out. "Uh."

"Emelie?" Kristian pressed, panic rising in his voice.

She shook her head, clearing her eyes. "Oh gosh, I'm sorry, Kristian. Shannon Eve is your female's name, and she's from Midgard—in Alabama. I think I'm seeing that she works in a tire store?"

We all felt Kristian's relief when he breathed an alleviated sigh, then met our eyes. "Thank you. All of you."

"Thank us by going to find her!" I exclaimed, laughing when he managed to pull the shifting stone from his pocket before I finished speaking. A second later, he was gone.

Emelie dusted off her hands and grinned. "Another crisis averted."

"Your modesty is admirable," I teased.

Jakob bowed. "Safe journey, Emelie."

"Sure thing, Jakob, and Erin?" She eyed my bathrobe. "I want details as soon as I see you next. Scratch that, before I see you, 'kay?"

I grinned. "You got it, Em."

CHAPTER EIGHT

I woke to Jakob's strong arm pulling me snug against his erection. Smiling into the pillow, I hummed a sigh of contentment as elation bloomed inside of me. I was mated to the sexiest male in existence.

"Good evening, älskling," his deep voice mumbled into my ear.

Yawning, I rolled over in his arms, resting my cheek on the light sprinkling of hair on his chest. "Good evening, my mate."

He kissed the top of my head. "You honor me."

"I don't know how you can say that. I fell asleep on you this morning." A glance at the clock told me that I'd slept most of the day away.

His hands slid down to drag me on top of him. "Apologies are not necessary. It was my fault. I did not allow you to rest."

No, he hadn't. He had ravished me. We made love so many times that I had already lost count before I passed out with him still inside of me. I ground myself into his hardness, my hips moving in slow circles. "You know, I'm feeling pretty rested right now. How about you?"

He drew his hands up my ribcage and let his thumbs graze the hardened peaks of my breasts. "Incredibly rested, my love."

My next words were interrupted by the excruciatingly loud crash of the door being blown off of its hinges. Screaming, I scrambled off of Jakob to cover my nakedness a second before Soren strode into the room.

Jakob stood up naked, ready to defend me, his green eyes glowing with the power he was prepared to unleash.

Soren's eyes moved from Jakob to me with disgust. "I thought you might want to see today's headlines." He threw a green-inked newspaper onto the foot of the bed and stalked out of the room.

"Fuck!" was Jakob's only response to the picture on the front page. It showed the two of us on the garden bench, my fangs buried into his neck while his hands were planted firmly on my ass. The headline, in big block letters above it, read, *PRINCE JAKOB VÄSEN HAS AFFAIR WITH FIRE-WALKER.*

"Shit!" I added. "I'll talk to him and tell him that we're mated."

Jakob shook his head. "It will not matter to him."

"I have to try." I stood up to get dressed, quickly realizing that I'd left my clothes in the harem and that my robe was in shreds on the floor. In desperation, I wrapped the sheet around me, kissed Jakob, and ran after my brother. I caught up to him in the foyer and yelled at his retreating form. "Soren!"

He stopped but didn't turn around.

"Please don't go without hearing what I have to say!" I pleaded.

His eyes widened when he finally spared me a glance. "Have you any shame?"

"Jakob is my mate. We had our bonding ceremony this morning. I've done nothing wrong."

He snapped his fingers, and the sheet I wore was replaced with traditional elven garb. "Of course, you have not." Reaching out, he stroked my cheek. "With your endearing naivety, I should have known someone would try to take advantage of you. I blame myself."

His pious attitude pissed me off. "This is no one's fault! I love him, and he loves me!"

Ignoring my outburst, he tenderly took my hand. "Are you so sure that it is you that he loves?"

His question confused me. Who else would he love? "What do you mean?"

"I cannot believe he has not told you."

I didn't like his tone. It immediately put me on the defensive. "If you mean about his ex-mate, yes, he has."

"Has he told you that his 'ex-mate' is your mother?"

A sharp jolt flashed across my chest, and I gasped out at the pain. Disbelieving and numb, I asked, "Viveka was his mate?"

"In the eyes of the council and the whole of the Norselands, he is her mate."

I felt dizzy and nauseous as I thought back to Soren saying that Jakob knew her best. How blind I'd been not to have seen this.

Soren wrapped an arm around my shoulders. "Allow me to escort you to Ásgard."

"No, I need to be alone for a minute."

"You cannot stay here, Erin. I will not allow it."

In the history of wrong things to say to someone who is broken-hearted, that must have been among the top ten. It pushed me right over the edge. "You know what? Fuck you, Soren."

"Pardon?"

"I said. Fuck. You. I'm tired of your hypocritical bullshit. Our situations are almost identical! You didn't worry about Emelie's honor when you were trying to fuck her two years ago."

He sucked in an angry breath. "Emelie is not my sister."

"And that makes it any better?" I yelled, the fire within me begging to be let loose.

"No, it does not." He sighed. "Can you not see that I wanted better than this for you? You should be treated with respect, Erin."

I pleaded with my eyes. "Jakob is your best friend and my true mate. Who could treat me with more respect?"

"A male that respects you would never subject you to the scrutiny he has. Your face is plastered halfway around the Norselands!" Turning toward the door, he said, "Say your goodbyes, Erin. I expect you back at the apartment soon," and then he left.

That was it, the straw that broke the proverbial camel's back. It was time to leave. I couldn't stand another minute of Soren or this situation. If I didn't get out of here soon, I was going to lose my mind. Closing my eyes, I concentrated on my apartment, willing myself to shift there. I knew I had the power to do it if my brother did.

Jakob yelled from the top of the staircase, startling me into opening my eyes. "Erin, stop! Do not leave!"

He was too late. The familiar weightless feeling that accompanied shifting was already upon me. I didn't know how to stop it once it was underway, and right now, I didn't want to. I couldn't believe that he would keep something like this from me. My own mother! Regardless of me telling him I didn't want details about his mate, he should have told me it was Viveka. Tears of anger and hurt rolled down my cheeks as Jakob's anguished face disappeared from my view.

I sensed that something was off the second I appeared in the darkness of my apartment's hallway. Tiptoeing my way to the living room, I found that my instincts were dead on. My apartment was in disarray. Every book on my bookshelves had been searched and thrown unceremoniously to the floor. All of my cabinets and kitchen drawers were open in the kitchen. The place was ransacked, and ... oh shit, dusted for fingerprints.

Dread filled me. I hadn't listened when Emelie reminded me to call Chase, and she had freaked out and called the police. Honestly, what else had I expected her to do? Ignore her boss and best friend not showing up to work for days? Oh, this would be bad. She was going to be royally pissed at me for not telling her I was taking a little vacation ... to get mated ... to an elf. Even I didn't believe it. How would she?

I hurried to where the phone should have been and found it missing. The police must have taken it in as evidence. Evidence of what, I have no idea. The answering machine hadn't worked right in months. Stepping over a pile of scattered books and DVD's, I made my way to my bedroom and grabbed a jacket from the closet. I needed to get to the shop, now. What was I thinking, shirking my responsibilities like this? I was the worst friend and boss—ever.

The short walk to the store seemed like a monumental task. I didn't remember it being so bright, or painful. Pulling my jacket above my head. I tried to shield myself from the worst of the sun's rays, but eventually, I gave up the pretense that I was not burning to a crisp and ran the last two blocks to the safety of the store. Crashing blindly through the opened door, I collapsed between the non-fiction sections and started to cry, cradling my badly burned hands. They'd taken the brunt of the sun's assault when I held my coat up to protect my face. How could I have forgotten about the dark elves inability to withstand sunlight? My skin felt like it was getting stung by a million tiny pricks of a needle at the same time. How stupid could I be?

A soft, soothing voice sounded to my left. "Erin?"

Through my tears, I could see Chase's solemn eyes looking over the various spots of smoking flesh. They were as wide as saucers. "Hey."

She crouched down on her knees, fat tears rolling down her cheeks. "Oh, Erin. I thought you'd been kidnapped! The police said that the first forty-eight hours were the most critical time. I didn't think I'd ever see you again."

"I'm okay. Just give me a minute to catch my breath." And for my flesh to hopefully mend itself.

Chase's forehead was etched with worry. "What happened to you? You vanished without a trace. Your checking account, credit cards, bus pass, none of them were touched. It was like you dropped off the planet. Where were you? What happened to your hands?"

I looked around the store from my prone position. "Are there any customers?"

"No. Why?" She was understandably confused. "Are you in some kind of trouble? Tell me what's going on!"

For a moment, I debated telling her the truth. She was the best friend that I'd ever had in my life. If anyone would believe something like this, it would be her, right? I really, really hoped so.

Bracing myself for the worst, I began. "There's something unbelievable that I need to tell you. Can you lock the door? I don't want anyone to overhear this."

"Okay." She did as I asked and then sat at the counter, nervously chewing her thumbnail and looking more scared than I'd ever seen her. Soren probably wouldn't approve of me sharing my secret with her, but even he could understand that I didn't have anyone else to confide in. I certainly couldn't talk to him about it. That was out of the question, and Emelie was grossed out by the mere thought of Jakob being intimate with me. There was no one else.

Gritting my teeth against the agony, I struggled to my feet and shuffled to the counter, where I sat staring mindlessly at my wedding ring, wondering where the best place was to start.

Chase leaned across the countertop and smiled. "That's a beautiful ring, Erin. Elven made—the clothes, too. Am I right?"

Stunned, I jerked my gaze to her. "You know?"

"Well no, not about the ring, but about the Norselands, yes. I'm a faery."

I exhaled a deep breath as sweet relief filled me. I didn't have to convince her of anything. She already knew.

She cocked her head and narrowed her eyes in suspicion. "Are you engaged to the King? Who else in Svartálfaheim can afford a rock like that? Spill, lady. Where exactly have you been?"

"You'll have to give me a second to wrap my mind around the absurdity of anyone being mated to Kristian, and then I'll happily tell you where I've been."

Arching an eyebrow, she asked, "You're on a first name basis with the king?"

"I spent some highly memorable time at Väsen Castle before I came back to Midgard."

True to form, Chase looked suitably impressed with my little adventure. "Memorable time at the castle, huh? I just bet it was."

Feigning ignorance, I drew a halo around my head with my rapidly healing hand, then smiled like the cat who ate the canary.

She grinned. "You've been a bad girl!"

"Maybe," I conceded.

Her smirking, mirthful face suddenly became pensive. "Wait a minute."

Anxious at her strange tone, I sat up straight. "What is it?"

"Which of his brothers gave you that ring?"

"Jakob did, we …" I trailed off and shot my eyes to her chagrined face. "Damn it, Chase! You've known Viveka was my mother this whole time? Why on Earth … I mean, Midgard, didn't you tell me?"

She bristled at my anger. "Yeah, right! So you could go off all half-cocked to find your faerytale mother and live happily ever after? No, thank you!" Noticing my indignant look, she added, "We both know she would have had you brainwashed and doing her dirty work, long ago, if I had told you."

Laying my head on the counter, I moaned. "That is so true. I would have run off like an idiot."

"Yes, you would have. Even as a small child you were headstrong." She patted my head. "It hasn't been easy to keep you hidden."

131

I peeked out from my folded arms. "Small child? How long did you watch over me before we met?" We'd only been friends for a few years.

"Since you were seven. It has been a great honor to be trusted with the safekeeping of Odin's child. The job would not have been awarded to anyone who wasn't up for the task, so there's a fair amount of prestige involved." She frowned. "Well, until now. I'm in so much trouble because of your disappearance."

I scooted my chair away from her, just in case she decided to get any payback for me forgetting to call her. "I'm so sorry, Chase. I had so much going on that it just slipped my mind." Stiffening with a horrible thought, I asked, "Who are you in trouble with? You aren't with Odin, are you?" I didn't want to have to fight my best friend, but I would if it meant that I wouldn't be served up to my father on a silver platter.

"No!" she said vehemently. "The faeries serve no one but our queen."

"I'm glad. I really need a friend right now."

She examined my healed hand. "So, sleeping with your Mom's old male, huh? How's that going?"

I smirked. "Well, if my brother, Soren, weren't trying to cock-block me, it would be so much better."

She shook her head. "I can't believe you're speaking of Soren in that way. It's so weird. He's revered, you know. As in, he's the mightiest of Odin's sons regardless of Thor's popularity. Everyone knows the real strength lies with his first son."

"Whatever!" I said disgruntled. "Soren may be powerful, but he can be a real hypocritical dick, and I have my own talents now, I'll have you know. Magic that Soren doesn't have, damn it. We'll soon see who is the most powerful."

She slapped her palms on the counter. "You seriously have to spill, Miss Powerful. I want to know everything. Start from the beginning and don't stop until you get to right now."

"Well, the biggest news is that Jakob Väsen and I are mated."

Her mouth dropped open. "How?"

"Do you remember the spell book … the one with the runes?"

She nodded. "Hell yeah, I remember it. It came up missing at the same time you did. I figured that if you weren't kidnapped, your disappearance would have something to do with the book."

"It did. Jakob was summoned when I recited a spell. He scared me so much that I almost sprayed him with pepper spray, but then he called my brother and his mate, and they came here to meet me. Emelie is really sweet, but Soren makes me want to pull my hair out one strand at a time."

She shrugged. "Sounds like typical brother stuff to me. So, what did the spell do? I mean, besides call him to you. I wonder if it was a spell to find love."

"I don't think so. Jakob read over it and said that he and all of the dark elves on Midgard are mine to command. Whether that's really true, I have no idea. So far, nothing else has happened, at all."

"Okay, that doesn't sound ominous or anything. What happened after you met Soren and the Norn?"

I smiled, remembering what happened in front of Jakob's bathroom mirror. "Jakob took me to his house on Álfheim."

"And gave it to you pretty damn good, if I'm to judge by that goofy smile."

"Not right away," I said, a blush filling my cheeks.

"Wow … but Prince Jakob makes a stick in the mud look exciting. Why him? Why not the Mad King? He's freaking hot. Those eyes. They're just downright drool-worthy."

"Mad King? Kristian? Please, the only thing mad about him is the way he screws with his brother. I'm telling you, it's a testament to Jakob's patience that Kristian isn't six feet under somewhere. He and his right hand are quite the practical jokers."

She shook her head in amazement. "Look at you—standing up for your male. You're smitten, aren't you?"

I couldn't deny it. I was in love. More than that, I was in the kind of love that made me wonder what Jakob would look like caring for our young. "He's my true mate, Chase. It's impossible not to love him."

Her disbelieving smirk faded at the mention of him being my true mate and was replaced by a look that could only be described as crushed.

"Chase, what is it?"

She stared at the Mystery section with unseeing eyes, her mind somewhere far away. "I found my true mate a few years ago," she said after a while, smiling bitterly to herself. "He was ruggedly handsome, a giant of a male. I worshipped him, Erin. He was my … everything." Bringing her eyes back to me, she sighed. "As much as I craved this male, as much as I knew that he was for me, he didn't reciprocate my feelings."

I was floored. How could anyone not love Chase? She was stunning. The male had to be blind … and stupid.

She shook her head. "I can't believe I told you that. I thought I would carry it to my grave."

"I'm glad you did, Chase. I just wish I didn't feel so shitty about shoving my happiness in your face."

"Don't be. I don't see him anymore, so it's easier for me than it used to be. I'm happy for you, Erin. You deserve this after the life you've had."

I nodded and pulled down the shoulder of my top to expose my back and veer away from the subject. I didn't want to make her uncomfortable by asking anything else about him. No sense in dredging up painful memories. "I got my valknut the second we left Midgard. It hurt like hell."

She laughed and showed me hers. "We have matching tattoos!"

"Badass!"

"Yeah, well. I think we lose a little street cred because there are millions of others with the same one."

"Maybe you do," I huffed. "Damn, I wish I would've had the chance to meet Odin. I'd love to tell him how much I love this new body art of mine."

"You considered meeting with him? Are you insane?"

"Soren didn't think denying his request to see me was wise, and he is my father."

"So, then why didn't you meet him?"

"Your queen, oddly enough. She stopped us in the woods once we arrived on Ásgard and advised us not to."

Chase froze. "Who did?"

I furrowed my brow and sighed, readying myself for more bad news. "Why do I feel like I'm about to learn something that is going to piss me off?"

"Because there's no way that my Queen could have been on Ásgard."

Slamming my now healed hand down on the counter, I let out a yell of frustration. "Viveka, you bitch!" That female was evil incarnate. I hoped she could hear me curse her in whatever corner of hell she lived in.

"Easy, killer. What did she say to you while you were there?"

"She berated Soren, but she also told us that Loki had been freed and gave me a shifting stone."

She sprung to her feet. "Let's have it. There's no telling what magic has been put on the stone."

Terrified by her words, I dug it out of my pocket and flung it on the counter as if it were poisonous.

She grinned at the girly squeal that accompanied my throw. "Relax," she soothed, holding the stone up to the fluorescent light and then handing it back. "The Queen will examine it to determine what damage it has done. Are you ready to meet the real Queen Layla?"

"We're going to Faeryland?"

"It's called Älvornas Rike, and yes, we are. Don't get your hopes up for something exciting. We are much like the humans."

"Sure you are. Except for the whole flying and turning into a foot tall version of yourself. Which, by the way, is super cool."

"Yeah, except for that."

"Well, is there anything I should know before we go?"

Her perfect, bee-stung lips pursed in thought. "Look down when we arrive. It's bright to outsiders."

"Gotcha." I moved to stand up but hesitated. "They aren't going to think that it's weird that you're bringing an elf home, are they?"

"I don't think anyone would call you an elf. Not with you being Odin's daughter."

The sudden, worried expression that graced her face alarmed me. "That's not a reassuring look on your face."

"Nope," she said, with a half-smile.

"Ugh. This should be fun," I griped, as we linked arms and popped out of the shop.

CHAPTER NINE

There was no blinding white light on this journey, only blackness and then an explosion of color. I shaded my eyes with my hands and stared down at the vivid green grass on the sides of the well-worn path Chase was all but dragging me down.

"How can you see?" I demanded of her, tears leaking out of the corners of my eyes.

"I'm used to it. You will become accustomed to the intensity in a few minutes."

That was a huge relief. "Where are we going?"

"To the castle. Layla needs to know what's going on."

Ten or so minutes later, my eyes adjusted, and I was able to see my surroundings. It was amazing. The area around us was teeming with both tiny and human-sized faeries that all bowed and then skittered out of our way, chattering with delight as they skirted the many brilliantly colored bunches of flowers lining the path.

Waving to a shy, young female that was hiding behind her mother's leg, I smiled, enchanted with everything around me. "It is so gorgeous here, Chase."

She grimaced. "I suppose it is."

Our walk ended at a gleaming castle with turrets so high that they were obscured by the fluffy, white clouds that were scattered across the perfect azure sky above us. It was magical in every sense. Mostly in the sense that the castle was pulsing with power. I had a feeling that if you threw a rock at it, it would either throw it back, or it would be sucked in, never to be seen again. Not too terrifying.

The second the guards at the ornate entrance saw Chase, they let us in without question, leading us up a massive white marble staircase to a double door. One slipped inside while the other told us to wait. Chase looked ready to jump out of her skin when the doors opened, and the real Queen Layla appeared.

"You have found her. Excellent."

I dropped to my knee to bow the way Soren had shown me and dipped my head down.

"Rise, daughter of Odin."

I straightened. "Thank you."

"Your majesty, Erin came back to Midgard on her own accord. She has learned of the Norselands."

Layla's brows furrowed as she studied me. It was eerie. She didn't seem to remember me at all. "That does make things easier. Doesn't it, my daughter?"

"Yes, mother. However, I have additional news.

She nodded. "Come into my chamber, quickly."

I mouthed, "Mother?" to Chase as we followed the queen into the next room. She answered with an indifferent shrug of her shoulders. This was going to be bad. I just knew it.

The queen's chamber was an enormous room with windows that lined the wall ahead of us from floor to ceiling. I was sure that this was the best view of Älvornas Rike. "How amazing it is here!" I exclaimed, drawn to the view.

Layla joined me at the bank of windows and peered out over her kingdom. "It is, child. As is that elven ring on your finger. Who is the lucky male?"

For a second, I thought about lying. I wasn't sure if I should tell her, though I doubted that she would care that I stole the mate of a female that had impersonated her. Besides, she might have read it on the front page of the Faery paper, if Älvornas Rike was anything like Svartálfaheim. "Jakob Väsen is my true mate, your majesty."

Her lips curved into a sly smile. "Jakob is lucky to have found you, but tell me, how does your wicked mother take the news that her daughter is consorting with her mate and longtime lover?"

"I don't think she knows." I lifted the ring to the light, trying not to show how sickened I was by the thought of Viveka being Jakob's lover. "I've only met my mother once, and during that time, she was pretending to be you."

The Queen whirled to her daughter for confirmation. "Chase, is this true?"

"I believe so, mother."

"Show me now," she insisted of me. "But take care not to burn me. Your eyes are aflame."

Embarrassed, I nodded and took her hand. "My magic is so new to me. I don't have it under control yet."

"Don't trouble yourself, child. It takes years of practice to achieve perfection, and for some, that never comes."

Closing my eyes, I focused on every moment of my trip to the forest of Ásgard and was relieved when I heard her surprised gasp. I was doing it right. I hoped she wouldn't go ballistic after she saw what I had to show her.

Layla spoke before I had a chance to display everything, prompting me to open my eyes. "Daughter, call Kalig and Fedrus to my chamber."

Chase curtseyed and eyed me with a worried look. "Right away."

"Come with me, Erin," Layla urged. "And give me that tainted stone you're carrying. It must be destroyed. I have no doubt that they have been using it to track your movements. It's quite clever."

I dug the stone out of my pocket and followed her, despite Chase's worried expression. Upsetting the Queen was not on my agenda today. She was pissed enough as it was.

Leading me into a small, cozy room with two chairs in front of a fireplace, she gestured that I should take a seat. "This is my thinking spot," she explained.

"I bet it's a great place to read a book with a cup of coffee, too."

She settled across from me. "It is, though I prefer ambrosia to coffee."

"I tried it a couple days ago," I gushed. "It's fantastic. I wish that I could afford to have it come out of the tap instead of water."

She laughed and nodded in agreement. "That would be more convenient than traveling to Álfheim every time I get a craving—which is daily. Did you try it at the market? I've heard tales of a beautiful, but unknown, dark elf female with Prince Viggo and the Norn there."

"Nothing gets past you, huh?"

"You'd be surprised. It never occurred to me that it might be you, though you were missing. How did you find your way to the Norselands? Was it the book that Chase mentioned?"

"Yes. The spell I recited called Jakob to me. He introduced me to my brother."

She eyed the ring again. "It is a hasty decision, your engagement, but you have made a fine choice. Viveka portrayed me well when she said that Jakob should be king. I have long thought it so."

"Thank you, your majesty."

She tsked. "There is no need for formality. You may call me Layla." Noting my surprised expression, she added, "Viveka's portrayal of me was so accurate, that it makes me wonder if she has been spying on me."

"I hope not."

"I, as well, my dear. I, as well." She gave me the same narrow-eyed look Chase had given me back at the store. If I wasn't so terrified of her, I might have laughed. "So, Erin of Midgard, tell me, how do you find your brother?"

"He can be a bit...irritating."

"Then, you have spent a minute or two with him," she said, with mock seriousness. "That is all the time it takes to figure that out."

We shared a laugh. It was hard not to love Layla, despite the initial scariness.

She tucked her feet under her and got comfortable. "So, does your little rebellion know about the temple yet?"

I tried to keep my face neutral. "Rebellion?"

"Oh, come now. As you said, there isn't much I don't know."

I caved under her stare. She was quite intimidating when she wanted to be. "We do. We just haven't found it yet. Jakob, Nils, and Loki have searched for it with no luck."

Her eyes widened. "Loki, you say?" She cackled with laughter. "What an idiot Odin is. Ordering that male to do anything has no logic. Not after he has suffered by his hand for a thousand years." She shook her head. "Odin is acting in desperation. That is never a smart move in battle. He should know that Loki will never do his bidding after his torture, and honestly, I am surprised that Loki did not set out to kill you on sight for revenge."

"Jakob doesn't trust him," I confided. "But I think he's okay to a degree. He seems to be a big fan of my grandmother."

"Weren't we all?" she sighed. "Alva was a wonderful female. Jakob may not be her biological son, but he is very much influenced by her. I am not surprised that he has decided to take the smartest course of action. Loki does have a long reputation of defecting to gain what he desires. He would abandon your rebellion if it gave him an opportunity to kill Odin."

I nodded my agreement and wished Jakob was here with me to hear this. "Can I ask how you found out about the rebellion? I know Soren has gone out of his way to keep it a secret."

"Of course, you can. Myrgjöl told me."

"Emelie's grandmother? I haven't met her yet."

"She sees a victory for your little rebellion ... well, if you have us as allies, that is." Her eyes lit up. "Kicking Odin's ass ... that is such an intriguing thought. It almost makes me want to join forces with your dreadful brother."

I grinned at her devious expression. "It does have something, doesn't it?"

She chuckled. "I am told that Odin has grown complacent in his defense, that he is letting creatures that are run by selfish gain and insanity control what he should have command of. It will make defeating him almost too easy."

"How do you know all of this?" I asked, hoping that she would share what she knew. The rebellion needed her information—like yesterday.

"It is simple, child. I have spies. Every kingdom does. Some are just ... better than others. Though Myrgjöl's information is invaluable, it can be a little erratic in coming. It is important to me to stay abreast of the happenings within the realm." She turned her head toward the room we'd just come from and smirked. "Ah, here are two now. I placed them in Álfheim to watch over Soren's rebellion, but by your memory, they were far away, were they not?"

"They were," I answered with some hesitation. Where was she going with this?

The two males that had given me the shifting stone, now both six foot in height, walked in single file to stand before us. They looked from me to their Queen with nervous faces before bowing their heads.

Layla stood to greet her spies. "Chase, come."

I looked behind me and saw Chase hovering at the door. She appeared reluctant to join us but obeyed the queen's request with a heavy sigh. "Yes, mother?"

"You may take Erin and leave. There is much to be done."

"Yes, your majesty." There was no emotion in her voice.

I stood and curtseyed. "Thanks for having me, Layla."

A warm smile lit the queen's features. "You are most welcome at any time. However, that invitation does not extend to your brother—any of them."

"Yes, Ma'am." Grinning, I joined Chase, and together, we made our way to the exit.

She raised her eyebrows at my smile. "That went well, I presume?"

"Why? What were you expecting?"

"One never knows with my mother. She has this calm before the storm thing going on. I am afraid for the ones we've left with her. If she finds that they have crossed her intentionally, we will never hear from them again, and I'm not talking banishment."

I pondered that scary thought as Chase laced her fingers with mine and shifted us back to the store.

The second we materialized into the back room, I called to Jakob. Mad or not, he needed to know what had happened.

His relief came through the connection before his apologetic voice did. *"Erin, please forgive me."*

"There's no time for that, Jakob. You have to warn everyone!"

"What is it?" His tone was all business.

"The 'Queen Layla' Soren and I met on Ásgard was Viveka in disguise. She's tracked everywhere I've been by the shifting stone she gave me."

"Do you still carry the stone?"

"No, the real Queen Layla has had it destroyed."

"How did you come to meet the faery queen? Älskling, where are you?"

"The bookstore, with Chase, the freaking faery princess."

"Ah ... pardon?"

"Chase, the one that works at my store, is ... wait for it ... Queen Layla's daughter."

His astonishment washed over me. *"Chase ... but she is a warrior."*

"Yeah, a warrior assigned to watch over me for the last eighteen years."

"That is ... an ingenious way of keeping a close eye on a potential enemy, is it not?" There was a bit of humor in his response.

"I wouldn't put anything past Layla. She was enraged when I told her she's been impersonated."

His chuckle filled my head. *"Indeed, I thought that she might be. Anything less than that would be out of character for her. She is a singular creature, with a mind as sharp as her tongue."*

"Remind me never to piss her off."

"Let us hope I never have to, my love," he said in a serious tone. *"I believe dusk is fast approaching in New York. Will you wait for me at the store with Chase? I do not care if your brother has forbidden it. I will not feel at ease until you are safe in my arms."*

"Are you going to tell Soren where you're going?" I couldn't keep the sarcasm out of my voice.

"No."

"He will be angry with you, won't he?"

There was a pause as if he was choosing his words with care. *"I wish the circumstances were different, Erin. Believe me, I do. However, this obstacle with Soren is minuscule when compared with our longevity, and it changes nothing for me. He may oppose our love, as is his right, but if it is your desire, I will leave the rebellion, and we can be together on Midgard or anywhere of your choosing. The 'where' of it matters little. I will have you as my mate in any fashion if you choose to allow it. I leave the choice to pursue what we have found together in your hands, not Soren's."*

It must have hurt him to offer an escape route to me. I could feel the desperation and sincerity come through the connection in waves. He couldn't bear to lose me. And I couldn't … no, wouldn't, let that happen. *"You're pretty much stuck with me forever, you know."*

"Beloved, I am not stuck with you. I am blessed to be your mate. I love you, and I will join you in five minutes."

"Me, too. Hurry."

When Chase realized my conversation was over, she bombarded me with questions. "What did my mother say while I was gone? Is she going to join the warriors in their rebellion?" Her eyes shined with genuine excitement at the thought.

"She did say that she was tempted to join, but she didn't give a definite answer. What I do know is that she doesn't like Soren or Kristian."

"That is so not a newsflash. I've known it for at least a thousand years."

I stopped and stared at her youthful face and pink hair. She looked like she could still be in high school. "How old are you?"

"Twelve hundred and three."

I sat down at the counter and sighed. "All of you are so … old."

Chase laughed and walked to the other side of the counter. "Gee, thanks. You say the kindest things."

Mortified that I'd said something so unfeeling to her, I backtracked. "I meant that I feel like an infant compared to all of you. Is there anyone in the Norselands besides me and Emelie that are under five hundred years old?"

She switched off the espresso machine with a bemused smile playing at her lips. "Not one."

"Really?"

"No. Of course, there are, silly girl. There are millions, and not just on Midgard."

I sighed in relief. "Good."

"So, who'd you call to?"

"Jakob. He'll be here in five minutes."

"I am already here," he said, coming out of the darkened back room.

"Jakob!" I exclaimed, before throwing myself into his waiting arms.

He held me tight for a moment and then bent to kiss me, hungrily taking my lips with his. "Please, forgive me, älskling. I should have told you."

"It's okay," I said, snuggling into the wide expanse of his chest. "I should have let you."

"Whoa," Chase muttered, her voice ringing with disbelief.

I looked over to find my friend's mouth dragging the floor. She looked like a cartoon character. "What are you staring at?"

She walked up to Jakob and took his face between her hands. "Yep, green eyes. You're not Kristian. I think you might be channeling Kristian's sexy persona though." She flicked the collar of his shirt. "You're a hottie, Jakob. Who knew?"

Jakob laughed and gave her a hug. "That is the closest I have ever come to getting a compliment from you, so I will take it as such. How are you, Princess?"

"Never been better. You?"

He glanced at my inquisitive face and smiled. "I know the feeling, my old friend. Erin, did Chase tell you that we were comrades in the Elven War?"

I jerked my gaze to Chase. "You were a soldier in the Elven War?"

"Sure. It was fun." She waved away my questions. "So, what's the plan, Jakob? Is Erin staying here with me or with the rebellion?"

His raised eyebrows told me that he hadn't expected Chase to know about them.

"Nothing gets by Layla," I reminded him.

His lips quirked. "Indeed. Chase, it is my hope that Erin will consent to join me at the castle. Because of the breach, the rebellion has relocated there. You are, of course, invited to accompany your charge there."

"Is Evangelina still cooking for the royal family?" There was a hopeful note in her voice.

He grinned. "She is."

"I'll come then. Erin, you haven't lived until you try her ambrosia cake. I can almost taste it now."

Jakob secured me to his side by a hand at my waist and held out the other to Chase. "Shall we?"

Chase took his hand and gave me a wink. "We shall."

The courtyard of Väsen Castle was deserted when we arrived. Even the torches that had illuminated the area in the past now stood without their cheerful green flames.

"What's happened?" I whispered, afraid to speak aloud.

"Dark elves can see better in the dark," Jakob explained. "While we are at war, the castle is on guard." He hurried us across the paving stones and into the safety of the kitchen.

Squinting out of the doorway, into the vast darkness of the forest beyond the castle, I tried to make out the guards I knew were hiding there. There was nothing but blackness. "I guess I don't have that talent."

"Ha!" Viggo's taunting voice cried behind us. "There is something I can do that you cannot!"

I ignored him until I sat at the empty kitchen table, then extended a choice finger. He didn't notice. He was too busy taking a turn around the countertop with Chase in tow, a goofy smile plastered to his face. It was clear that they were buddies, even before he spun her, laughing, into the chair next to me.

A bark of mocking laughter erupted from the doorway. "I get the next dance," Nils growled. "At least, I know what I'm doing with a female." He leaned against the doorframe and pegged Chase with a questioning glance.

If I hadn't heard the tiny, pained squeak from Chase, I might have never looked up to see the devastated expression on her face. But I did, and it slayed me. Nils was her unrequited love.

Panicking, I scrambled up to my feet. "Chase, can I show you something … uh, privately?"

Her voice wavered when she answered, "Yeah, sure. Lead the way."

I led her down the servant's hallway, instead of taking the shortcut through the parlor Nils was blocking the passage to, much to Viggo's amusement.

"You are acting like a queen would already, poppet," he pronounced with authority, the joyous grin still stretched across his face. "No lowly servants polluting the air in our hallways, by Gods."

With a weak, "Shut up," Chase followed me into the narrow passageway with Jakob right behind her.

Looking nervous, he implored, "Forgive me, Chase. I concealed Nils being a member of the rebellion out of fear that you would not accompany Erin if you knew."

"No. There's no need to apologize. You are right, as usual. You've saved me, once again, from making a fool of myself. My superiors would have been appalled at a second desertion. They still have not forgiven me for leaving the Elven War, even today."

Uncomfortable with her teary-eyed gratitude, Jakob stammered, "Please do not allow yourself to … uh, vex about the circumstances, my lady. All will be well. You shall see." After he gave Chase a pat on the back that was full of awkwardness, he kissed me on the cheek and went back the way we'd come.

I stared at his back as he walked away. He was the most perfect gentle-male, and to me, that was incredibly hot. *"Jakob?"*

He didn't turn around, but answered, *"Yes, älskling?"*

"I'm rewarding you for the kindness you showed Chase."

"Indeed, my love?"

"With my mouth."

He shook his head and laughed. *"I look forward to returning the favor."*

Smiling a loopy grin, I hurried a pale-faced Chase through the upstairs hallway and into Jakob's chamber, which (thank goodness) bore no signs of the enthusiastic athletics we'd almost enjoyed just a few hours ago.

She sank, boneless, onto the end of the bed. "I don't think I can do this, Erin."

I sat down next to her, hugging her close. "How long has it been since you've seen him?"

"I have not met with him since I left my post in the war. I couldn't be around him, Erin. I couldn't concentrate on my duties. My mother assigned me to your detail right after. It gave me something to focus on … something other than Fenrir, and since Midgard is largely ignored by the creatures of the Norselands, I haven't had to endure seeing him—until today."

I marveled at the length of time she'd lived with her sorrowful misfortune. Eighteen years might seem like far too long of a time to pine over a lost mate to an outsider, but I'd already experienced what it felt like to be so close to your mate and not be allowed to do anything about it. It must be agony for her to see him now. All of those resurfaced emotions—I did not envy her. "How did you meet him?"

"He, the Väsen princes, and I were in the same guard during the war." She paused, her anguish clear in her expression. "Though, I did meet him once as a young faeryling, when he had a short affair with my mother."

My jaw dropped. "Are you kidding me?"

"I wish." She stood back up and faced me. "That's it! I just need to look at this from a different view—a soldier's point of view. I'm assigned to watch over you, and damn it, that's what I'm going to do. As far as I'm concerned, Nils doesn't exist while I'm here."

I refrained from rolling my eyes. Sure, that would work. "Did you guys ever … uh, you know?"

"No, but I remain chaste for him, as is our custom."

Well, if that wasn't the most depressing thing I've ever heard. I will never, ever, ever utter another word about feeling like a spinster at twenty-five. A virgin for over a thousand years? Was there anything crueler than that?

"I don't get it. You're you," I gestured to her loveliness. "And he's … him. Why would he reject you?" Chase was not just pretty; she was also royalty. Was Nils insane? Wait. Of course, he is. This was Nils we were talking about.

She sighed and stared at her shoes. "He doesn't view me as a sexual conquest."

I was baffled by this. "But … you have lady parts."

Her face was deadpan. "Believe me, I know."

A light knock sounded on the door, and we both looked wordlessly at each other. Shrugging, I shook my head, indicating that I wasn't expecting anyone. "Yes?" I ventured, hoping for a good outcome.

Emelie's almost inaudible voice answered. "It's me. Say, do you have Nils' true mate in there, by chance?"

I yanked open the door and tugged her inside.

She made a beeline for Chase, holding her hand out to her. "Hi, I'm Emelie, Soren's mate. You must be Chase."

Chase took the hand that was offered with a skeptical look. "I am pleased to meet you, Emelie. I've long known your grandmother. Is she well?"

"Oh yes. She's fine, just fine," Emelie answered, distracted by what she was seeing behind her shining, metallic eyes. No doubt, she was seeing Chase's future.

I giggled at her strange actions. "Uh, Em? You're freaking her out." Chase's face held the same expression she wore when the little old ladies that frequent the bookstore tried to engross her in a conversation about times gone by. Now that I knew how much older she was than them, that look made a lot more sense.

Emelie blushed and relinquished her hand with reluctance. "I'm so sorry. It was rude of me."

"It's fine. As I said, I know your grandmother. She is a little … uh, overzealous sometimes, too."

I huffed. "Yeah, yeah, moving on. Get to the good stuff. Em, what did you see?"

She smiled. "Nils, of course. God, he's a moron to have not noticed you. He … um, notices you in the future."

I giggled again. "See, Chase? It's just like I thought. He's a dumbass. That's all."

"Total dumbass," Emelie agreed. "You look hot as a brunette. It suits you."

"I have the appearance of almost every other faery in Älvornas Rike with brown hair," Chase pouted. "You're serious? I give up the pink for him?"

Emelie smirked. "Yep, but it doesn't bother you much— eventually."

Sighing, she steeled her shoulders. "Well, the things you do for love, right?"

"Right!" Emelie and I said in harmony.

"Well then, let's go brunette! Where's a mirror. You have to help me decide on the shade."

"Yay!" I exclaimed. I was excited to see a glimmer of hope in my friend's eyes and to do something that the future of the Norselands didn't depend on. "The bathroom is through here."

CHAPTER TEN

I t didn't take long to find the perfect chestnut brown for Chase. If Nils didn't notice her now, I would hit him with something a little harder than a clue by four. She was stunning, the epitome of a bombshell pinup girl.

"Are you sure I don't look ridiculous?" Chase asked, fidgeting in my pencil skirt and crimson red blouse.

Emelie and I gave each other commiserating looks. She'd asked us that a hundred times since we started playing makeover. "Yes, for the millionth time, you're gorgeous. You make us normal females look like homely spinsters. Geez, Chase, you're aware that you're in desperate need of a healthy dose of self-esteem, aren't you?"

"Shut it, Erin. I'm not used to all this girly stuff."

Emelie clapped her hands together after she finished arranging the last of Chase's long curls and grinned like a fool. "Okay, let's go show her to the guys. Nothing is as sure to get Nils's attention as competition."

Chase's eyes widened with fear. "Are you sure that this a good idea? What if they all laugh at me?"

"They won't," I assured her. "They'll be busy trying to hide their hard-ons."

"Erin!" Emelie screeched, laughing at my boldness.

"What? You know I'm right. All these single males, waiting thousands of years for their mate to just breeze in and save them from a life of loneliness. You couldn't ask for a group of males more appreciative of the female form than these guys are."

"That's true," Emelie said. "Stay away from my mate, Chase."

She slipped on the heels I'd loaned her, wobbling a little. "Not a problem. Moving in on a Norn's mate would be the ultimate in stupidity. Let me know if it ever happens though. I want to see what you do."

"I will," she promised, giggling. Then, she turned to face me, hands on hips. "And don't think I've forgotten that you still haven't told me what happened here last night, Erin. Soren hasn't stopped threatening Jakob's life all day. I'd like to know why I'm restraining my mate from kicking his best friend's ass."

"I was going to tell you, Em, I was. But ..." I motioned to Chase.

"I know. I'm kidding, though I am dying to know." She made a noise of excited glee. "This is so much fun! I can't tell you how glad I am to have females to hang out with again. Living with males is so boring. All they do is talk about war and argue about who has the biggest dick ... metaphorically speaking, of course. Well, most of the time."

"That's all males, Emelie," Chase agreed, shaking her head in repugnance. "Try being a soldier with all of that ego in your face. It's a friggin' nightmare."

"Hey!" I cried. "Don't mess up your hair! It's perfect."

She rolled her eyes. "You couldn't put a dent in this hair, Erin. Emelie put so much magic into the curls, I'm not sure they'll ever wash out.

Emelie scoffed. "I'll have you know that I put just the right amount of magic in there. Now, quit stalling and go put the charm on your future mate."

"This is going to scar me for life, isn't it?"

I grinned as the dinner bell pealed and put my arm around her. "Chase, it's pretty much guaranteed. Now get in there."

The males took to their feet when we entered the dining room, a low whistle escaping from Viggo. "Damn, Chase. You clean up well."

"Thanks. I spilled a bit of wine on my jeans." Her face was hot with embarrassment. "I am fortunate that Erin and I are close to the same size."

Nils smirked and motioned to her head. "Did you spill something in your hair, too?"

I gave Nils a withering look, trying to help cover Chase's little white lie. "Pink doesn't go with this color, Nils."

Jakob realized what we were up to right away. With a wink at me, he pulled out Chase's chair with a flourish. "I am sure that Nils did not mean anything by his comment, Princess. It must have been an unexpected shock to him to see you with the beautiful shade you have chosen, as it was to all of us. We have only known you to have pink hair in the past." He glanced at our resident asshole. "Is that not right, Nils?" His voice held a stern 'you better not fuck this up' note.

"Yes," he answered, returning Jakob's glare with a bewildered expression. "That is it—if we were in some kind of alternate universe. What the hell are you on about, Jakob?"

Chase rolled her eyes. "Whatever. Let's just drop it, guys." To me, she added, *"I told you he wouldn't notice me."*

"He noticed your hair wasn't pink anymore," I reminded her. *"That means he was checking you out. Flirt a little. See what happens."*

Muttering, she said, *"Okay, I'll try ... and fail."*

After twenty minutes, I regretted ever pushing Chase into trying to lure Nils into a relationship. I watched as she fruitlessly tried to engross him into a conversation during dinner. She was even brave enough to bare her substantial cleavage to him while passing the mashed potatoes to get his attention. All of it was in vain. He ignored her, his indifference made clear to everyone at the table. To Nils, she was just one of the guys.

Staring at the dumb-shit wolf, I frowned. He was going to give me premature wrinkles if he didn't snap to it. *"What gives, Em?"*

With an almost imperceptible shake of her head, she answered. *"Your guess is as good as mine. I've never seen him reject anyone of the opposite sex."* Grimacing, she added, *"Mated or not."*

I glanced up at the future mates again. Chase was staring at Nils with desperation in her eyes like she'd never see him again. *"That's what I was afraid of."*

All too soon, I watched the males excuse themselves from the table and leave. Nils was one of the first to go.

"I'm sorry, Chase."

She shrugged in cool detachment, but I could see the hurt in her eyes. "I told you guys. This was pointless."

"It's not pointless. It is complete bullshit, and I'm getting to the bottom of it!" Emelie said, eyeing the direction Nils went with suspicion.

Chase sighed and stood. "Don't bother with it, Emelie. I need to go make a report to my mother, anyway. Are you going to be all right here for a day or so, Erin?"

I got up and put my arms around Chase. Emelie followed suit. "Of course, I will. Go do what you need to do."

"You'll call to me if you need me." It wasn't a question; it was a command.

"I will," I promised.

"Good. See you two soon."

When she blinked out of the room, Emelie and I locked eyes. "We have to do something, Erin." Her voice carried an edge of unsettling worry. "She's hurting."

"I know." Before our arrival on Svartálfaheim, I would have

wagered that Chase wasn't afraid of anything. Now, I knew better. She was terrified of the enemy that I'd never counted on—rejection. Wringing my hands, I started to pace the length of the table. "Can't you just work your magic on him? That's what you do, right?"

"I could, though it would be unethical if they weren't meant to be. That's not the case here. With true mates, their fates are made to intertwine together. The magic is already there!" Emelie fumed, pacing in the opposite direction. "Nils has to feel the pull. He's just hiding it for some stupid, inexplicable, ridiculous reason."

"Why would he do that?"

"I don't know, but I intend to find out."

When we didn't come to the parlor for after-dinner coffee and ambrosia, Jakob came in to check on us. "What are you two doing?" He was astonished by our angry, silent pacing.

"Nothing," we said in unison.

"Nothing it is," he conceded, smirking as he settled into a chair to observe our silent scheming. "But, before you do something to make the situation worse, shall I find out why Nils is not interested in taking Chase as his mate? I know you will both not rest until you know."

I stopped pacing to appraise my mate. This wasn't the kind of thing that he would do—ever. Nonetheless, he did look serious enough about what he'd said … and really, really sexy. I cocked my head to the side as a mixture of confusion, wonder, and desire filtered through me. Had Jakob ever looked like this to me before? His short, onyx hair almost appeared shinier, more alluring, above burning, electric-green eyes that matched his caramel skin to perfection. Even his usual no-nonsense, all-black stance on his attire seemed … well, perfect. He was resplendent, magnificent—a male from a dream.

"You'll ask him that for us?" I purred, making my way around the table toward him. I just couldn't resist touching him in some way, especially since Soren wasn't in the immediate vicinity to berate me for it.

He answered with a knowing quirk of his lips aimed at me. "Ladies, I would do anything for the both of you. Chase deserves every happiness, and though it may not appear so at times, Nils does, as well."

"How kind of you," I replied, distracted by the paradigm of masculine superiority sitting in front of me. I was almost to the point that I was considering asking Emelie to leave the room so that I could beg Jakob to forgive me for leaving him. In addition, the thought of fucking him right there on the chair was just too tempting not to do, and I doubted she'd want to stick around for that.

With an outraged huff, Emelie reached across the flower arrangement in the center of the table and smacked Jakob on his arm. "Stop influencing her!"

I tore my gaze away from his unnatural perfection (with difficulty) to look over to Emelie's appalled face. My body felt sluggish and slow like I was on the verge of being drunk. "Is that what this is? Why you seem so ... mouthwatering?"

His timid smile was answer enough for me.

"Mouthwatering?" Emelie shook her head in horror. "I think I'm going to be sick."

Ignoring her distaste, I sat on his lap and whispered, "I like it. Don't stop."

Emelie, looking a delicate shade of green, flung herself over the table to get out of the room. "You guys are freaking twisted. I am so out of here."

Even in my intoxicated state, it was pretty comical to see her half-sliding, half-tripping her way out with one hand shading us from her vision until the door slammed behind her. "You don't think she'll tell Soren, do you?"

"No, love. But, I do believe I will have to explain myself later. She will not let me go without being reprimanded."

"I get the feeling that she's bossier than she looks."

Jakob chuckled. "Your assumption is correct."

I nuzzled into him, placing delicate kisses on his neck and the exposed vee of his chest. "Where were we?"

"We were about to see how well you can defend yourself against my influence," he said, kissing my pouting lips. "Do not sulk, Erin. It is a necessary skill."

"I'm not sulking." I glowered. "I'm horny. Are you sure you wouldn't rather find one of the thousand isolated spots in the castle to make love instead?"

"I am not, by any means. However, you need to learn this skill." There was a gleam in his emerald eyes as he grinned. "If you can."

"What do you mean, if I can?" I scoffed, offended at his lack of confidence. "Of course, I can. I'm the daughter of Odin, which should be enough of a threat to get you naked and on top of me, but sadly, isn't."

"Erin, I can promise you that once the temple is defeated, I will be happy to make love to you whenever you wish, but right now, you need to concentrate on withstanding my power."

Smiling, I trailed my fingers from his shoulder to his belt. "I don't want to resist. I want to be naughty."

"You must," he said, stilling my wandering hands.

I gave up with a heavy sigh. "Fine, but you'll be making this up to me tomorrow morning. A lot."

His face fell. "My love, you know I cannot."

"But, you promised that you would tell Soren to fuck himself," I whined, lifting myself up to stand.

"I am sure I never used those words," he teased.

I took the liberty of smacking him on the shoulder for that one. "You know what I mean!"

"Yes, I am becoming quite accustomed to the subtle way you and Emelie get your thoughts across," he said, rubbing his arm.

"Do I need to hit you again?" I raised a threatening hand.

"No." He laughed and trapped my arms behind me. "You win, but might I remind you that it has been less than a day since Soren found out about us. I think it is wise to give him time to come to terms with the situation … and for Emelie to work a little magic. She is good at calming him down when he is angry."

"Must be nice. I wish I had someone to do that for me."

He cupped my face, peppering it with soft kisses. "You are so adorable when you are cross."

I kissed him back, much more thoroughly, until we were both out of breath. "Do you think so?"

"Yes. I also think you are a natural at offensive magic, as well as defensive. You haven't felt my influence for several minutes have you?"

Huh. He was right. I hadn't even noticed. That intoxicated, sensual feeling was gone as soon as I got mad. "No, I haven—"

"Incoming!" Emelie screamed in my head.

"Soren's coming!" I hissed.

He moved toward the door to leave. "Shift. I'll find you later."

"I love you."

"I lov—" His reply was cut off by my disappearance. I really needed to learn to time the shifting thing better.

Much to my disappointment, Jakob didn't return to the castle for the rest of the night. To their credit, Nils, Viggo, and Emelie tried to keep me from noticing his conspicuous absence, even managing to persuade me to play Monopoly and Scrabble with them, but at four in the morning, when Nils suggested Hide and Seek, I gave up on the hope that I would see him and excused myself to walk the long trek back to the room Axel had shown me earlier. My room, of course, was in the wing opposite of the wing Jakob's chamber was in. No doubt, my brother had a hand in that. I would bet money that Soren and Emelie's room would be right next to mine so he could keep an eye on me.

After a quick shower, I climbed into bed alone, wide awake, and going over everything that had happened in the past couple of days. So much had changed, I hardly recognized the sad existence that I was once used to. I had everything I'd longed to have in my human life. Well, almost everything. I didn't have my mate.

I woke the moment someone tore the thin sheet off of my body and put a hand over my mouth. Screaming for Jakob in my mind, I struggled against the strong arm, kicking and punching out as the huge male settled between my legs, his massive erection pressed tight against my most intimate flesh. "Submit to me!" the male growled.

There was no mistaking the scent and the intoxicating influence he was using. Whimpering in desperation, I reached for his belt, unbuckling it as he ripped my panties off and pushed two fingers into me. Crying out behind his hand, I enclosed my mate's wide girth in my palms and stroked his length, moaning as his fingers moved in rhythm with my hands.

"Shhhh, älskling. Soren's room is across the hall."

I nodded, not giving a shit where he was at the moment, and rose my hips in silent invitation. He guided himself into me, groaning out his relief. "I tried to keep busy tonight," he whispered. "To keep myself from thinking about you—the sight of you on your hands and knees, screaming for more of my cock, your swollen bottom lip clenched between your teeth as you came … it's impossible. I crave you—your body, your blood, everything. I want all of you." His every word was punctuated with intense pulses of the same sensual influence he was using earlier. I closed my eyes and let myself drift away in pleasure, intoxicated by his magic until barreling back to reality in the throes of orgasm.

161

Eager to join me, he set a frenzied pace, driving himself harder and deeper, before growling out his release through clenched teeth, then collapsing in exhaustion on top of me.

"Wowww," I breathed when I could speak.

"Have I impressed you?" he panted, lifting himself onto his elbows to look into my eyes.

Devious smile intact, I shook my head. "Uh, no. I was going to ask you if you call that lame attempt, 'sex'. Because it felt like you kind of phoned it in."

He dropped his head onto my shoulder and chuckled into my hair. "Do I bore you, Erin?"

I grinned at the ceiling. "Exceedingly."

"Enlighten me as to how I shall entertain you to your satisfaction, my hard to please älskling."

"Oh, Jakob. It's so cute how you think you can."

"I see," he said, pushing himself up. "Then I will be on my way. To be frank, I do not have the time to devote to one of you insatiable type females as it is. There are only so many hours in the night." The springs in the mattress creaked as he stood. "I bid you good day."

"All right then. Thanks for the…uh, experience."

He didn't respond.

"Jakob?"

Nothing. I slid off the bed and fumbled along the wall for the light switch.

Hands grabbed my arms and held them to my side. "Looking for someone?" His breath tickled my ear.

"Maybe," I admitted.

"Do you know what I think?"

"No." But I knew what I thought. I wanted him. He knew how

to make me desperate for his touch.

He slid an arm across my stomach to pull me closer. "Hold on. I am taking you somewhere where we can be alone."

In a blink, we materialized into the middle of a candlelit corridor somewhere in the castle I'd never been before. I didn't recognize the deep blue of the tapestry against the brilliant gold of ... everything else. "Where are we?"

"This was my father's wing—our wing, now that we rule in Kristian's absence." His fingers skimmed the edge of the t-shirt I wore. "But never mind that for now. I think we should play a game."

My curiosity was piqued. "A game?"

"Hide and seek, to be exact. Nils said that you declined to play earlier, but I think that you will enjoy it if you play by my rules."

"What are the rules?"

"There are but two. Rule number one—no clothing allowed." He lifted my shirt over my head and tossed it to the floor. "Rule number two—you will hide from me." His hands grazed the hardening peaks of my breasts, coaxing a moan from my lips. "Then, I will find you."

I shuddered against his warm chest. "What if you can't find me?"

He slid his hand between my legs. "Rest assured, I will."

"Hey!" I whined when the hand disappeared.

His laughter came from my mind. *"Hide. I will count to fifty."*

"Jakob, you tease!" Screw the game, I just wanted him.

"Fifty, forty-nine ... you are not hiding, älskling."

"Yeah, because I'm not six years old."

With a chuckle, he materialized behind me and kissed the nape of my neck, and then had the audacity to swat me on the ass and say, "I said, hide."

163

"Fine," I said, through gritted teeth.

"Twenty-nine, twenty-eight," he called after me

"Damn you, Jakob Väsen!" I took off running down the corridor, turning down the first hallway I came to, hoping it held a good place to hide. One look down the hall told me I'd made the right decision. There were at least twenty doors on either side. The likelihood of him finding me on the first try would be slim. I could find a better hiding place while he searched. I just had to be quiet.

"Thirteen, twelve, eleven ..."

Shit! I had to pick fast. Heart pounding, I jerked open the sixth door on the left and threw myself in, while trying to close the door without making a sound. Okay. Now, where to hide? There was moonlight to see by, but with my terrible night vision, I couldn't make out anything, except the shape of a giant chifferobe, a bed, and behind me, a closet. Great choices, if you want to be found right away.

"Ready or not, here I come."

There was no time. Closet, it was. I turned the knob, trying not to make a sound. The door popped open with a loud creak, and I froze, listening for footsteps. I breathed a shaky sigh of relief when I didn't hear anything. Tip-toeing into the closet, I closed the door before I realized what was behind me. It was amazing. It was a room of clear glass—ceiling and all. The moon was luminous, shining through the glass, touching everything with an eerie, magical glow. A spiral staircase twirled up toward the sky, where an open-air room was perched in the center. Drawn toward the stairs, I started to wind my way up, wincing when the staircase shifted with my weight. What I found at the top surprised me. Books, of all types, were lined on circular shelves surrounding a chaise filled with beaded and tasseled pillows. This was someone's reading nook. And someone had the most luxurious, decadent reading nook ever!

"Did you know that your magic is so potent that it's calling to me? You could never hide from me," Jakob said, showing me that

he was in the hallway I'd chosen. *"I know I'm close. What could be behind door number two, I wonder."*

Smirking at his cockiness, I sat on the chaise. *"Keep guessing, Mr. Väsen."*

"Mister, is it? Can your 'mister' get a hint?"

"No hints. You're on your own."

"Have I mentioned that you are an evil, evil female? I think I shall have you punished for your insubordinate behavior."

I giggled. *"You've mentioned it a few times."*

"Door number three it is."

"You're getting warmer."

"You have no idea," he said, in a way that made me shiver with anticipation.

"That's quite the way with words you have there, Jakob."

"You should see what else I can do with my mouth."

My mouth dropped open. By now, I should be used to him surprising me with the dirty things he says. That kind of thing tends to happen when you're mated to a certified sex god.

"No witty comeback? I'm surprised, Erin."

I didn't say anything. My mind had gone blank with just a few words from him.

"Little elf?"

"Jakob?" I asked.

"When I find you, I'm going to eat you up."

Whoa. Would I even be able to survive this mating?

"Are you sure you have no hints for your mate, älskling?"

Again, I didn't answer. He was here, in the outer room. And he was toying with me. Holding my breath, I eased down into a lying position on the chaise and arranged the heavy velvet pillows in front of me until I was covered. There was no way he would see me unless he frequented this space and knew how they'd been left.

"I can sense you. Come out, come out, wherever you are."

My heart palpitated. He was too close. I could almost pick up on the intoxicating scent of his skin. Or, was that his influence? That cheating bastard! He knew that I couldn't call him on it. I'd give my location away. Well, two could play that game. Sucking in long, slow breaths, I closed my eyes and sent out my own influence on every exhale. Jakob groaned below me. No wonder I could smell him. He was in the room!

"Erin, you set me on fire."

The stairs shifted, and I forgot to breathe. The silence was deafening as I listened for movement. For a few agonizing heartbeats there was nothing, then the pillows were yanked away and thrown unceremoniously to the floor down below. Jakob, looking wild, jerked me to my feet by my hands. "I win," he said, growling, before clamping his mouth to mine.

I took the hardness brushing my navel in my hands and stroked him. "Only because you cheat." Kissing my way down his stomach, I winked at him as I ran the flat of my tongue up his shaft.

Steadying himself, he gripped the railing until it groaned, and then in one lightning-fast moment, released it to capture me in his grip and toss me onto the chaise.

"Hey!" I squealed, surprised by his urgency. "Wha—"

He didn't let me finish, muffling my response with a finger on my lips. I peered up at him with my eyes wide.

"Are you frightened of me?"

"A little," I admitted.

A demonic smile crossed his lips, causing me to have an inescapable urge to push myself away from him.

"Going somewhere?" he asked, kneeling on the edge of the

chaise to wrap his long fingers around my ankle. He tugged me closer. "You are mine."

I tried to answer him, but my tongue-tied voice couldn't seem to utter even a single syllable. I was frozen in both fear and lust. Prowling up the short distance, he covered my body with his own, dragging his mouth over every surface along the way. "Please," I panted, arching into him.

Drawing the pads of his fingers down the side of my breast, he asked, "Is there something you want, älskling?"

"Yes," I breathed, so hungry for him.

"There is something I would like, as well."

"Anything, Jakob."

Pressing his lips to mine, he kissed me, then said, "My turn to hide! Count to fifty!"

Before I realized what he was doing, he was down the stairs, and the door was slamming behind him. *"Jakob, hand to God, if I find out this is a trick to make me practice finding you with my magic, I will make you suffer!"*

"Not if you cannot find me."

Yep. I was about to do bodily harm to my mate. Not what I expected for our honeymoon period, but hey, he wasn't what I expected in a husband.

"Forty-one, forty, thirty-nine. Ready or not. I'm kicking your ass."

I woke alone in bed, pleasantly sore in all the right places. This morning had been … I didn't know what words could describe how it had been, or the things we did together. It was almost as if it was an amazing dream. But dreams don't leave tingling, healing bites on your neck and thighs.

Stretching out in the pillows, I looked over to find the t-shirt I'd been sleeping in folded next to me. Thoughtful. I breathed in the unmistakable scent that was ingrained in the shirt. What wasn't perfect about him?

A sharp rap at the door brought me back to reality. "Who is it?" I asked, yawning and stumbling to my feet to pull the shirt on.

Axel's voice sounded from the other side. "Chase is in the kitchen for you."

"Thanks," I called.

"Of course, princess."

Princess. That was going to take some getting used to. Hurrying to dress the rest of me, I ran down the hallway to find Chase looking a nervous wreck and staring at my mate over the breakfast table.

I looked at her with question. Nervous wasn't in her nature. "What's up?"

She didn't react at all. She didn't even look up, just answered, "I invited someone."

"Here?" I asked. "Who?"

Her reply was interrupted by the entire kitchen wall of the castle being ripped away. I threw my hands over my ears and screamed just as a handsome blond male was revealed. A second later, Jakob channeled his inner linebacker and tackled me. We landed on our hands and knees in the tall grass of the hill overlooking the castle. The first thing I noticed was that the kitchen was engulfed in fire. Smoke was billowing from where we just stood.

"Call to your brother," Jakob said, not taking his eyes off the courtyard. "We need a head count."

I tore my stare away from the smoking wreckage and screamed silently for my brother. *"Soren! The castle has been attacked! Chase is an imposter."*

"Where is my mate?" His voice was frantic.

Oh God, Emelie. *"I don't know. I haven't seen her tonight."*

168

There was a moment of silence.

"I cannot reach her. Are you safe? Where are you?"

"I'm with Jakob on the hill that overlooks the courtyard."

"Stay there. I will join you as soon as I find my mate."

"Okay."

Bursting into tears, I said, "Soren is coming. He can't reach Emelie."

Jakob pulled me into his arms. "Freyr and Viveka have gone. All is well, my love. The staff and soldiers have been evacuated, and Viggo and Axel will arrive to await instructions in a moment. No one was injured." He used the pads of his thumbs to wipe the tears from my cheeks. "Do not cry, älskling. Emelie will be found."

I nodded and leaned against his chest, breathing in his unique scent to help calm my jangled nerves. I felt so safe in his arms. He would die before he let my mother touch me. "Where have the soldiers gone? Don't we need them to protect the castle? And where are Loki and Nils?"

"The guards are on the outskirts of the kingdom, looking out for more unwanted arrivals. Fenrir and his father have gone in search of an audience with Surt."

"Who's Surt again? I can't remember."

"Surt is a Jötunn. Humans would call him a giant. He resides on Múspellsheim and is a master of the flame. He will teach you to scry using your fire if it is possible."

"He can teach me to see visions with my fire?"

"I hope so. We need to find Odin's temple. This tyranny must be stopped." He smoothed back my tousled hair. "I am sorry for manhandling you. I thought I would lose you if I did not move fast."

I melted into the safety of his embrace. "Jakob, feel free to manhandle me anytime. Thank you."

169

He kissed me with such tender emotion that it brought fresh tears to my eyes. "I could not bear to part with you, Erin."

Viggo's snicker sounded behind us. "The castle is burning to the ground, and you two are out here making out?"

"Careful Viggo, your jealousy is showing!" A familiar, pissed off voice said.

I hurried off the ground and bowed to Queen Layla. "Your majesty, have you spoken to Chase today? My mother—"

"Yes, child. Viggo has told me about the situation, which is why I have come. Chase did not report to me last night. I thought that it was because of her re-acquaintance with that tasty Fenrir Wolf, but he informs me that she went home to Midgard alone." She turned to a newly arrived Soren. "What will be done to find my daughter? She has not answered my summons."

Soren bent to kiss me on the forehead. "Emelie is safe with Myrgjöl."

"Good." I breathed a huge sigh of relief.

"Soren!" Layla demanded. "My daughter?"

"Erin will go to Surt. We will find her."

Walking to me, she laid hands radiating heat on my shoulders. "I've given you the greatest gift of Faery. Just think of us, and you will find yourself in Älvornas Rike. I want to know the moment you see her. Promise me that you'll come to me if you are ever in need of my assistance."

"Of course, Layla. Thank you for your generosity."

"You are most welcome. Good luck." With a disparaging glance at Soren and Viggo, she disappeared in a rainbow-colored burst of sparkles.

"How nice of the queen. You are fortunate to have received such a gift, Erin," Viggo said, with sarcasm dripping from his voice.

A rustling of the grass below the hill alerted us to Nils striding toward us. "It's been my experience that Layla can be very nice," he contradicted, his slight smile indicating that she had left a lasting impression on him. "If you know what I mean."

"A gentle-male never tells about those experiences," Viggo chided, not entirely hiding his cringe at the thought of the two of them together.

Nils's eyes crinkled at the corners with merriment. "Is that right? What would you know of it?"

I jumped a little as an irate, disembodied voice scolded the bickering pair. "I can see you two were really worried about me! Sheesh!" Emelie materialized in between Soren and me.

"Em, this is my worried face," Nils said, thumbing in the direction behind him. "What's the word on the castle?"

"Everyone is safe," Soren answered. "The damage can be repaired." He appeared annoyed by their banter. "How did the meeting with Surt go?"

"He is anxious to meet her."

"Excellent. We leave now."

CHAPTER ELEVEN

In the end, no one volunteered to go to Surt's world, except for my brother and Jakob. Apparently, Surt's temper was as hot and unpredictable as the flames he commanded. With just a second's glance at Múspellsheim, I couldn't blame him for feeling surly. It was Hell. Like, literally. The landscape was a rock-strewn stretch of barren wasteland. Steam sizzled out of cracks in the red-tinged, blistering hot sand every few feet. What kind of creature could survive in this desolate, miserable place?

I soon found out. A seven foot tall male with a long fiery red beard, burning green eyes, and a huge sword strapped to his back stood in a large slate courtyard outside a massive stone castle. His elongated arms were held out wide in welcome. Despite the genuine smile he wore, I knew right away that Surt would be every bit the mighty warrior books portrayed him to be. He was built to destroy anything in his path

"Ah," he bellowed. "Here is the son of Odin, how far you have traveled to see me!" His voice was deep and forceful.

Soren dipped into his unusual bow, and Surt mimicked the motion. "Hello, Surt. It has been many years. How does your part of the realm fare?"

Ignoring Soren's question, he peeked around my brother and grinned at me. "You have brought a dark ..." His forehead furrowed as his words drifted off. "Is this lovely female a sister to you, Soren?"

I leaned to the right and waved my fingers at him with my brother's protective shoulder between us.

"Yes. Forgive my rudeness, Surt. It has been an arduous day, and I thought Fenrir would have mentioned our relationship during his visit." He gestured to Jakob. "I believe you already are in the acquaintance of the dark elf prince?"

Surt eyed Jakob, who was standing silent, a half-smile gracing his handsome face. "I have heard the news of your mate's deeds. It is disgraceful, the path she has chosen. Have you requested an audience with the council for an annulment?"

"I have broken the bonding without the council's consent. They no longer govern my actions."

The male nodded with a sage expression. "I understand your choice, Prince Jakob. I have an even greater dislike for the council than I do for the elven female you mated—though it is a close thing."

"I'm pretty sure that is something we all have in common," I said, smiling at his hatred of my mother and my father's corrupt government.

Surt's laugh boomed throughout the isolated valley. "She speaks!"

Soren chuckled at his excitement. "That, she does. Allow me to introduce my sister and granddaughter to Queen Alva, Princess Erin Väsen of Midgard."

I started at the name Soren gave me. It was true on two counts, of course, but it was still shocking to hear it spoken out loud, even more so coming out of my stubborn brother's mouth. I thought for sure that he would call me by my human surname.

"Well met, Princess." He glanced at my shuffling feet. "I seem to have misplaced my own manners. Please, come into the coolness of my home and rest from your long journey."

I accepted with a small curtsey. "Thank you, Surt."

He waved away my thanks. "It is but a trifle, and it is a pleasure to me, indeed. Few take it upon themselves to venture to this part of the Norselands, and it is my belief that none have been as beautiful as you are, princess."

Blushing, I knew that my eyes would betray my flame. I couldn't help it if I wanted to. His home seemed designed for invoking fire. With cement walls and floor, and minimal furniture, it wasn't much to look at, except perhaps, the monumental fire pit in the center of the room. I was drawn to the circular monstrosity as soon as we entered. Running my fingers down the unusual blood-red stones that decorated the outside surface, I beamed. "This is magnificent, Surt."

"Thank you, young one. I cannot tell you how splendid it is to meet with another who is one with the flame, though I am surprised your protectors have brought you here. It is dangerous. You are a priceless treasure that many will covet once your power is known."

"Yes," Soren agreed. "We feel the same. That is why we have come to you. Erin requires instruction that we are unable to supply."

"You want her to scry. The wolf said as much."

"That is it, exactly."

Surt's laugh rumbled through his massive chest. "Is that all? Nothing could be simpler." He moved to the window and glanced out. "I suspect you will ask me not to delay in this. The rumors of war follow you."

"Do they?" Soren asked with caution.

"Yes. They speak of war with this young one's father."

"It is true, Surt. We will soon fight our father. Can our rebellion count on you as an ally?"

"You needn't ask. How can I deny protection to one of my own kind? I am not capable of such a shameful deed."

I could almost feel the tension leave the room upon his words. We were all aware that the rebellion would soon need all the help it could get.

Learning to scry wasn't as simple as Surt had insinuated. After a light dinner of an unknown animal, he taught me the 'basics'. Which were so far from basic, I didn't think I'd ever be able to concentrate hard enough to accomplish them.

After several hours, I was only able to see a tiny glimpse of the temple. Surt said it was because of my human-like fear of fire, and I couldn't disagree with that. After a lifetime of *'FIRE BAD'*, the prospect of picking up a burning ember with your bare hands to see some smoke-filled vision is beyond terrifying.

Nonetheless, here I stood with that big, scary ember merrily crackling in my palms, while a crystal clear vision of the four of us gathered around the fire pit was perched above it. In the vision, everything seemed normal—Surt was standing to my left, smiling with approval at my progress while I wasn't looking, and Soren stood watching with his usual non-expression plastered to his face, but Jakob? He was staring at me with undisguised lust. No, staring wasn't accurate enough of a word for his actions. He was entranced. I hoped Surt couldn't see the unguarded attention I was receiving.

"Jakob, you're staring at me."

"I ache for you, älskling," he said, in a matter-of-fact voice. *"Now, please pay attention to Surt."*

"I will never get tired of hearing that."

He chuckled at my preoccupation. *"Love, he is becoming agitated."*

"Fine!"

"Erin, I promise you. I shall never stop saying it."

I grinned. *"You are so getting laid the next time I find somewhere horizontal."*

"Why wait for that, love?"

Surt's irritated voice interrupted my next words to Jakob. "Erin, if you don't mind."

Chagrined, I whispered, "Sorry."

"You must focus, Erin. Push your magic into the ember. It cannot hurt you."

"I'm sure that's true, Surt, but I have a problem with the thought of burning off my eyebrows." Because of the temple's faraway location, the flames were igniting, burning higher and hotter to let us see over the distance. I'd hastily slung the flames away from me, in reflex, every single time we'd tried, so far.

His lips twitched. "You will not lose your eyebrows if you concentrate."

"You could be doing this for me," I told him, through gritted teeth.

His serene smile widened. "I do know that. However, I will not. How else will you learn? You are being a—what is it they call a coward on Midgard?"

"I believe the word you are searching for is chicken," Jakob supplied with a smirk.

I bit back the 'blow me' comment that was on the tip of my tongue and gripped the ember. I was not going to let him call me a chicken. I could do this. I was the daughter of Odin, for Pete's sake!

Urging the flame higher, I called to it with my magic and heard an electric snap of connection when it responded. I smiled. The vision now in the ember I held would wipe the smirks right off their faces.

"Aha! You have done it!" Surt exclaimed, clasping his hands together in joy. "Look, gentle-males, and you will see what you seek."

I heard Soren suck in a breath over my shoulder as he saw the temple's crude stone walls against the background of a blazing orange sunset. "Erin, can you pan out over the water a bit?"

"Sure."

The sudden baritone of Jakob's voice on my left made me jump. "It is Vänern Lake."

"Where is it?"

"Sweden."

Surt waved the vision away. "Yes, yes. Go to Sweden, but first, Erin, you must learn to scry without touch. Though it is doubtful that you possess the amount of control that it would take to accomplish such a feat, I would feel that my teachings were incomplete without at least showing you how it is done."

"Okay." What did I have to lose? Eyebrows grow back, right?

He scooped the now small fire from my hands and cast it back into the pit. "It will be more difficult to command the fire to share its secrets in this way. Nevertheless, it is the most effective way to scry. Are you prepared to start?"

"Yes."

"Good. First, I will show you how it is done. The fire must be coaxed in a particular way." He clasped my small hand in his large one. *"I do not want your brother to overhear this. He seems out of sorts tonight."*

"Jakob is my true mate, but Soren is being irrational about my choice."

"Are you so sure that he is? Your protection is first and foremost in his mind. Look into the fire, and you shall see." He waved his arm and the same view of Soren and Jakob I'd seen before arose, but this time my brother was in high focus. *"Do you not see the fear in his eyes?"*

Before, when I saw this image, Soren had on his usual mask of disdainful arrogance, but now, his furrowed face had worried eyes. It didn't make sense. *"When I saw this before, he didn't have an expression at all."*

Jakob's lustful visage moved in front of Soren's pained face. *"Did he not? Or, were you so preoccupied with your lover that you could not see his fear?"*

Embarrassed, I shrugged. *"I don't know."*

"Fire was never meant to be a way to spy. It was meant to be

a way for our kind to communicate. If you concentrate on one thing, such as your mate, you will miss the important things that you should see."

"Our kind? I thought the gift of the flame was a rare elven gift."

"And so it is. In the way that it is rare that an elf is born with the talent."

"That means that we are related, right?"

"Yes, though it must be deep in your lineage. You do not have an inkling of our signature." He looked at me with a wistful expression. *"It is a shame that you are already spoken for. It is hard to find a beautiful female who has the talent."*

I didn't doubt his words. He lived in such solitude that it would take a miracle for him to find a mate … or to make a friend who is sister-in-law to a Norn. I squeezed his hand with a burgeoning feeling of excitement in my belly. *"Have you considered having a Norn find your mate?"*

"I have heard stories about the Norns. Are they common where you are from?"

"No, but my brother's wife is one. I'm sure she wouldn't mind casting your fate."

His somber face lit up with hope. *"It is a pity that she did not accompany you here today."*

"Why don't you come back with us? You could teach me to scry anywhere, right?"

"Yes, but do you not worry that this scheme will not sit well with the males who brought you here?"

"No. I'm not worried, at all. They want you on their side, and I'm sure that Emelie can spare a few minutes for a new friend."

Releasing my hand, Surt pulled me into his strong arms for a hug. Our flames ignited in fiery unison as we embraced. Mine a bright blue and his an orangey-red to match all that outrageous hair.

"Thank you, Erin. No one has ever shown me the kindness you have."

I smiled up from somewhere around his ribcage. *"We're family, and family sticks together."*

Holding me by the shoulders at arm's length, Surt returned my smile with an affectionate one of his own. *"I believe that you became beloved to me the moment I met you, dear Erin."*

Stepping back, he reached out as if he were going to caress my face, but instead, he pressed a gentle thumb into the center of my forehead. From the point of contact outward, heat radiated so intensely that I screamed in agonizing pain until blessed unconsciousness overtook me.

I awoke with a startled gasp. Unsteady and dazed, I sat up and looked around the silent, unfamiliar room I was in with what I knew were eyes of blazing blue flame. My fire was closer to the surface than it had ever been before. I felt fevered, powerful—wrong. Panicked, I untangled myself from the luxury linens I'd been sleeping on and ran to the closest open door, praying that it was the bathroom.

By some miracle, it was. Hurling myself into the marble shower stall, I huddled into a corner and trembled. I didn't want to burn the place down—wherever I was. God, I hoped that Jakob would show up soon. Hyperventilation seemed to be imminent. Wrapping my arms around myself, I hugged my knees to my chest, staring at the chrome fixtures, before realizing that I was wearing a black t-shirt that Jakob had worn in Surt's world. Breathing in his scent seemed to relax me a little, or maybe, it just gave me hope that he would return soon. I doubt that he would've gone far shirtless.

"He didn't," a female's ethereal voice said, from across the room.

I jerked my gaze toward the voice but saw nothing. "Who's there?"

A stunning silver-haired female substantialized on the edge of the adjacent bathtub, her face strikingly similar to Emelie's. With a grin that crinkled the corners of her bright silver eyes, she spoke again. "I believe that Emelie's face is like mine, not the other way around, my dear."

"You're Myrgjöl, Emelie's grandmother?"

She smiled at the mention of her granddaughter. "I am, and you must be the beauty that has swept the king off his feet."

"I'm not too sure that I had a choice in that," I told her. From the moment I met Jakob, I knew that I would be willing to stay with him for the rest of my life. There had been more of a connection between the two of us in the first thirty seconds we were together on that sidewalk than I'd ever had with a human man, even the ones that I'd had long-term relationships with.

"It may not seem so, but there is always a choice, child. You could have chosen not to cast that spell, or you could have chosen to stay on Midgard, instead of going to Álfheim with Jakob. Or you could have even chosen to mate with Kristian instead of his brother. These were all possible futures for you."

I was horrified. "Mate Kristian? Are you kidding me?"

"He was Emelie's choice for you, was he not?"

"I guess so. She mentioned the castle numerous times, but—"

"But, she made a mistake, didn't she?" she interrupted.

"I'm not following." I was more confused than ever. How did Emelie make a mistake?

"She gifted you with a bit of her magic. On accident, of course. You have a unique talent that she didn't foresee."

"What talent is that?" I asked, discouraged. Another ability? I was doomed. There was no way that I could handle another one. How did Soren make all of his magic look so effortless?

"Your brother has had thousands of years to perfect his magic," She reminded me, smiling. "But I am not here to talk about that stubborn, pig-headed, pain in the ass male. I'm here to talk about your talent for absorption."

"Absorption? What does it do?"

"What it implies. You can absorb magical talents from other creatures. Next to the Norn's ability to cast fates, it is the rarest gift of the Norselands."

I thought back to Axel and Kristian's dropped jaws at dinner the other night. "I shook Kristian's hand."

"Yes, you did. You have touched many creatures since your arrival."

She was right. What powers did I have that I didn't even know about? I mean, who hadn't I shook hands with or touched in some small way?

"You have not touched Viveka," she said in answer to my internal pondering. "Make sure you touch her when you see her, no matter what. Her talent should not be wasted."

"Wasted? You mean, she's going to die?"

Myrgjöl climbed into the shower and slid down the marble wall to sit next to me. "She will."

Shocked, I didn't know how to respond. I knew she was the enemy and that she was mad as a hatter, but she was still my mother. I guess I hadn't thought she might actually die.

"It is a pity that she became mad with her quest for power. Things could have turned out so differently."

"Would she still be with Jakob?" I blurted out like the words were burning a hole in my tongue.

Myrgjöl saw right through my transparency. "You should never doubt Jakob's love for you, Erin. You are his true mate. Emelie's gift to you made sure that your fates recognized that, even if the two of you didn't, though I suspect the power of

181

influence that you borrowed from him may have been the thing to make him accept it. He is stubborn to a fault about doing the right thing, you know."

I laughed, in spite of the tears building in my eyes. "He can be … infuriating."

Smiling a soothing smile, she handed me a lace handkerchief. "Yes, Erin, he can be. However, he is also one of the best males in the Norselands. You've been blessed with a good match. He will protect you with his life." She paused in thought, her eyes glazing over in silver. "And he will have to. Now that you are such a coveted commodity, everyone will want you to join their ranks. It will be a constant struggle, Erin."

Tears slipped down my cheeks before I could catch them. "I don't think I can handle all of this so soon."

She wrapped a companionable arm around me. "You can, and you will. There is no reason for you to fear. You are powerful enough to defeat anyone, your father included. I promise." Glancing at the doorway, she stood. "Shit. I have to go. Here comes your Mr. Tall, Dark, and Hung." She winked. "Good luck, Erin."

"Thanks," I said to thin air, wondering if I'd just had the weirdest dream of my life.

Jakob strode into the bathroom a millisecond later, his hand on the sheath situated on his belt. "Who were you thanking, Erin? Why are you dressed in the shower? Are you crying?" Crouching down next to me, he tilted my chin up to peer at my tear-stained face. "Älskling?"

"I'm fine," I replied, far too cheerful for the way I felt. "Just a few hundred years of therapy and I'll be A-Okay."

He gathered me in his arms, tucking my head under his chin. "Tell me what has happened."

"Myrgjöl just left."

"What news did she bring?"

"The news that I have the power of absorption, and that I have to touch Viveka before she dies."

His face betrayed his fear. He was worried about the prospect of me getting close enough to my mother to touch her. "I find that I am speechless, Erin. You have touched so many—Emelie, Soren, Nils, Viggo, Surt, Chase, me...you must be overwhelmed with power."

"Overwhelmed feels a little understated, Jakob. Have you noticed that we're in the shower stall?

"Yes, love. Is it Surt's magic?"

"It was terrifying, Jakob. My fire felt like it was out of control when I woke up."

He chuckled and leaned down to kiss me, lingering for a moment. "You will soon learn to master it. Surt will help you. He is quite smitten with your charm. I have endured hours of his constant praise of you."

I scoffed. "Poor you, having to hear about how great your mate is while I was rendered unconscious then left to wake up scared and alone. That must have been awful for you."

"Terrible," he assured me, laughing at my unhappy face. "Erin, you amuse me."

"I'm glad someone is amused," I grouched.

He stroked my pouting lip. "It was only terrible because I cannot bear to hear another male sing your praises. You are mine. I, alone, should be able to speak of your perfection."

Stunned, I mumbled, "Oh."

With a bittersweet smile, he lifted me from the shower and carried me back into the bedroom, laying me on the bed and stretching out beside me. "I am sorry that you woke alone. Stay angry as long as you like."

I nestled into his warm chest. "Where were you?"

"Smoking on the balcony."

Looking up, I wrinkled my nose. "I wish you wouldn't."

"Erin, I've smoked for hundreds of years. It will not kill me," he reasoned.

"I guess we all have our vices," I conceded. "Want to know what my vice is?" Stretching up, I peppered his mouth with soft kisses that he returned with a deeper version of his own until I was panting for breath.

"I love you, my mate," he said, nipping at my lip.

"Enough to tell me where we are and if I can expect my brother to come through the door to interrupt us?"

He chuckled. "We are on Midgard, in Lincoln, Nebraska. And yes, your brother could come through that door, or any door for that matter, if he sets his mind to it."

"You're hysterical. Can I ask why we're in Lincoln, of all places?"

"Viggo owns a large acreage just outside of town. We are using it as a ... I suppose you could call it a base of operations. The rebellion will stay there until we plan an attack on the temple, and the open fields are ideal to teach you to use your magic as a weapon."

"Who's going to teach me that?"

"I will, morning and night until my heart does not feel as if it is being ripped out when I think of you in battle. I cannot lose you, Erin."

"Aw, that's sweet, Jakob. And graphic. But how will you ..." I trailed off as I realized what he was implying. "Whose blood will you drink?"

He reached into the pocket of his jeans. "Emelie's. She gave us each a vial, in case of emergencies."

"I see," I said, making a not so valiant attempt at hiding my feelings about him drinking another female's blood. Even though she was my friend and Soren's mate, I had a twinge of irrational jealousy streak through me at her mention.

Jakob tucked my hair behind my ear and stroked my cheek. "Ease your mind, love. I do not cherish the thought of drinking another's blood."

"Good, because I despise it."

"I, too, wish that there was another choice."

"I wish that I could do it for you," I admitted, a little ashamed of my greed in this. "It's stupid, but even with all of the other magic I possess, I hate not being the one who can do that for you."

A look of concentration crossed his features. "Erin, Myrgjöl said that you had the power of absorption, did she not?"

Sitting up, I gave him a wide-eyed look, understanding what he implied with his question. "Uh, bite me, Jakob."

He laughed. "You know, out of context, those words could be a little unsettling to hear."

"Then I'm glad that no one else is here to hear it," I teased. "Come on, do it. Wait. You won't burn up right away if it doesn't work, will you?"

"Not right away, no. It would take an hour or so," he replied, his fangs peeking out, past his smile.

"So, it's like what happened to me when I went back to the shop? The thousand needle pricks of hell and smoking flesh?"

He sat up. "You could have been injured, Erin. Why am I just hearing this now?"

"I forgot. I had a lot going on with the whole Soren, Chase, Älvornas Rike, Queen Layla, and the Nils thing."

"If you burned, I doubt you have the light elves ability," he said, clearly upset with himself. "I am sorry, my love. I should have thought to caution you after your elven magic emerged."

I rolled my eyes at his martyred expression. "You have to stop blaming yourself for my stupidity, Jakob. You did try to stop me, remember?"

"Yes, but I have not made myself available to you in the ways that are important, as I should have. You must have questions about your magic, and concerns about your expectations, now that Kristian is gone, and you shall be Queen of Svartálfaheim. Please believe that I will be more attentive to your needs ... all of them, from today forward."

I shook my head. "All of my needs, huh? Oh, Jakob. You've got it bad, don't you?"

He pulled his borrowed shirt over my head, leaving me in just my panties. "At the moment, nothing bad comes to mind, älskling, but to answer your question, yes, I do."

"Jakob, I understand that your responsibilities keep you away. And, I mean, sure, I have questions, but when faced with the option of having mind-blowing sex, or having a serious conversation about current affairs, I will always pick sex." I stood to slide my underwear off. "Every topic pales in comparison with your dick."

"Forgive me, Erin," he said, surging up from the bed with me in tow. "I have never wanted to 'fuck' anyone, but you bring out the animal in me. I want you on my cock. I have to be inside of you." He backed us to the wall and kissed me, teasing at first, then with an overwhelming intensity I struggled to match. Breaking the kiss, he panted through sharp fangs. "I have too many clothes on."

Desperate to give my mate what he wanted, I successfully made his jeans disappear on the first attempt. Jakob smiled at the turn of circumstance, but instead of congratulating me on my new found talent, he didn't say a word, just lifted me up, so that I could wrap my legs around him. Breathing heavily, his single-minded determination made his face appear almost cruel as he impaled me against the wall and groaned out his pleasure. Over and over, he drove into me, never taking his eyes from mine. His fierce gaze was hypnotizing. So much so, I couldn't be sure that he wasn't using his influence on me. Mesmerized, I watched as he brought my palm to his mouth and bit down, drawing on the fresh wound until we reached our peak together, both of us crying out in uninhibited ecstasy.

Jakob collapsed onto the mattress with me still clinging to him. "You have no idea how much I have missed you being in my bed."

I pushed myself up on my weak arms and sprawled next to him. "I do have some idea. It's about as much as I miss being in your bed. It's heaven—one of the most comfortable beds I've ever slept on."

He arched a bewildered eyebrow and turned his head toward me. "Sorry, what?"

An involuntary giggle escaped from my lips. It was impossible not to laugh at the lost look he had on his face. "I'm infatuated with your bed."

"Then I shall not stand in your way of sleeping there."

"That's all I ever wanted," I teased. "Can you get Soren to do that, too?"

He grinned. "It will be my next endeavor."

"Seriously, I think we should give Soren an ultimatum, and if he doesn't like it, we should just leave. Not the rebellion, of course, just from his society until he can grow up. It may take a few thousand years, but he will eventually accept our mating, right?"

His face was skeptical. "We shall see about that. Soren is..." He groped above his head for my discarded shirt and shoved it at me as a knock sounded at the door. "Here already."

I leaned in to kiss him before he could get up, tracing my finger through the dark hair of his chest and downward toward his still heavy erection. "Soren has a sixth sense for interrupting what has the promise of being an extremely satisfying night."

"It does seem that way," he agreed, catching my wandering hand. "Älskling, you little devil. Your brother will suspect the worst if I do not answer the door soon."

Arching a devious brow, I purred, "I know. I'm counting on it," and gave him a light squeeze with my free hand.

Groaning, he shot up from the bed. "I should have been warned that my mate would be so evil." He motioned to his dick. "What am I going to do with this?"

"Ask the male that's trying to make me a nun out there. And tell him I'm taking a shower before I go anywhere, while you're at it."

"Of course. Nils retrieved a few belongings from your apartment while you slept. You will find them in a satchel on the dresser."

A sudden vision of me having to walk out of the hotel room in the prostitute's outfit I'd wore last Halloween filled my head. "I can't believe you let Nils pick out my clothes."

"It was not as if I wanted him to go through your private things. I would have sent one of the staff if it had not been too dangerous. I doubt that it will give you any relief, but I did ask him to be tasteful and practical. There may have been several threats involved."

I picked up a tiny black thong that lay on top with a finger. "I guess you could consider this practical. I could fashion it into a slingshot if I had to."

He closed his eyes and took a deep breath. "I am going to kill him, and then I want to see you in those and nothing else, though the ones you had on earlier were…more than alluring. And speaking of those, where are they, and where are my jeans? I will need them if I have any hope of Soren not beating me into a bloody stain on the carpet."

"Oh, yeah. Is now a good time to talk about my—" I did quotation marks with my fingers. "Emerging magic? Because I have no idea how I pulled that one off."

He barked out a laugh and flinched when the insistent

knocking turned to pounding. "Soren wishes the clothes into being. It should not be hard."

I closed my eyes and thought about the customary pair of black jeans he'd been wearing. When I opened them, he stood dressed but looked a little disheveled. "Are you okay?"

He smiled and pulled me into his grasp, tracing the curve of my bottom with his strong hands. "Perfectly, and I was serious about the panties. I want you in those and nothing else."

With a seductive grin, I murmured, "Anything you want, my king. Now please go get the door before Soren breaks it down."

He bent to kiss me, his green eyes growing brighter with his mounting lust. "I will remember that you said that, Erin."

"Then I hope you have a good memory," I replied, kissing him back, then heading to the bathroom with the bag Nils had better hope included more than lingerie.

CHAPTER TWELVE

V iggo's farm was situated far off the county road, about thirty minutes outside of Lincoln, judging by my annoyance level. The trip had been so monotonous. Cornfield after never-ending, mind-numbing cornfield. "Are we there yet?" I asked, ready to jump out the window just to get some excitement.

Soren laughed at my petulant tone. "Yes. That is the house in the distance."

Slowing down to turn on a hidden dirt road, I spied the white house I'd been praying would materialize. I couldn't stay in this car with Soren's smug face a second longer. I was so pissed at his refusal to accept Jakob and me as mates. Even after spending so much time traveling on the trip to Múspellsheim, he still wouldn't budge.

Soren caught my attention in the rearview mirror, a pleasant smile, which was every bit out of place as Viggo owning a farmhouse in corn country, spread across his face. Cue the creepy movie music. This was starting to feel like one of those low-budget slasher flicks that come on late at night. "Am I ever going to leave Nebraska, Soren? Which is it going to be? Huh? Buried behind the barn or fed to the pigs? Because if I get to choose, I'll just start digging now."

He scoffed at my crossed arms. "Are you serious, Erin? Viggo would never own pigs."

I sighed, more exasperated than I was thirty seconds before. "Well then, what's the smile about, Soren?" Why had I ever wanted a brother?

"Nothing particular," he answered, in his irritating, cryptic way. Still smiling, he started humming as he guided the car to a stop behind the house.

"Are you humming a merry tune? What the fuck, Soren? Can someone tell me what is going on?" His attitude was a complete one-eighty from the way it was just a couple of hours ago.

Emelie smacked him on the forearm. "Stop it. This is not a vacation."

"It almost feels like one," Nils supplied. He'd been so quiet, I'd forgotten he was stretched out across the far back seat of Soren's SUV.

"See?" Soren asked.

"Both of you, shut up!" Emelie warned, crossing her arms. She looked at me with pursed lips, shaking her head. "Ugh, males, you can't live with them, and you can't feed them to the pigs."

Axel and Viggo stood waiting in front of the house as we pulled into the driveway. Damn, they were so handsome. I'd have to talk to Emelie about a 'males of the rebellion' calendar for next year. Maybe we could make some extra cash before they annoyed us to the brink of insanity.

Emelie opened her door and jumped out, holding up a hand in the universal stop motion. "Nope. Erin and I are having a quick chat. You can see her in a minute, okay?"

"Please, do not delay her any longer than necessary," Axel said, bowing.

Bewildered, Emelie responded, "Of course not, Jörmungand. We won't be long."

Just as confused as she was, I followed her into the cozy old house and into a parlor adjacent to the living room.

As soon as I was settled, she asked, "So?"

"Hmmm. Whatever could you be talking about?" I replied in a sing-song voice.

"Spill, Erin."

"It's no big deal, Emelie. I spent the day with him. We had sex."

"Yeah, about that. Soren told me that he walked in on you two."

"If you consider kicking in the door and catching us buck naked, then yes, he did."

She was grim. "I suppose I should have expected Soren to omit that tiny, little, insignificant detail."

"Well, he did seem pretty embarrassed once he'd done it."

She rolled her eyes at her mate's antics. "I'm sure he did, the hotheaded idiot, but forget about that for a minute. There's something I've been dying to know since Soren told me about what happened."

"What's that?"

"I'm wondering if Mr. Serious penciled you in for a sex appointment, or did he just narrate and correct your form the whole time?" She straightened and spoke in a stern, accented voice. "Erin, remember your posture."

I burst out laughing at the scholarly way she portrayed Jakob. Sure, he was sharp and focused, but he didn't act like the uptight dullard they all thought him to be. At least, not with me, he didn't.

"Emelie, it was incredible," I answered in truth. "Wild and out of control." I lowered my voice to a whisper. "We did it on the carpet and once in the shower before we ever made it to a bed."

"The carpet?" she asked, in astonishment. "Let's just back up a minute here. We are speaking of the same male, aren't we? Tall guy, dreamy green eyes, stick up the ass personality?"

"Yep. That's him."

She looked impressed. "Jakob Väsen … the carpet, really?"

In a blink, Axel popped into existence behind Emelie and stole a kiss from her cheek. "She is indeed serious, my lady. Evangelina even asked me if she needed to make breakfast for the females, thinking that they were new ones in residence."

Emelie dragged her horrified gaze from Axel to me. "Oh, Erin.

Please, tell me you didn't!"

I grinned, unable to contain my excitement. "I did, and it was hotter than hell."

"It's true," Axel agreed, winking at me. "It would have been the hottest thing I had ever overheard if Jakob hadn't been involved." He shuddered as if reliving the memory. "That part was quite disturbing."

Emelie held her hands over her ears. "Hush, you two. This is Jakob we're talking about."

"I wouldn't bother with that, kitten," Axel said, dismissing her disgust with a self-satisfied smile. "Now that Soren knows about the harem part, you'll be hearing plenty about it, I am sure. He was furious upon hearing the news."

My stomach plummeted, and Emelie took off for the door, shouting instructions behind her. "Give me some time to calm Soren down!"

"What are you going to do?" I called after her.

"Damage control!" she yelled. "Fuck you very much, Axel!"

He chuckled and sat down at the table. "That was ... excellent."

"Why did you tell him about the harem?" I demanded, pissed and confused by his smugness. Why would anyone that had met my brother try to anger him? Soren was sure to kill Jakob over this.

Axel was unabashed. "I was bored."

I sat down and smacked him in the back of the head. "What the fuck, Axel?"

Viggo walked into the room just as Axel caught my hand. "Abusing the king's servants already, huh, Erin?"

"He deserved it. That, and a swift kick to the ass," I answered, glaring at Axel, daring him to say different.

Viggo laughed at our power struggle and pulled my hand from

his friend's grasp. "Take care that you avoid his touch, Erin. He can be quite persuasive."

I nearly laughed. How well I knew how compelling Axel's magic could be. "He is not the only one with the power of influence."

"Indeed. I could hear Soren yelling at Jakob about the harem from my bedroom. Axel that was a real dick move, telling him about that. What could you have gained from incriminating my brother?"

"Dick move!" Axel spat. "It is funny that you would choose those words because those are the ones I would have chosen for the situation Saint Jakob put us in. You should have seen him, parading her around like he'd won first prize in a true mate contest, and then, to top off the insult, he sent her around the dinner table to put the king and me under her sway. I am sure that even you will agree, Viggo, that to wave Erin's supple beauty under our noses and then to fuck her senseless within earshot is the definition of a 'dick move.'

"Oh, fuck." I bent my forehead to the tabletop and gave it a quick whack. "Fuck." Whack. "Fuck." Whack. "FUCK!"

"Erin, what the hell? Viggo exclaimed, grabbing my shoulders to keep me from doing it again.

"This is all my fault!"

Viggo smoothed back my hair and examined my reddened forehead. "How could any of this be your fault, poppet?"

Tears slipped down my cheeks. "Myrgjöl told me tonight that I could absorb magic from others, which makes me the dick in this whole mess."

Axel understood what I was implying. "Kristian gave you his magic when he took your hand."

"Yes. I'm so sorry. I had no idea what I was doing ... or taking."

He sighed in relief. "I am just glad to hear that there is an explanation for the urges I had after dinner. The need to pull that straight-laced know-it-all off of your naked body and show you how a real male fucks was relentless."

"Axel!" Viggo scolded. "Watch your tongue when you speak to my niece, or I will cut it out!"

He waved off Viggo's stern reprimand with a wave of the hand. "Ask Kristian, if you do not believe me. We both suffered until Evangelina made us leave the east wing."

"Is that why he was drinking in the kitchen that day?"

"It was either that or go insane. Did you have any idea how much influence you were using on us?"

"None, though I'll admit that I was hoping to give you a little bit of payback for the influence you were both using on me. I just wanted to wipe the smirks off your faces. That's all."

"Well, what a surprise," Viggo said, sarcasm dripping from his words. "The king and his right hand used their talents for evil instead of good. You two are a couple nefarious deeds away from getting your own HBO series."

"It was harmless flirting, Viggo. I can assure you. How was I to know that she would steal his magic and use it against us?"

Incensed, I sprang from my seat. "Uh, asshole, I wouldn't have done anything if you hadn't started it! And do you think that I want that power? Why couldn't it be something useful?"

"You think his magic useless?" he asked, astounded by my harsh honesty.

"Okay, maybe useless is a bit cruel," I acknowledged. "I just find it ironic that someone who will never need it would have the power of sexual influence."

"Likewise, Erin," he growled, lifting a sensual eyebrow.

"Gross," Viggo and I muttered in unison.

Axel stood with a sigh. "I believe that I am starting to see the family resemblance. Good day to the both of you.”

“Good day,” I said, echoing Viggo again.

Axel turned back to us, looking bothered. “One Viggo is quite enough, Erin.”

I watched, bemused, as Axel stalked out of the room. “Wow. Grumpy-pants is in a foul mood.”

“Ignore him. He’s always in a mood when his king is away.”

“Yeah, well, Kristian has an uncanny knack for driving me bonkers when he’s in town. Before he returns with his mate, I plan on booking my room in the asylum. You know, before the rates go up.”

“Make it a double room. I will need someone to wipe the drool off my chin for me.”

“Deal.”

Emelie returned right after Viggo, and I decided to make a pot of tea. She was in a complete funk. “Soren is a disconsonant ass,” she said.

“Nice word choice,” I congratulated. “And?”

“And, he won’t listen to reason. But then, why would he? I’m a Norn ... who can see the future ... and knows exactly what’s going to happen ... and could help put things to right,” she muttered, sullenly pulling out a chair and flopping down.

“Why am I not surprised?” I asked.

“He’s pissed about the harem thing. I mean, beyond pissed. I’ve never seen him so angry.”

Viggo poured her a cup of tea. “Here. You’re trembling. Both of you just need to calm down. This will all blow over soon. It has to, now that you and Jakob are mated.”

“Yeah, about that, Erin. What the fuck with the not telling me? I could have been a little more prepared for World War III if you had."

"Chase got me all distracted the night I saw you," I explained, hoping she wasn't as angry as she sounded. "I just haven't had the opportunity to tell you since."

"What do you call that thing your neck is holding up, Erin? You can talk to me anytime," she muttered, pouring copious amounts of sugar and cream into her tea.

Putting a comforting hand on both of us, Viggo said, "Now, now, ladies. Let's just try to get through tonight without the idiot males in this house driving us insane. Okay?"

"Okay," we agreed, both of us trying not to laugh at his feminine tone.

"That's my girls! Now, Erin, the first thing I want to know is what magic spell you put on that 'paradigm of everything that is good and right' brother of mine to get him to step foot in the old harem. "

"No spells. Believe me, Jakob put up a good fight," I said, polishing my nails on my shirt. "But, uh … I always get my male."

Emelie laughed. "You are a terrible influence on our Jakob. I love it!"

Viggo nodded in agreement. "As do I. He needs someone like you in his life … before he bores someone to death."

"I don't get it. You guys see him so differently than I do."

Emelie passed me a plate of spiced cookies. "I said that exact thing to Viggo after Soren and I were mated. If I recall, he wondered if I had a brain tumor."

"I'm still wondering that myself," I teased. "I mean, Kristian is so hot, and Soren is so ... Soren."

She smiled. "He isn't like that all the time. Can I show you?"

"Am I going to have to bleach my eyes after this?"

"No. I don't think so."

Against my better judgment, I let Emelie grasp my hand in hers and closed my eyes. At first, she filled my mind with her pouring over photo albums, mooning over a picture of the mysterious white-haired male that her parents told her stories about. She was more than enamored. He was her first love. In the next scene, Soren was holding her frail, sick body as he healed her. Then, the vision morphed into a desperate Soren telling her that he would find a way to stop her marriage to Kristian and kissing her passionately as he lay atop her naked body.

"Liar!" I cried out.

She laughed, tears leaking from her eyes. "Now we're even for you not telling me."

I stuck out my hand. "Truce? I won't talk about sex with Jakob if I don't ever have to see or hear anything like that horrible, horrible vision again."

"Truce," she agreed, shaking my hand in a business-like manner with a grin.

"I'm down with sex from either one of you," Nils said, from where he leaned on the doorframe listening to our conversation. "And with me, you won't have to be embarrassed about it later when you tell your girlfriends."

Emelie rolled her eyes. "I'm pretty sure that no female would remember having sex with you. You're pretty much an 'I'm too drunk to make good decisions' kind of fuck."

Nils smirked at the vulgarity he seemed to bring out in Emelie as he sat at the table. "I'm hurt, Em. It has been but two years, and already you have forgotten how you begged me for my cock."

I gasped. "Emelie, you slut!"

"I was out of my mind," she said, in her defense. "Freyr cursed me!"

She was mortified, and I felt terrible for laughing, but when something this caliber of hilarious came along, it was mandatory. "And here I was thinking you were so innocent."

"Bite me, Erin."

"Are you sure that you don't want Nils to do that?"

Viggo chuckled. "Good one."

Emelie gave us an evil glare. "Erin, if you don't forget everything you've heard in the last few minutes, I will tell Soren about you doing it on the harem floor. I'm not even kidding."

I sucked in a breath. "You wouldn't!"

Nils stopped laughing and stared at me in disbelief. "Oh no, Em. Let me tell him. Just let me find my cell phone first so that I can take a video of his reaction."

Emelie shot daggers at him. "You shut it, wolf! Before I tell your daddy on you."

Viggo roared with laughter. "Oooh! Burn!"

The male we spoke of cleared his throat at the doorjamb. "What is it that you would like to share with me, Emelie?"

She paled when she realized whose voice spoke behind her. Looking like she'd rather be anywhere else, she turned around to face Loki. "N-nothing. I was just joking around."

He nodded. "I see, my lady. Son, have you began Erin's training?"

"Relax, father. I'm getting to it," Nils said, ignoring Loki's stern expression until he turned his attention on someone else.

"And you, Emelie? We haven't much time."

Nils scoffed. "Emelie? What is she going to teach Erin? How to knit?"

An incredulous Emelie stood from the table. The look in her eyes was straight pissed off. But it also bordered on 'someone ate the last bite of Chicken Parmesan'. "What did you say, mutt?" She spat out the words with hot venom in every syllable.

Grinning like a fool at the drama unfolding, Viggo was delighted to help jog her memory. "He said that you were incapable of teaching Erin anything but how to knit."

Emelie gave a nasty smile to a now wary Nils and snapped her fingers. He disappeared.

"What just happened?" I asked, taking the teacup from Emelie's trembling hands.

She turned her eerie silver eyes on me and sat with a deep sigh. "I put the dog out."

Loki put a fatherly hand on Emelie's shoulder. "It was deserved, my lady, and indeed, I hope it proved to be therapeutic for you. Fenrir's personality must be taxing to one so young. I imagine patience can be a hard virtue to learn when you are subjected to one so annoying at such regular intervals."

Emelie nodded in commiseration. "You are so not wrong about that, Loki."

Viggo was beside himself with laughter. "What I want to know is, where is out? You only tremble when you send someone a long distance away, and you've never had a reaction like this before. Come on, Em, where was it? Múspellsheim? Niflheim to visit that hot sister of his?"

She smirked. "Nowhere in particular."

Seconds later, Nils reappeared. Rivulets of melted ice puddled under his four feet as his fur thawed. He seemed to be semi-frozen as he spoke, but all the way incensed. Canines chattering, he snarled in our heads, "Antarctica, Emelie? You sent me to fucking Antarctica!"

With more of a smile than I'd ever seen him wear, Loki said, "Take form, son, you are destroying the carpet," and then left the room.

If a wolf could have rolled his eyes in exasperation, Nils would have. Instead of following his father's advice, he shook his coat, sending flecks of ice and water shooting toward us. I screamed and ducked, but none of the slush hit me. Peeking up from the other side of the table, I saw a wondrous sight—Jakob.

He stood stock still just outside the doorway, his eyes burning a bright, concentrated green as he held every drop of water and ice motionless in the air—including the ones still attached to Nils. His countenance exuded pure, unadulterated rage. I knew that if I didn't get him out of here soon, there would be words between him and Nils. Many, many violent words.

Eyes wide, I stepped through the crystalline minefield to stand next to my mate. "Jakob, can I interest you in a night out on the town? I mean, after …" I gestured to the cleaning nightmare waiting to happen. "This is over?"

If he was surprised at my suggestion, he didn't show it. He just took out his shifting stone and offered me his arm. "Of course," He didn't take his eyes off a frozen Nils. "Emelie, I will hold him still for a minute while you make your way over here."

Her evil grin was downright scary. "Be right there, Jakob."

I grinned at the childish behavior they were engaging in and felt a streak of pride filter through me. These two...okay, three friends were my family. They were all so different, but they were also the same, and I loved them for it—for all of their quirks and craziness. As I watched Jakob count to three, I knew at this moment, without a doubt, that I would do anything to keep them safe, even if that meant I would have to kill the ones that shared my DNA. There's nothing like a werewolf's antics to bring a family closer together.

We didn't wait around to see if Nils would retaliate for Jakob turning the tables on him, but we could hear his rage as he screamed, "JAKOB!" in a window-rattling timbre.

Emelie snickered. "Well, that's my cue to leave."

"Chicken!" I yelled at her retreating form.

Jakob grabbed my arm. "We should go. Now."

Grabbing Soren's car keys from the table in the foyer, I jingled them with a devil may care grin. "I have a better means of travel."

He raised his eyebrows. "Stealing a car is a better idea?"

I nodded. "Today, it most certainly is."

It was official. I was a terrible influence on Jakob. If I'd been surprised by his acceptance of my wicked invitation to steal a car, that was nothing when compared to the shock I felt as I watched him levitate Soren's SUV out of Viggo's driveway, over the cornfields, and onto the deserted highway. It was far beyond anything I ever expected him to do for me.

"Erin, there is nothing I wouldn't do for you," he responded, in answer to my thought.

I clucked my tongue. "I seem to remember you promising to stay out of my head, Jakob. What happened to that?" My shield was easily kept up when others were around for the sheer embarrassment factor. However, when Jakob and I were alone, I often forgot. I mentioned it to Emelie once. She told me that I forget to block because, secretly, all females want to be heard by their mate. I disagree. I think it's because I trust him to keep what he finds up there a secret. Besides Em and Chase, who else could I say that about?

Pretending to be admonished, he replied, "I will endeavor to remember your privacy in the future, my princess, but in the meantime, your chariot awaits."

I curtseyed with a slow, sensual dip and slipped my hand into his. "Thank you, kind prince."

Once we were safely ensconced in the car and speeding down the highway, I decided to busy myself with changing the presets on the radio to news and Spanish channels to curb my boredom.

"Erin? What are you doing?" Jakob inquired, observing my in-seat Salsa dancing.

"Hmm?" I asked, pressing a button until it beeped.

"Why are you torturing your brother? You know he listens to

Classical music."

"Actually, I didn't know that. I haven't spent much time with him. Probably, because he's been a dick about ninety-nine percent of the time."

"How will you ever learn who he is if you keep avoiding him?"

I paused in my oh-so malevolent deed and turned to my mate, who was bewildered by what I was doing. "Look, you can be cavalier about what he did to us, and that's fine, but I don't have five thousand years of patience built up under my belt. Besides, I'm Soren's little sister. I'm pretty sure there's a chapter on annoying him to death in the handbook."

A slow grin spread across his face. "You know, I am sure that you are right. Carry on."

"You got it." With thoughts of the other mischief I could get away with in my mind, I continued flipping through the channels.

After a couple more miles, Jakob asked me what I knew he'd been wondering since we left. "Can you explain why we are stealing your brother's car when we could be shifting wherever we like?"

Shrugging, I leaned back into the seat. "I just need some time by myself."

"I hate to be the one to point this out, love. You are not alone. You see, alone is when there are no others around you."

I shot him a baleful look, but there was no real heat behind it. "Thanks for the tip."

He inclined his head, trying not to laugh. "Of course."

"What I meant, ass, is that I don't count you as someone else. You're a part of me. My right arm, as it were."

In a surprising move, he pulled the car into the tall grass on the side of the empty road. "Erin, I am perplexed by your choice of words. However, I believe I understand the sentiment." He smoothed my hair back from my face and kissed me. "I love you, too."

"Do you love me enough to tell my brother to leave us alone?" I asked, looking past him to the livid, white-haired maniac standing in the middle of the highway, glaring at us.

He nodded to Soren and turned back to me. "I should not have stopped."

"No, I should have given him an ultimatum. Either he deals with what is, or he won't have to deal with me at all. I'm thinking now is the perfect time to do that."

"Give him time to calm, my love. Nothing can be accomplished while you both are so angry."

I slumped in my seat. "You're right. I'm sorry I talked you into this, Jakob. It just made the situation worse."

"I am not sorry," he whispered. "I look forward to spending time with you."

"Tomorrow, we talk to him, okay? Promise me."

"I promise."

CHAPTER THIRTEEN

The next evening, I stumbled downstairs from yet another day without my mate in my bed to find Nils and Viggo finishing up their breakfast in their typical fashion—like they'd never eat again. "Uh, guys, you're supposed to chew your food before you swallow it," I reminded them.

"Good evening, Erin," they replied in harmony, ignoring my sarcasm.

I sat and stared them down, not yet awake and feeling more than a little angry at any and everything. "What's going on?" They didn't just ignore sarcasm. They picked it apart, stomped all over it, and then gave it back to you ten times as bad.

"What do you mean?" Viggo asked, taking a break from stuffing his face to pour more coffee.

"What. Is. Going. On?" I reiterated, holding out my cup for him to fill.

"Well, Soren and Em are at home 'resting', Jakob is using his kingly manner to convince the elves of the kingdom to drink light elf blood for their safety, and the rest of the motley crew are in the backyard practicing," Viggo informed me, around a mouthful of toast.

I wrinkled my nose. "Whose blood are they drinking?"

Nils laughed. "Don't worry. Em isn't supplying the entire kingdom with her blood if that's what you're thinking."

"Well, no. Call me crazy, but I doubt my brother would drain his wife of blood, even if it would save an entire race."

"You are right about that," Viggo said, smirking. "Though, he did give me this vial of her blood for you. He is hoping that her Norn magic will trigger more of your talents when you drink it."

205

"More talents? I don't know how many more 'gifts' I can handle!"

Viggo patted my shoulder. "Do you want some milk for that granola you are pouring all over the table?"

I looked down, sighing at the mess I was making. "Are you sure I don't have the magic to produce my own milk?"

"Someone is pissy today," Nils observed.

"Blow me, wolf boy."

He perked up. "Well—"

Viggo held up his hand to silence him. "Stop. Whatever you are about to say, just stop."

"Yeah, Nils. Do I have to remind you that I can sic Emelie on you at any time?"

"Funny you should bring that up, Erin." Viggo's smile was wide as he poured my milk. "Nils just returned from another impromptu trip to Antarctica this evening."

I choked on my cereal. "What?"

"Emelie has been a little touchy lately. Actually, for the last few weeks."

"I know the feeling," I muttered, pushing the cereal away and standing. Just thinking about the battle to come made me lose my appetite.

"Worried?" Nils asked, getting up from the table. "You won't be after you train up."

"That's where I'm headed."

"Good." His eyes yellowed, and he bent down to a low crouch. "Are you ready for this?"

"What—" I started, before Nils half-phased in a blur of motion and pushed us both through the plate glass front window. My breath was knocked out on impact, and I gasped what little curse words I could get out before sitting up and trying to get my bearings.

Nils stalked in front of me, more dangerous than I'd ever seen him. His eyes glowed, a sure sign that his wolf was close to the surface. "Get up, Kvinna," he growled, circling me as if looking for a weakness.

Was he serious? I gingerly lifted my bruised body from the ground, dusting the dirt off my clothes. "What the fuck, Nils? Are you high?" He would be lucky if I didn't kick his ass for making me ruin my new shoes.

"I will attack you at your weakest, Erin. I suggest you stand and fight me."

I didn't understand. Why would Nils do this? Warily, I held my hand out and focused my flame in case he decided to attack again.

"Come on, Erin!" he bellowed into the night, the last word ending in a long, soulful howl. Phasing into his wolf, his attack came too fast for me to follow. Screaming, I panicked and struck out, hoping to catch him in the ribs with my foot. That succeeded in making him growl a throaty chuckle from ten feet away. Frustrated, I crouched down, my fingers resting on the grass in front of me. I would get the upper hand the next time.

The moment he sprang in my direction, I pivoted my body to the side, spinning myself out of the grasp of his outreached paw. Or, I would have, if I wouldn't have overestimated my turn. He used my momentum against me, slinging me into the tall grass on the other side of the driveway. As I lay there, I decided two things. One, I was glad to have accelerated healing because everything from my head to my feet felt bruised, and two, next time, I would just throw myself to the ground to save him the trouble. Even with all of my magic, I could never best him. He had thousands of years of experience in battle.

"This is madness!" he screamed into the night, stalking to the place where I lay recuperating in human form again. "Fight me!"

"Fine!" I roared, sitting up with bared fangs. I was beyond

tired of playing 'Let's get my ass handed to me'. If he wanted a fight, he was going to get it.

He bared his long canines. "Well then, let's go, little girl."

With a growl and a powerful burst of energy, I exploded up from the ground, gathering my fire in its most concentrated form. It was my only hope to overpower him.

His laughter filled my mind at an annoyingly loud decibel. "You think that will stop me?" he taunted, stopping me in my tracks.

The distraction of his usual egotistical jackassery was all it took to break my plan of retaliation into a million pieces. Taking advantage, he attacked as soon as my fire died down, knocking me off my feet and pinning me down. Before I could even think of a way to buck him off, he was already across the yard, sitting on his haunches and wearing a smug little, 'I'm a gigantic jerk, and I'll take any opportunity to point it out' wolfy grin.

I hated him … really, really, really hated him. In truth, the more I looked at his big dumb dog grin, the more I wanted to kick his ass from here to next Tuesday. My fire was a white-hot presence in my senses, connecting with my rage and coaxing me to unleash it on him. And far be it for me to deny my magic when our acquaintance is so new, and I so desperately wanted to punch him in the throat. I wasn't an unfeeling female, after all.

Standing, I freed my fire, letting it cover my body. In response, he tensed, readying himself to spring. I waved him forward.

On this attack, the previous lightning fast moves seemed to come slower, his bounding leaps shorter. In fact, the hypnotizing reflection of my blue flames in his widened eyes didn't entirely mask the new look of abject fear they held. At the last possible second, he veered to the side to avoid me, not able to get his hindquarters to follow his front. Whether he was afraid of getting burned by the fire that consumed me, or whether he didn't have the heart to hurt me again, I didn't know, but his poor planning caused his back half to crash violently down onto the gravel driveway, pelting my face with rocks as he skidded toward impact with my legs.

With an ear-piercing shriek, I jumped upward using agility I didn't know I had and started to panic when several unexpected things happened at once. A blast of scorching heat seared outward from my body, launching me to a height I could have never reached without magic, and at the same moment, my arms stretched to impossible lengths, easily steadying my balance. Around me, everything had become a strange ultra-violet, brighter, and more vivid than I'd ever seen before. It was amazing ... and terrifying.

Seeing my fingers flatten to long, electric blue feathers caused me to cry out in confusion, and another ear-shattering shriek rumbled up from my throat. Then, realization hit me. I was a bird—a bird on fire that was on a collision course with the ground.

"Erin!" Emelie shouted from the front porch, holding her hands over her ears and wearing an astonished look that marred her normal smiling visage.

I tried to answer her frantic call, but another shrill squawk came out of my ... uh, beak, before I had to brace myself for the imminent crash-landing behind the house. I flapped my wings to try to slow my descent, and amazingly, it worked. I landed on my feet ... err, talons, stumbling over my too long stick legs and turned to face a fast-approaching Emelie.

"Oh, for the love of the Norse," she said, pinching the bridge of her nose, sighing, and then smacking Nils, who was still in his wolf shape, for all she was worth. "Phase, right now, Nils."

Obeying her command, his fur rippled and stretched until he stood tall and naked next to her. "What'd you do that for," he asked disgruntled, rubbing his shoulder. "I did what her brother asked me to do."

The lines of her young face were harsh in the blue glow of my flames. "Soren told you to push his sister through a window, then attack her until she changed into an animal he wasn't sure she would be able to turn into?" she retorted with sarcasm. "Yeah, that sounds like him."

Exasperated, Nils explained, "He might not have been sure, but I was, Em. I could smell it on her. Like I can on him. Like I can with all shifters."

I turned an eye up to him and glared. Why hadn't he told me this sooner—the jerk. My heart felt like it was about to pound out of my chest.

"Stop staring at me, Erin," he shivered. "That bird eye thing creeps me out."

I retaliated the only way I could think of … by pecking him on his bare foot. "Ow!" he howled. "What the fuck? I did what I was supposed to do. Why am I getting tortured for it?"

"Oh, shut up. You deserved it," Emelie said, tiptoeing toward me with wide eyes. "Holy shit, Erin! You're like a … help me out here, Nils."

"I was hoping you would know."

Those weren't the reassuring words I'd been looking for. I mean, this bird thing was a hoot, no pun intended, but I was ready to change back into my usual form and forget that this was something I could do—for the rest of my life.

"She appears to be a firebird if this is anything to go by," Viggo said, joining the others with a long feather, glowing in the night like a fading ember. "Though, there hasn't been a firebird sighting since medieval times in Eastern Europe. In all probability, she is the last of her kind."

"Definitely, the last," Emelie agreed. "How many fire-walkers have a shapeshifter, like Odin, for a father?

"Just one?" Nils guessed.

"Yep, and she's standing here, looking uncomfortable with all our jabbering. Erin, honey, Soren does this all the time. Just relax and close your eyes. Try to imagine yourself in your usual form. It should happen right away."

I closed my eyes, grateful that I wasn't in this alone, and did as she said, thinking of my usual tall self, then held my breath.

The change was as immediate as all of my magic had been, thus far. I blinked to focus on their faces in the pitch-black night. My eyes didn't work as well at seeing in the dark as they had while I was in my bird form. When I finally made out Nils, standing with his arms crossed to the side, I stood. "You suck, Nils."

"Awe, come on, Erin." He stuck out his hand. "Friends?"

I took what he offered with a vicious grin. "We were never friends. You know, on account of you being a dick, but I will promise not to kill you for pushing me out of the window. Oh, and for almost paralyzing me."

He waved away my anger. "Soren would have healed you up. Besides, how else would I have been able to get you mad enough to bring out the animal in you?"

His words chimed in my head. "That's what Soren sent you out here for. Not to teach me combat, but to see if I could transform?"

His smile was telling. "You're as smart as you are beautiful."

I looked down in embarrassment. Nils had a way of making every woman uncomfortable with his questionable way of speaking…and dressing. He was still buck naked. "Wait a minute. How am I still dressed but you're nude?"

"She's as smart as she is beautiful," Viggo chided. "Time to fess up."

Nils put his arm around me and led me toward the back steps. "I have nothing to confess, Viggo. So what if I choose nudity over artificial fibers. It makes everything much more accessible when I need it."

I threw off his arm. "Ugh, Nils. You're disgusting. You know that, right?"

He shrugged, smiling a boyish grin that could charm the knickers right off of any single female in the Norselands. "You still love me. I can sense it."

"Can you also sense that the next time you do something like this, I won't be pecking you in the foot?" I asked, squinting my eyes, then glancing downward with a meaningful look.

"Not only do I sense it, but I also anticipate it," he answered with a lewd smile. "Tell me something? Are you always this hot when you threaten someone's male-hood?"

"Oh, fuck off, Nils."

"What's all the excitement?" Axel asked us from his hidden spot near the steps.

I spun my feather between my fingers. "Nothing much. I found out that I can turn into a giant, loud bird, and that your brother is a masochist. But that was just the last five minutes or so. Wait around. I'm sure something else will push me over the brink real soon."

He arched an eyebrow at the words that didn't match my nonchalant tone. "Indeed?" He motioned to the piece of my plumage that I held. "Is that your feather?"

I handed it to him. "Yep."

"I am astonished. It has been six hundred years since I have heard of a firebird in the Norselands. They are extinct."

Nils clapped him on the shoulder. "Not anymore, brother. Behold, the giant, glowing peacock of death."

I reared back to hit him, but he sprinted away too fast for me to catch. "I'll get you later!" I yelled at the back of his head, as he went up the stairs toward his room. "And put on some damn clothes. There's only so many times I can look at your dick in an hour!"

"See! It's not just me," Emelie said, stepping in the back door with Viggo right behind her. Grinning, she asked, "Is there tea?"

Viggo grabbed the teapot. "I'm on it. Want to get the ladies a cup, Axel?"

He bowed. "Of course, my prince. It would be an honor to serve you."

The teapot clanked to the stove. "You know how I hate that subservient shit, Axel."

"I do," he answered, placing a cup and saucer in front of each of us. "That's why I haven't stopped doing it."

"You are spending way too much time with Kristian," I observed. "You're twins, at this point. Where is your brother from another mother, anyway?"

"Still looking for his mate." Axel sighed. "He hasn't had much luck."

"And my brother?"

"He's checking out a lead on Chase's whereabouts."

Nils came down the stairs wearing a towel over his wet hair and nothing else, right on cue. "Don't lie for Soren, brother. He may not want to tell them, but I do. It is what is right."

"Tell us what?" I asked.

"We know where Chase is."

Everyone was stunned. Well, not everyone. Just Emelie and I reacted. Grinding my teeth, I swore to myself that I was going to start kicking several someone's asses if they continued to keep essential secrets from me. Emelie? Well, I could see why they didn't tell her. She was trembling like a leaf and looking as if she would faint at any moment. I counted to ten and asked as politely as my temper would allow, "Nils, how do you know where she is?"

"Chase has been rambling to me about Viveka and Freyr for the last day and a half. She's disoriented, but she is lucid enough to know that Freyr is using her power to keep their whereabouts hidden."

When Emelie's tremble became an all-out shimmy, I pulled out a chair for her. She eased into it, looking like a lost puppy. I could hear her teeth click together as she gasped out, "She is alive," speaking more to herself than to any of us. It was clear that tonight had been a little more excitement than she could handle.

I filled a glass with water and pushed it at Emelie. "Okay, since Emelie is out of sorts, why don't you answer a few questions for us, Nils?"

"What do you want to know, Kvinna?" He laid his towel over a barstool before he sat on it, all the while managing to look like an old-time villain. All he needed was the mustache to twirl. Nils was just so … weird. I'd never met someone so strange and normal at the same time. Well, except for Chase. No wonder they're fated mates.

"Three things," I said. "One, how do males shower so fast? I would still be in there trying to find a towel in the three minutes it took you to take yours. Two, have you told my brother about this? And three, why am I just hearing about this?"

He breathed out a pained sigh. "To answer your questions in order, as boring as they are, I shower fast because I'm not a female, and yes, I notified Soren the second I heard from Chase. The not telling you part, you'll have to take up with your brother."

"But, I don't get it," I complained. "Why would she call to you, but not to her mother or me?"

"Whatever magic she is being forced to use is blocking her from contact with you. Believe me, I'm positive that she would rather talk to anyone else, and I probably would not hear her at all if she were not my true mate."

Emelie and I both shot our widened eyes to Nils. "Your what?"

Viggo shook his head at us in awe. "You guys are so scary when you talk in unison. I freakin' love it."

"He's about to find out what scary looks like," I said. "You're a fool, Nils. What the fuck?"

Serious for what must be the first time in his long life, he said, "Stay out of it. I can handle it."

"Then handle it!" Emelie snapped.

"I have been handling it for the last twelve hundred and three years," he bit back in anger.

Axel cleared his throat. "I believe that you have been 'handling' it for a lot longer than that, brother. Remember that time you got caught in th—"

"Shut up," Nils interrupted. "You promised me your silence."

"No, I did not. What I said was something along the lines of … I will save this humiliation until such a time that it suits me to use it against you. That time is now if you are wondering."

Jakob arrived and took a seat next to me, shaking his head in undisguised distaste. "For the love of the Norse, Fenrir. Put some clothing on. Allow me to apologize for my friend's appalling behavior, ladies. He is an embarrassment to our gender. It is almost as if he was raised by wolves."

"I give zero fucks about what you think, Jakob."

"Enough!" Soren commanded, sweeping into the room. "Nils, don't let me see you undressed before my mate and sister again."

"I could give him something to wear," I said, smiling at Nils. "You like polka dotted dresses, right?"

"I know for a fact he does," Emelie confirmed, watching her mate leave the room. "Soren wants to speak to you, Erin."

"Ugh … do I have to? I've just seen my mate for the first time today. Can't I, at least, tell him my exciting news first?"

"Yes, you have to, because this time I think that you're going to approve of what he says. I'll fill Jakob in on your fancy new ability to burst eardrums."

"You're a terrible liar, Em."

She threw an arm around my shoulders. "I know. Now go and make up with Soren, so he'll stop driving me bat-shit crazy."

"Fine!" I whined, stomping my foot in petulance. "I'll be right back."

Pouting, I made my way out into the hall and called to my close-minded, hypocrite of a brother.

"Soren?"

He answered right away as if he'd been waiting on me to speak. "Will you join me in the library?"

"Sure."

It felt like I was on trial, and Soren was about to judge me. "Dead elf walking," I muttered to myself.

Soren stood when I entered the room, ever the gentleman and no doubt ready to read me what I'm sure would be an enlightening riot act, but I didn't let him speak first. It was time to lay my cards on the table, and this time, I wasn't going to bluff.

"Soren, today will be my last day with the rebellion."

"You cannot mean that," he said, aghast. "Surely, you do not think that Odin's rule must continue."

"No, of course not. It's just that—" I broke off, afraid to finish. What if he tried to force me to stay? Emelie did say something about a locked tower.

He took my hand, his eyes imploring me. "What is it, dear sister?"

"I just can't be here. Not when you cling to this absurd chivalry notion the way you do. I will no longer be prohibited from seeing my mate. I'm a grown female. I make my own decisions."

"Is it so absurd that I want my sister to be spared from the ridicule that will follow you after a shameful affair like this?"

"That's just it! It's not shameful. His mating is over in every way, but paperwork filed with the council and a hastily thrown together bond. Everyone in the Norselands knows that she is an escaped criminal." I closed my eyes and tried to reign in my anger. I couldn't look at him without wanting to roast him alive. Why couldn't he see reason?

When I felt calm, I opened my eyes to find his face expressionless, and that pissed me off all over again. "Even with all of that, you would still begrudge him the happiness we've found in each other? It's cruel! You're cruel. I'm fucking out of here."

He sat quietly for a moment and then sneered. "Do you think that the faeries can protect you out there?"

"No, nor would I ask them to. I do, however, think that I am capable of taking care of myself."

"Odin will find you."

His sullen, petulant tone struck a nerve. "He's already found me! Viveka planted the fake stone for that reason alone!"

"Perhaps, that is true," he seethed. "We have no way of knowing, even less of a chance if you leave us. We need to take down the temple before anyone else gets killed, Erin. Cedric's death will not be in vain!" His heavy breathing was still loud in my ears, even after he turned away. "Erin, I may be new in your life, but I already know you are not selfish enough to sacrifice others for your love."

"No, I am not. I would regret it for the rest of my life if I did, but Soren …" I looked him square in the eyes. "I refuse to stay away from Jakob any longer. We're mated. End of story."

His crimson eyes shot to someone behind me. Following his stare, I found my determined mate in the doorway. Soren stormed up to him. Electricity crackled as it arced from its conduit to the metal fixtures in the room. "Why are you lurking in the hallway? Do you not trust me to have a conversation with my own blood?"

"No, Soren. I came here because I am concerned about your safety. I do not trust her anger. She is in a volatile mood."

"She is not alone in that," he said with contempt. "I cannot believe that you would let her leave the safety of the rebellion."

"If she chooses to leave, I will honor her wishes. I would follow her anywhere," Jakob answered, tranquil as usual.

My eyebrows rose at his response, and I tried, albeit unsuccessfully, to keep the smugness from my expression. That wasn't what I'd expected him to say.

"I see," Soren said to him, and he left without another word … and then came right back with Emelie hot on his heels.

Emelie joined me near the fireplace, laced her fingers with mine, and smiled. "I was going for slow and steady, Erin, but this works, too." She turned to her mate with a hard glare. "Soren, swallow your pride for once in your damn life, and tell them what you told me."

"Little one," he soothed. "This is unnecessary."

"Is it? Because it looks to me like they're headed for the nearest exit."

I slipped my engagement ring out of my pocket and put it on in defiance. Brother or not, he wouldn't keep me from Jakob.

Soren's eyes bulged with rage, prompting Emelie to step between us and put a light hand on his chest. "My love, I get it. You want to protect your sister, but can you not see how this is doing the opposite? You're pushing her into the clutches of danger. No offense, Jakob."

Jakob inclined his head with a slight smile. "None taken, Emelie. As always, I bow to your wisdom."

Soren didn't miss the hidden insult in his words. "Do not dare to insinuate that I do not heed my mate's advisements, Jakob. I am faithful to her … in every sense. Can you say the same?"

"Careful, Soren!" Jakob seethed, looking murderous.

With a weary sigh, Soren looked at his fellow warrior. "I did not mean it. Forgive me."

Jakob nodded his acquiescence. "Of course."

Soren sat as if his legs would no longer hold him upright. "When Myrgjöl foresaw Odin's death, she saw you both as his replacement." His eyes were wild with worry as he glanced up at me. "I fear for her, Jakob. If we kill my father at the temple, is she prepared? What if an unknown enemy tries to usurp the throne? How can she protect herself against warriors trained for eons?"

Jakob put a reassuring hand on Soren's shoulder. "She will not be alone in this. You would not abandon her in a time of great need. I know this as a truth. I do not need a reminder of how much you care for your sister."

Watching Soren's forlorn expression as he nodded in agreement made me realize something I'd missed before. When Emelie warned me about an obstacle in my relationship with Jakob, I'd thought that it was Jakob's mating. Now I wondered if it wasn't Soren's fear that was the impediment.

I extricated my fingers from Emelie's grasp and walked to my brother. Everything was so obvious now. I couldn't believe I didn't figure it out sooner. "This is why you've tried to keep us apart, isn't it?"

Soren's bowed head was confirmation enough.

"Oh, Soren."

"I am so sorry, Erin. You may hate me for what I have put you through, but just know that I could not bear the thought of another person I love dying. You are so new to your magic, so innocent. It was my friend, Cedric, all over again."

My heart ached upon hearing his earnest words. "That won't happen, Soren. Right, Em?"

She grinned. "Nope."

He stared at his mate for a long moment and smiled. "Jakob, when the kingdom speaks to the elves about the upcoming war, tell them the truth about your mating. It is time we announce our plans."

I threw myself at Soren and squeezed his middle tight. "Thank you!"

He enveloped me into his embrace and bent to kiss my forehead. "Do not make me regret doing this. You are my most beloved sister. I could not bear to lose you."

"I won't," I promised, then watched him take his leave with Emelie, but not before he cast one last stricken look in my direction.

Stunned, I sat long after they left the room. I couldn't believe that Soren had done everything he had done out of the fear of losing me. He seemed so … invincible. Hell, even Chase had said he was revered as Odin's most powerful son. If he was this afraid for my safety, I knew that I was in for a bumpy ride.

Jakob crouched down and laid a warm hand on my knee. "Are you well, älskling?"

I had to think about the question a bit before answering. I wasn't sure. On the one hand, I was glad that Soren's opposition to my mating was over, but on the other, I longed for the naiveté I enjoyed up until a few minutes ago. I was now more terrified than I'd ever been in my life. Whatever creature came up with the term, ignorance is bliss, was obviously a kindred spirit, or an offspring of insane parents, like Viveka and Odin, such as myself. Either way, they knew what they were talking about.

With a deep sigh, I threw up my hands. "I don't know how to feel," I admitted. "Just when I thought things couldn't get worse."

He took my hands in his and kissed them both. "That only means that things will get better from hereafter."

CHAPTER FOURTEEN

The evening of the full moon, we left the farmhouse as a group, armed to the teeth with both magic and weapons of the mundane sort. The most noticeable of all of them being the flaming broadsword on Surt's back. Last night, he'd spent an hour entertaining us all with stories of the fire-walkers in our family, all while sharpening and re-sharpening that gigantic blade of his, until it was deemed ready for battle.

Soren had listened, from his spot in the shadows of the bonfire, with apparent interest, but then later warned me not to put much stock in my flames. He didn't think that I could defeat Freyr with them. Truth be told, I knew he was wrong. I could melt them where they stood with the intensity of my heat. I doubt even Odin could come back from that.

As excited, amped up, and boisterous as the males were for the upcoming battle, Emelie and I couldn't join in. Terrified, we held each other's hand in a death-grip, glancing at each other with crazed looks every few minutes. Unlike the males, this was our first battle, and we were afraid for what we stood to lose, regardless of the foretold victory. The not knowing was killing me. And judging by the twitch in her left eye, Emelie wasn't feeling much different.

She gripped my hand even tighter when Soren called us to attention. "Is everyone clear on their part in the invasion?" A chorus of yeses answered him. "Good," he sighed. "It is time. Remember, we meet at the giant ash on Midgard in one hour. I do not give a shit if your leg is stuck in a bear trap. You bring it with you if you have to. Just get there."

Nils huffed indignantly as every eye turned his way. "What? When have I ever been caught in a snare?"

Viggo was quick to answer. "Twice, if memory serves. Once, you weren't wearing pants. Does that ring a bell?"

He grinned. "Nope."

Soren ignored their conversation, continuing on. "On the count of three, we shift. One. Two. Three."

All I could see was darkness. "Jakob," I whispered, a little panicked.

"Right here, love." He laced his fingers with mine and pulled me snugly into his side.

Viggo laughed behind me. "You are the most pathetic dark elf, Erin."

"Shut up," I growled. "Or the next time I can see, you'll be pulling my foot out of your ass."

"Someone is touchy," he muttered.

Axel's deep voice rumbled to life. "Can you blame her, my prince? She may see her mother hurt tonight. Indeed, both of her parents hurt. Regardless of the circumstances, a creature would have to be heartless not to care about the only parents she will ever have. Have a little empathy."

"Uh, yeah, Axel. That speech might be a little more touching if her parents weren't lunatics, with a side of narcissistic psychopath."

"Quiet!" Soren ordered. "Emelie, does any of this look familiar to you from the dream Freyr visited you in?"

"I can't tell. I can't see well either. Care to comment on that, Viggo?"

"Uh, nope, can't say that I do."

Nils snickered. "Smart male.

Surt spoke up. "Allow me, my lady."

An instant later, two torches, on either side of the vine-covered steps, blazed to life. Her breath caught. "Those are the steps from the dream."

Soren turned to Loki. "You know what to do."

"One hour," Loki said out loud, more to himself than us, then disappeared.

"To your positions!" Soren ordered, eyeing Nils until he came to stand next to Emelie and me. "Do not leave them under any circumstances, Fenrir."

He wrapped an arm around each of our waists. "Do not worry. This will be an easy victory. Em, you want to do the honors? I have my hands full here."

"I'm on it," she said, waving goodbye to a fading stoic-faced Soren.

We materialized to the top of the steep, stone staircase. At Nils' urging, Emelie and I tip-toed down winding stone stairs with him, careful not to make a sound. It wasn't easy. Nils could barely move with Em and me bravely clutching each of his arms in fear. Warriors, we were not.

At the bottom, there was more darkness. "Do you think Chase is down here," I asked, my voice quivering. Damn this lack of night vision!

"I am positive," Nils whispered. "Viveka, too. I can smell her."

"Very good, Fenrir," a female's unfamiliar voice said.

I was temporarily blinded when the lamps on either side of the room blazed to life. When I could see, I found my mother standing in front of us, a smug smile spread across her face. I should have expected this.

"Hello, Viveka," Nils offered, all the while sending us a silent message to give him the use of his arms. "I believe it is time that you return to your cell."

Viveka scoffed at his words. "How dare you speak to me as if we are on the same level, mongrel?"

Her cold superiority made me snap. "Hey!" I exclaimed, pissed on his behalf. "Why don't you shut your fucking mouth? Nils may be a wolf and an immature prick, but he's our immature prick. You, on the other hand, I loathe." Lowering my voice, I took a step closer. "And, if I had my way, I'd let my fire steal the oxygen from your lungs and watch you die." I paused to let her see the fire swirling in my eyes. "Just give me a reason to."

Nils merely chuckled at the death threat to my mother, but Emelie gasped in surprise. I knew she'd be shocked. Hell, I was shocked. There was no way I could have anticipated how I would feel when I met Viveka. Meeting her today had brought all of those old feelings of anger and abandonment to the surface. How much I hated her! Everything about her—the lip curled in repugnance, as if she couldn't stand to be near so many below her class, the beautiful long, black curls so like my own, and most of all, the ring on her finger that my mate had put there. How could Jakob have ever loved this female? She oozed hatred and contempt.

"Oh, Erin," she simpered. "That vulgar speech is beneath you. As is the company you keep. Do you think Soren's group of misfits can defeat Freyr and his allies?"

Her ignorance made me smile. She had no idea who she was dealing with. "No, mother. I think I can defeat Freyr and his merry little band of sycophants."

"I think so, too," Emelie informed her, smiling nastily with her silver eyes narrowed. "You, yourself, will have the pleasure of spending the rest of eternity in Svartálfaheim's prison. But don't worry, you'll have the thought of how you abandoned your only child to keep you company."

A flicker of fear crossed Viveka's face before her usual disdain won over. "Jealous, Norn? Are you regretting your decision to enlighten the king to our plan? It is not too late to join us." She glanced at me. "Either of you."

Nils took a step toward her, ready to pounce. "I think my feelings might be a little hurt by the exclusion, Viveka."

I was so distracted by Nils' mocking conversation, so caught up in the heat of the moment, that I didn't notice Freyr sneaking up behind us, until Nils fell forward at Viveka's feet, unconscious. Throwing myself away from Freyr, I huddled against the wall, screaming silently for Soren and Jakob, while Emelie's very audible scream filled my ears. She was frozen with fear. A fact that she was making known by berating me in my head. *"Don't just stand there! Help me, idiot!"*

Straightening, I steeled myself and said, "What the hell was that, Mom? Do you always have someone else fight your fights for you?" She ignored the jab. Instead, she watched Freyr as he undressed Emelie with his hungry, leering eyes. "Uh, hello?" They both ignored me. "All powerful ass-kicking chick right behind you," I told them. Still no response.

When he ran his knuckles down the side of her face and her neck, I barked out, "Get your hands off of her!" and grabbed him by the arm. Did he think I'd just stand here nonchalantly as he tried to round second base with my brother's wife? Uh, no … not going to happen.

Freyr shook off my hold, hurling me to the floor. He sneered down at me. "Bind and gag your offspring, Viveka."

I growled at her as she approached. "Touch me, and I will break and burn every appendage on your body, female."

She retreated, unwilling to take me on. What a surprise, just one more thing she depended on someone else to do for her. How in the worlds could this weak, entitled female be my mother?

"Are your words true, daughter of Odin? Are you a fire-walker?" Freyr dragged Emelie to his side as he stalked closer. It was clear that he would use her as leverage if I didn't cooperate.

Smirking, I said, "First, I have a question for you, Freyr."

He arched a perfect, golden eyebrow. "And what might that be?"

"THIS!" Surt yelled as he thrust his sword through Freyr's

back until I could see its flaming tip come out of his chest.

Laughing, Freyr looked down at the smoldering wreckage of his chest. "Do you honestly think this will kill me?"

"No," I answered, giving Surt a meaningful look. At his nod, I grabbed the end of the sword, pushing my fire into it. Freyr's shrieks of pain rang across the room as his clothing caught fire, blackening his skin. He was dead within seconds.

Viveka's wide eyes looked from my triumphant face to what was left of her meal ticket. "Nooooo!" she roared as she rushed toward us, now angry and desperate enough to attack.

"STOP!" My voice boomed in the small space, startling everyone. "Or you're next." I let go of the sword, watching with perverse satisfaction as Surt yanked it out of a charcoaled Freyr without mercy and cut off his head before he collapsed the floor. Turning to a stunned Viveka, he seized her arm and pulled her up the stairs, dragging her when she refused to walk.

Emelie sagged against the wall in relief. "Oh my God, Erin. You were amazing … and fucking scary. You charred Freyr to a crisp!"

I skirted around what was left of Freyr and knelt down to check Nils' pulse. I didn't even want to think about what I'd just done. I had a feeling I'd be speaking to a therapist about it for the next hundred years or so. "Yeah, well. I'm sorry for not reacting faster, Em. I just froze."

"Me too," she admitted, breathing out a heavy sigh. "I was so stupid coming here, thinking that I could defeat Freyr just because I'd done it before. What if he had hurt the baby?"

My jaw dropped. "The baby? Are you saying what I think you're saying?"

"If you think that I'm saying that you're going to be an aunt, then yes, I am."

"Holy shit!" I squealed. "Does Soren know? How far along are you? Do you know what the gender is? Come on, give me some details!"

"I'm—"

Viveka's angered screeching interrupted her reply. I rolled my eyes. "How is it possible that she gave me life?"

"One of the universe's great mysteries," she replied. "Let's find Chase and get the hell out of here. Freyr's corpse is freaking me out."

Me and her both. "Lead the way."

We walked shoulder to shoulder down the freezing cold corridor until I heard a weak cry—Chase's cry. With a glance at each other, we sprinted to the source of the sound. Through a barred cell door, we found Chase huddled in the corner of a walk-in closet sized room.

Emelie tugged on the cell door. "We need a key, Erin."

"No, we don't. Hang on, Chase. I'm coming." I grabbed the door handle, melted it, and then kicked in the metal door.

"Nice," Emelie said, impressed. "Chase? Are you okay?"

Battered and bruised, Chase made her way over to us. "I am now."

"Emelie, take her to the farmhouse, and for the love of the Norse, stay there. I can't believe you came here in your condition."

"I'm pregnant, not disabled, you twit," she said crossly. "Besides there's no reason for you to stay."

I glared at her. "I'm going to blame hormones for that twit remark. I'll meet you there in five, okay? Nils needs attention." I chuckled. "Nothing new there."

Emelie laid a hand on my arm, stopping me. "Please, Erin. Don't go."

Panic's sudden attack struck, making my heart pound. "Is it Jakob?" I asked, not waiting for an answer before running back to the anteroom and past Nils' still sleeping form.

In the crowd at the top of the steps, Jakob's deep voice was music to my ears, although what he was saying didn't inspire much confidence. Pushing my way forward, I saw my mother, cornered, holding the jewel-hilted dagger from Surt's belt to her stomach. Jakob stood in front of her with his hands up in the upright and 'I won't hurt you' position.

"Viveka, will you not listen? You do not need to do this. Do you believe that Kristian's prison will be so terrible for you? He is not an unkind male to any female. Please, give me the blade."

"You could help me," she countered. "Take your rightful place as king. Free me, Jakob."

"So that you could do this again and again with Odin?" He shook his head. "No, Viveka. I cannot."

"Then you give me no choice." With those words said, she plunged the dagger into her belly twisting it to inflict greater damage, then fell to her knees, before collapsing against the stone wall.

"Noooo!" I screamed, rushing forward to pull the knife out before she could do more harm to herself. "Soren, hurry! Heal her!"

Soren didn't move. He only said, "My magic will do nothing if she will not accept it, Erin."

"Please, mother," I sobbed. "Please, don't do this."

Jakob crouched beside us, his face hiding the seething rage that lay open to me in his mind. He was angered by her selfishness and the blatant disregard for the child she had given birth to. "Viveka, for the sake of your daughter, allow Soren to heal you."

Blood trickled from the corners of her mouth as she spoke. "My king, she has been my curse, the ruin to all of my plans and our mating. I owe her nothing."

Seconds after her cruel statement, the spark faded from my mother's eyes. Stunned, I carefully moved my mother's lifeless torso from my lap and stood, shaking with rage. I could feel my eyes burning with heat, my flame begging to be set free, to set things to right. "Get Nils, and get out," I said to the group, my voice was calm and without emotion.

"What of Thor and Odin?" Jakob asked, reluctant to leave me.

"Now!" I screamed, causing dust and debris to fall from the cracks in the ceiling. I didn't want them to get hurt by my barely controlled magic. They had to go now.

Axel hurried down the steps to fetch his unconscious brother. "Jakob, father drove them away. I saw them after we arrived in the feasting hall. All three shifted at the same time." He eyed the impatient flames covering my body. "I suggest we follow their lead."

With one long last look at me, Jakob left me alone.

Making my way to the now deserted main hall, I stepped up onto the dais that held the three 'god's' thrones. Glancing around in disgust at the view, I could see why Nils had urged us to go downstairs. He was trying to protect us from seeing the massacre the temple's belly held. It was an awful place. Dozens of creatures hung with their throats slit around the perimeter. Below them, a trough stood overflowing with their blood. Bile rose in my throat. How could anyone do this to a creature?

From the darkness of the void that surrounded me, a male's lyrical voice asked, "Do you think that you are above this honor?"

I backed up to the wall. I couldn't tell where the voice originated. "Who's there?"

"I would hate to think you a greater fool than your brother," the voice continued.

"Show yourself!" I demanded, ready to give whoever this was a taste of what my flame could do.

Out of the blackness, a grey-haired male stepped into the sliver of moonlight that lit the room. My fire reacted, covering my body with an audible whoosh. It was Odin. I had no doubt. I could feel the same pulsating energy I'd become accustomed to feeling when I was around Soren. "Hello, father."

He inclined his head. "Daughter."

"I thought you were gone."

He disappeared and reappeared in front of me in a split second. "I did not have what I came for."

"You're going to be disappointed if you mean me," I warned him, amping up my fire's intensity to volcano hot.

Smiling, he wiped the beads of sweat off his forehead and continued, "Erin, my own blood, have a care. I am not the evil dictator the Norselands will have you believe I am. How can you ally yourself with Soren without first hearing my side of the story? He may be my oldest child, but he is not an infallible creature. He has made unforgivable mistakes of judgment, just as I have. You are an intellectual sort of female. Do you not desire to know why these sacrifices have to be made?"

"Intellectual sort of female, huh?" I huffed. "You're right. I'm not a fool, so don't treat me as such." I took a step closer to him. "There can be no just reason that you could ever give me that would sway me to your side. Who are you to kill any living creature? You're not a god, nowhere near it. All you are is a megalomaniac and an asshole."

"You will submit to me, daughter! I command it!" His voice was like thunder, the rumble making the stone foundation sway beneath our feet.

"Make me!" I growled back, pleased when stones started toppling from the ceiling. I would bring this whole place down on top of him if I had to.

Odin laughed. "You are but a child. Your powers cannot compare with mine."

I smiled at his arrogance. "Yeah, you're right. Our magic would be impossible to compare … because I'm stronger."

"Erin, you will obey me!" Odin screamed, all traces of humor now gone.

Not bloody likely. With a warrior's cry, I leaped toward my father, my anger bringing my fire into a tight column of magma hot heat in my hands. There was no disguising the satisfaction I felt as I watched it shoot like a laser into the face of the only father I'd ever known. Fear made his face young for a fleeting moment, then he appeared resolved. It was sick, even depraved of me, but I wanted to see the life leave his eyes. I wanted revenge. The taste of it was thick on my tongue.

My revenge, however, was not to be. When my magic hit its mark, the room imploded. Screaming, I covered my head, too shocked to think to shift away from the danger that never came. Laughing a hysterical little giggle, I looked up to my unexpected savior, the faery queen, and pushed myself up to my knees.

She stood fiercely in front of me, looking over the debris for any movement. "Rise, child. We must take our leave."

With a wobble, I got to my feet and threw my tired arms around her. "Layla, I can never thank you enough."

"There's no need," she assured me, brushing the plaster from my cheek and helping me to my feet. "You brought my daughter home. I was in your debt, not the other way around."

"Is she okay?"

"Perfectly. If not a little peeved at missing the action."

She could have it. I would give every magic I had in the worlds to know that I would never have to use it again in violence. "I'm more of a lover, I think."

Smirking, she shook her head. "With a mate like yours, who could blame you?"

I gave her a weary smile and glanced at the rubble. "Is he dead?"

"Gone, but injured, I would say. It will take some time for him to recover from that kind of damage, and my dear, he will not thank you for it."

"Then, it's over … for now, at least."

"For now. However, something must be done about this temple. We can't let Thor come back here. It must be destroyed."

"Leave it to me."

"I was going to, child." She disappeared in her customary burst of sparkles, her laugh still lingering in the air for several seconds after she was gone.

After several moments of deep contemplation, I decided that the best way to destroy the temple was from the sky. Almost being pummeled once was enough for one night. Taking a running leap into the air, I felt my arms lengthen to the strong, rigid wings that would carry me to a height low enough to blast this atrocity to kingdom come, but high enough to keep myself safe from the debris. Shooting through the opening created to allow sunlight, I flew straight up until I was above the tree line and hovered, taking stock of the situation. I could see fires smoldering on most of the grounds, and the vine-covered stairs we'd seen at the entrance now stood in a jagged pile at the base of the temple. Good. Closing my eyes, I concentrated on the staccato beat of my wings, imagining my fire pulsing stronger and hotter with every beat. It didn't take long for me to hear the roar of my flame surrounding me, as if I was standing in the eye of a hurricane. I felt calm, ready to end this nightmare, and when the fire's growl became too loud for my bird's sensitive hearing, I let everything I had go.

I came to with a gasp. Frozen in fear, I looked around me without moving. I seemed to be laying on hard concrete, in what looked like a deserted loading dock. Where was everyone? Wasn't I supposed to be at the tree? Oh, that's right. I didn't make it. Anyone could have brought me here.

Jakob appeared at my side. "Calm yourself, Erin."

"What happened?" I whispered, but a low squawk came out. I

was still in bird form. I hadn't even realized that I wasn't me. Well, the normal me.

Stumbling up onto the long stalks of my legs, I tried to relax. Two seconds later, I was pressed into the chest of my mate. "What was I thinking, letting you go into battle alone? Do not ever ask it of me again, Erin. I will not obey."

"Don't worry, Jakob. I was a fool. If Layla hadn't shown up, I would have been trapped under a thousand pounds of stone right now."

"We owe her a debt, my love."

I shook my head to get rid of the dizziness. "No. She says it's paid."

"Indeed, all of the rebellion's debt has been paid."

We turned to Layla's voice and found her and Soren smiling at us. "Good news," my brother said. "The faeries have joined our rebellion."

"Great," I replied with a note of hope tinging my voice. "Does that mean we can all go home now?"

"Home?" Soren asked, his expression masking his true feelings, per usual.

"To the castle. You and Emelie will stay with us, won't you, Soren?"

He dipped into the bow I'd become so accustomed to. "My Queen, it would be an honor to serve you."

"I don't need your service, silly. I need a brother." I grinned and stepped into his outstretched arms. "You'll have to do until I find a better one."

"I think that's my cue to leave," Queen Layla said.

I untangled myself from Soren's iron grip. "Layla, wait. I want to thank you ... for everything. We couldn't have done this without your help."

Her smile was serene. "Fear not, soon there will come a time when you shall return the favor."

I furrowed my brow. "Myrgjöl?"

Winking, she said, "Who else, my dear?" and disappeared.

I stood silent for a moment, staring into the space where she'd just stood. It was all over. Could it have really taken less than an hour to undo more than six thousand years of my father's tyranny?

"There was nothing easy about what you just did," Jakob told me, lacing his fingers with my left hand.

Soren offered me his arm on my other side. "He's right, sister. I'm proud of you."

"I'm proud of you guys, too. Most of all, you, Soren. I'm so excited to be an aunt. I can't wait to see if the baby has your hair and eyes."

Realization dawned on him. "Emelie is ... with child?"

I slapped my hand to my forehead. "Just go." He was gone before I finished speaking. "Oh God, Jakob. What have I done?"

"Made him a happy male," he supplied.

"You're hilarious."

He smoothed back my tangled hair, cupped my face, and pressed his soft lips to mine. "And you, my Erin, are perfect."

EPILOGUE

A couple weeks after what we'd been calling the 'temple incident', Kristian sent word that he wasn't coming back to rule. We all figured as much. With his mate now found, the allure of his solitary throne might as well be a punishment, though it was nice to have his blessing. There was an overabundance of other problems we couldn't escape so easily, and that was just one less thing we'd have to worry about.

Once the news of Odin's defeat traveled across the Norselands, it was amazing how many creatures flocked to Svartálfaheim for our protection, which we happily provided, of course. It was as predicted—Jakob and I were their king and queen. They no longer looked to Odin as their ruler, and this caused the balance of power (and magic) to shift to our side.

Our first appointment as the unofficial monarchy was to make sure that Chase stayed on as my right hand. I doubt Queen Layla would have stood for anything else. She had been more than helpful, but I knew she had her own agenda for the faeries of Midgard. She'd be keeping an eye on us, allies or not.

Much to Chase's dismay, Nils was selected as the most worthy to guard the king. I'm sure Soren would have been Jakob's first pick, but with Emelie's impending birth, he had become erratic. He was obsessed with the safety of their child. I knew that he had nothing to worry about. My nephew would live to marry Kristian's daughter with his human and see grandchildren of his own. My borrowed Norn powers assured me of that. All would be well … eventually.

After the Great War, Ragnarök, there would be peace. Until that day, we would go about with our planning and scheming, while keeping a watchful eye for anything astray. We didn't know when my father would strike, but we knew that he would. He had ruled for thousands of years. He wasn't about to hand over all of that glory to a daughter that had been here ten minutes. No way. He would come. And when he did, the rebellion would be ready.

THE END

Also by J.D. Nelson

<u>Wicked Ways Series</u>

A Night of Wickedness
All I Want For Christmas Are My Two Front Fangs: A Wicked
Ways Companion Novel
Wolves Will Be Wolves
Too Cute To Spook: A Wicked Ways Companion Novel

<u>Night Aberrations Series</u>

Night Aberrations
The Fire within the Night

<u>Stand Alone Novels</u>

Control: A Tale of Desire

About the Author

JD Nelson is a Bestselling Author of Fantasy Romance and Adult Paranormal Romance. An avid time-waster, JD enjoys watching TV and listening to audiobooks when she really should be writing. JD loves to hear from her readers. You can contact her through her website, AuthorJDNelson.com, or on Facebook, where she spends an alarming amount of time chatting with her many Author and reader friends, much to the dismay of her continually neglected manuscripts.

JD Nelson's Facebook
www.facebook.com/NightAberrations
JD Nelson's Twitter
https://twitter.com/authorjdnelson
JD Nelson's Facebook Fan Page
www.facebook.com/JDNelsonsNightAberrations
JD Nelson's Fan Club
http://www.facebook.com/groups/269730583130725/

JD NELSON BOOKS